couldn't put this book down – believable characters and ettings, an intriguing story and a great ending. It's a real page-turner."

e Johnson – poet, short story writer and novelist

Kingdom of Sanguel

Secret Mission

Alex Lee Davis

ISBN:
978-19999152-0-9 (Paperback)
978-19999152-1-6 (Kindle)
978-19999152-2-3 (Hardback)

Cover Design by Oliver Jobling (info@joblime.co.uk)

Acknowledgements

To the exceptional men in my life, my husband N[...] listening to the crazy plot lines and providing sob[...] guidance, my sons Jason and Warren, your bant[...] talk, and fun times were more than appreciated[...] me going - you guys are amazing.

Special thanks to Sue Johnson for her writing wo[...] advice and editing skills. To Oliver Jobling for cre[...] great book cover.

My gratitude and thanks go out to all those who [...] me throughout this project. Sincere thanks to Jer[...] Jackson, Barrington Mullings, Chevon Lindsay, Va[...] Barry Sinclair, Natasha Godfrey, Lynette Pienaar,[...] Need, Sue Nicholls, Nicky Smith, Oliver Smith, Jon[...] Omari Hutchinson and Paula Douglas. Your contri[...] are very much appreciated.

The library had dominated the corner of Albert and Queensway for decades. People marvelled whether the architecture was late Victorian or early Edwardian. However, the large pillars that marked its elegant exterior suggested otherwise. The welcoming pillars were not made of brick or mortar, but were metallic in feature; warming bronze, rippling tones, invitingly tactile. Whilst the public enjoyed the library's elegance, carved woodwork, high ceilings and beautiful archways, if they had thrown speculative eyes towards the staff, they would find someone rather intriguing. Mrs A Marquel, the head librarian, was someone quite special.

Chapter 1

The Reading Room

"We've got enough time. Calm down." Rafe laughed at his cousin's impatient excitement. They stood in the crowded main reception of the library. Two large posters advertised the reading room event. Parents and children purchased last minute tickets.

"Ray. Pleeease. Let's get in the queue now." Her black, braided hair, held back in a ponytail, bounced up and down, as she tugged on Rafe's arm like a five-year-old.

"Tia, it's so dark up that corridor - the ghouly man will get you!" he teased, as he inched his fingers across her hair as though they were spiders. Tia brushed his hands away. She was scared of creepy crawlies when she was younger. Now she was eleven, they didn't worry her, and she was now used to her cousin teasing her.

"I've never seen a ghouly man in my life. He's not real!" She folded her arms over the hand-made bag belted around her waist and pressed her lips tightly together. She wanted to reach up and ruffle Rafe's afro just to annoy him. Rafe noticed the change in her demeanour; Tia would normally shoot something witty back at him. He didn't want her to be upset, especially after the difficult couple of years she'd had.

"Ok. Come on then." With one arm around her shoulders, he guided her through the crowd.

The librarian followed them with her eyes, and cracked a crooked smile as they passed under the archway with a sign over the top that read 'The Land of Sanguel' - Enter if you dare!

Across the library, Ben and Lisa were supposed to be selecting books; something they did every Saturday morning. Ben couldn't find anything he wanted to read. He was busy watching the growing queue.

"Enter if you dare!" he said aloud and swept his mop of brown hair across his brow.

Lisa, in her particular adult-like manner, was trying to select a book - something she wouldn't be permitted to read at home. Ben strode up the aisle of books just as Lisa, on tiptoe, had taken down another romance novel from the shelf.

3

"Let's go and see what that Sanguel thing is all about," he said, as he approached and immediately tried to snatch the book from Lisa.

"Get off," she retorted. Swinging the book out of his reach, she turned her back so her rucksack would deliberately hit Ben. Lisa continued to read. Ben, undaunted and interested in *'Enter if you dare'* - a challenge he had to take on, said, "Come on."

Lisa pushed her glasses further up on her nose. Her hazel eyes gave a side-glance, wary of Ben's actions.

"I thought you were too old for baby stuff," she sniffed. Lisa was eleven, a year younger than Ben, but she felt and acted as if she were the eldest, not only because she was slightly taller than Ben, but mostly because she thought he was annoying and stupid. Lisa placed the book back on the shelf not realising they were being watched.

"I'm going to take a look."

"Go ahead. It's childish. It may just suit you," Lisa smirked, looking through another book entitled *'Joanna's boyfriend'*.

Ben knew that their mother expected them to return home together. He also knew that as soon as his back was turned Lisa would run home ahead of him to get him in trouble.

4

"You're coming with me now, or I'll give you a Chinese burn!"

Lisa laughed far too loudly, "Just because you learnt that at your stupid Xplorers Club – really? A bunch of boys running around in the bushes, playing with tents - what a waste of time."

"I can light a fire from raw materials and ride horses and.... Anyway, I don't go any more, I'm too old." He smiled proudly, but underneath it all, he missed it.

"Why couldn't the Xplorers be a pop band? Then I could tell all my friends. That would be so cool. Noooo - running around like an idiot, is more your thing." She turned her nose into the air, trying to extend her height and disdain, moved into another aisle. Ben marched behind her with his hands gripped onto the straps of his rucksack. Not to be hard done by, he pointed to the sign, 'Adult Fiction'.

"Look, you're in the wrong place. Yet again!"

"Well, what do you know - I can't read." Lisa didn't turn around. She allowed her eyes to wander over the book titles until she settled on something that caught her interest.

Sunlight warmed the area, coloured patterns danced on the books from the oval shaped windows adorned with yellow and green glass.

"You won't be allowed to take any of those out, you're too young - how many times do I have to tell you?" Ben's outburst met a chorus of 'Shush' from the people seated in comfy chairs in the reading areas behind them. This didn't deter Ben or Lisa. However, today would be different.

The steely eyes that were watching them closely belonged to Mrs A. Marquel. She had long dark hair, swirled neatly into a topknot and was dressed in a tailored navy-blue suit, white blouse and a light blue chiffon scarf, which flowed elegantly around her neck.

Ben and Lisa were so engaged in their disagreement that they only became aware of her presence when she spoke. A quiet, authoritative voice locked straight into their ears,

"If you don't lower your voices, you will be shown the path." Her dark eyes glared as she pointed her finger in their direction. Lisa stumbled backwards onto Ben's feet.

"Ow," he cried out and automatically shoved Lisa, who lurched forward and knocked Mrs Marquel off balance. Her neat, fitted clothing left little room for her to remain upright and she knocked several books off the shelves before landing clumsily on the floor.

Lisa and Ben froze for a split second. Mrs Marquel wasn't to be messed with. Ben tugged Lisa's jacket. They had to make a run for it or face her wrath.

They ran through aisles into the computer section, then dodged around a number of display units on the Viking conquests and just avoided a mother and child cleaning up a spilt drink.

Mrs Marquel was now in pursuit. She was unable to take long strides but progressed with short, wooden movements, her elbows tucked into her sides and her lower arms moving swiftly up and down like levers.

Lisa and Ben had managed to make it to the noisy children's section. Adults read books as children listened, others played with pop up books and games. They paid no attention to Lisa and Ben who hid behind a yellow wall with adverts promoting new book signings and special events. They took gulps of air and tried to hold back their laughter, which was almost impossible.

Ben peered around the corner. He saw Mrs Marquel hobble into view, her head working like a corkscrew trying to find them.

"She's heading to the exit," Ben said in dismay. "I thought she would head upstairs to our normal hiding place."

Lisa giggled. "She's stepped outside."

"Let's hide until she calms down."

"In there." Lisa shoved Ben in the direction of the event. He was more than happy to follow her direction.

They entered a dimly lit corridor packed with adults and children. All spoke in lowered voices apart from the few excited squeals. Green lights displayed fire exits. Lisa and Ben weaved swiftly through the crowd, upsetting several individuals as they bumped their way ahead.

They felt a sense of relief as they snuggled into the crowd, their pursuer out of sight.

The movement of the masses started to slow down. Ben jolted as he felt a hand grasp his arm. Horror swept over him as he tore his arm away.

"Don't be scared, it's all part of the experience," said a woman dressed in a white t-shirt and dark dungarees. A box of glasses with clear frames hung by chains in front of her. A tall teenage boy dressed in the same clothing handed out glasses beside her. He wasn't as friendly as the woman.

"You'll get thrown out if you act up," he warned, and placed glasses into Ben's trembling hand. "Don't put them on until instructed."

Ben gripped the glasses and apologised. He moved on quickly to catch up with Lisa.

They entered a cavernous room with a large stage. Dark walls, a domed ceiling dimly lit like the corridor presented a tranquil but eerie feel. In stark contrast, there were red, yellow and orange toadstools for chairs, wooden benches in between some of the toadstools; a distinct smell of grass and undergrowth greeted the crowd. The seating, arranged in semi circles faced the empty stage.

In any other circumstance, Ben wouldn't have anything to do with this type of surroundings. He felt he had grown out of fairy tales a long time ago, but for some reason - perhaps just staying out of reach of Mrs Marquel, this was quite appealing, especially as none of his friends were present. Lisa on the other hand still enjoyed fairy tales although she wanted to be regarded as a grown up.

Everyone filtered into the domed room, most of the adults headed for the benches as children squabbled for toadstools. Lisa was already inside talking to someone.

"A last-minute thing really…" Lisa was coy with her response.

"Last minute, you've got to be kidding. I couldn't wait." Tia was excited, "Look at all these toadstools. I think I'm gonna sit here. Come on."

"My brother is here somewhere. I'll come back when I've found him."

Lisa took her glasses off, placed them in a case in her rucksack then headed to the stream of people entering the room.

"Who's that?" Rafe asked.

"Lisa?" Tia looked up at Rafe to see if he was joking, but his blank look told her otherwise, "From school…?"

"I swear, you only started at my school and you know everyone there."

"Well… it maybe because I don't grunt at everyone and you seniors are always snotty and have no time for the juniors, anyway. Lisa only lives a few streets away." Tia gave Rafe a side glance of disbelief. "Notice I didn't introduce you, saves you wasting a grunt."

Rafe raised an eyebrow amused by Tia's come back.

"Talking's over-rated," he smiled.

The doors of the reading room closed with a slurp. The personnel who had been handing out glasses made their way to the platform and stood central stage, poised to speak as the stragglers finally shared seats. Lisa and Ben settled next to Tia and Rafe.

Silence swept through the cavernous room.

The crowd put their special glasses on as instructed. Soothing music gently resonated from the walls. The dimly lit room turned into a night sky, glistening with stars. Some of the audience tried to reach out and touch the stars. As they did this, the stars would vanish and delicate chiming sounds escape into the room as the stars reappeared. The instructors retreated slowly to the back of the stage until they gradually faded from view.

A little girl began to sing *twinkle, twinkle little star* which was soon muffled by the hand of an embarrassed parent.

"Whoow," Ben gasped, "We're in space."

"No, we're in fairy land." Lisa had forgotten all about being adult-like, and found pleasure once again in fairy stories.

"Oh, forget that. I want to see aliens, dinosaurs and bears, as long as we avoid the monstrous Mrs M...," growled Ben, and lunged towards his sister, imitating the claws of a lion.

"Ben you're scaring me. Stop it."

Tia giggled at Ben's antics. Rafe wasn't too impressed, but as long as Tia was having a good time, he was OK.

The stars faded away and dawn started to break over the stage and across the ceiling. A calm, audible voice narrated the scene.

"Hello one and all. We are going to take a journey to a land not so far away. Everyone there will be happy to meet you, but first, let's meet the animals. Please whisper so as not to frighten them away. If not, they may frighten you. (The voice chuckled at what seemed to be a joke.) *Please enjoy this unique experience."*

Clouds floated into view against a brilliant blue sky. In the middle of the toadstool arches, flowers came up from the ground. Someone reached out to touch a flower but it disappeared just as the stars did previously. Before the audience knew it, they were sitting in a woodland scene with trees, flowers, rabbits, deer and stags in the distance. They could feel a gentle breeze and smell the fragrance of the various flowers. Music floated through the air, complementing the movements of the animals as they appeared. Lowered tones of delight and amazement rose from the audience as they become engrossed in the enchanted environment.

Tia and Lisa were delighted with the animals, but Rafe was impressed with the whole scene change, while Ben anticipated the appearance of a dinosaur.

A magnificent white house, nestled in a hillside, came into view and took prominence. Below it ran fields with people of various hues dressed mainly in denims and loosely fitted tops (some of the women wore long flowing skirts and colourful headscarves), tending to cattle and crops. They smiled and waved at the audience. Most of the audience waved back.

A gathering of dark clouds came into view. Some of the audience became unsettled, wondering if they were really going to experience a downpour. The villagers looked towards the clouds with pleasure, clapped their hands and smiled at each other. This was short-lived when two bear-like beasts came bounding into the field. Their large, furry orange frames shook violently as their heavy paws thumped the ground. They rose up on trunk-like hind legs, their triangular shaped ears rotating like sails on a sea-tossed boat. Bodies now erect, side by side, they extended their white snouts upward and brandished metal jagged teeth. Eerie wails resonated from their jaws. Villagers scattered.

13

Panic descended on the audience.

The music came to an abrupt end. The harrowing wails echoed throughout the space. Flowers shrank and withered - their reduction faster than their appearance. Animals vanished, bird song ceased. Dark clouds spread across the sky. No rain came but a torrent of cold air blasted the room. Damp, musty smells overtook the fragrance of flowers. The room fell into darkness. Members of the audience huddled together. Some ran to the fire exits, tripping over toadstools and people's feet, their frantic bangs on the doors ricocheted around the room but the doors wouldn't open.

The narrator made a hurried announcement above the pandemonium: *"Please remove your glasses now"* – repeating this in a much calmer tone until the crowd began to follow the instruction and settle down.

Soothing music started to play, but there was still an unsettled edge to the proceedings.

The audience adjusted their senses as the room brightened to a blue sky. The voice came again: *"Because you have all been so good and not frightened away any of the animals, children will be given a token to say thank you from the inhabitants of Sanguel. Please be seated until your gifts arrive."*

The audience followed the instruction, although they really wanted to leave as quickly as possible. Except Ben. "Just as it was beginning to get exciting," he said.

"Really? It was frightening," Lisa said.

Rafe put his arm around Tia. "Are you OK?" he asked.

"Yeah, I wonder if the villagers are alright." She looked up at Rafe for the answer. Ben answered instead.

"Course they are. It's like being on the ghost train. It's just a scene, which means those beasty things couldn't have reached any of them. They were huge! Did you see how big they were? Like bears, but enormous. Metal teeth, those paws could have flattened any of us, and...," Ben was so excited he didn't notice the disapproving stares of some of the parents who were still comforting upset children.

Four individuals, along with those who had handed out the glasses, appeared beside the stage. They pulled three wheeled trollies behind them with similar sized presents wrapped in sky blue paper and colourful bows. They handed out gifts to children only and as they did this, they spoke in rhythmic tones:

"*This is your gift, and this is yours and yours. This is your gift, and this is yours and yours.*" Children joined in the repetition. Gifts received, the mood in the room lifted to a happier atmosphere, the abrupt ending forgotten.

Rafe didn't accept a gift. On seeing Rafe's refusal Ben did the same, but the teenage boy forced the gift into his hand. Ben dared not refuse this time. Lisa and Tia held their gifts and beamed at each other, they wanted to open them straight away.

"Open it when you get home. Let's get going," Rafe said and headed towards the exit with the rest of the crowd.

Tia quickly hugged Lisa and hurried after him. As they queued to leave, Mrs Marquel emerged and began to talk to Rafe and Tia. She escorted them to an exit the gift givers had gone through. On seeing this, Lisa and Ben hurried in the opposite direction, but couldn't dive through the crowd as they had done before. They had to queue like everyone else. As they approached the exit, they came face to face with a stern-faced Mrs A. Marquel.

She now wore several layers of orange, loose fitting clothing, but her blue chiffon scarf remained. Once she placed her hands on her, now ample, hips she blocked a considerable part of the exit. The children couldn't believe the increase in her size.

"And where do you think you're going?" she asked in a

voice filled with trickery and delight. This sent a shiver down their spines. It was clear to them they needed more than their normal skills to get away this time.

Chapter 2

It's all in a name

Ben's voice echoed in the now empty room, "We're going home!"

"That's what you think," said Mrs Marquel with a menacing grin.

"Please let us go home," Lisa begged.

"Not until you do something for me." She smiled, a much softer smile, but still with a hint of menace. "And now that you have one of my gifts, there is only one answer."

"Have it back." Ben threw the box at her feet.

Lisa was reluctant to do the same. She wanted her gift, so she asked, "What do you want us to do?"

Ben elbowed Lisa. She glared back at him holding her gift tightly.

"What about you Ben?"

"What?" He was still determined to get away.

"Don't play games. Would you like to do something for me?"

18

Ben felt like saying all sorts of things, things that didn't match what Mrs Marquel would have thought respectable.

Lisa looked at Ben. She leaned in and whispered, "We can say yes, but not mean it." She smiled weakly back at Mrs Marquel, who watched them keenly.

Ben shielded his mouth from Mrs Marquel's stare. "Let's push her over. Make a run for it."
Before Lisa could respond, Ben yelled, "Run!" He stormed forward, arms out in full thrust to push Mrs Marquel backwards. Instead, he fell forward and stumbled over his feet. The woman seemed to pre-empt what he was going to do and stepped to one side, which allowed Lisa to get past her.

Ben caught sight of Lisa dashing to the exit. This prompted him to jump up and sprint out of the room.

They ran down the corridor. Lisa clutched her gift and Ben begged under his breath for the exit doors to appear. To their dismay, as they approached what they thought was the exit, they re-entered the room they had previously come from.

Instinctively, they both turned, and ran back down the corridor, thinking they had missed the exit. The same thing happened again. They were back in the same room and this time gasping for breath. Ben put his hands across his

19

eyes to see whether he had really taken off the glasses. He had. He slumped to the floor next to a toadstool, feeling exhausted and sick.

Lisa fell next to him. Her rucksack felt like it weighed a ton. Her voice quivered, "This....is...a nightmare." She inhaled deeply.

Ben said nothing; he was trying to get enough air into his lungs to attempt the corridor again. He stood up as his legs gained strength and scanned the room quickly, "Come on. She's gone, let's go."

"This isn't fun. I don't think I can run anymore," Lisa groaned.

"Fun! At what point was any of this fun. It's all your fault we're in this mess! If you hadn't made her mad - in that silly adult section...," Ben tailed off, as Lisa got angry with him.

"My fault? You tried to push her over.... You made her angry.... You always make her angry."

As they continued to argue, a tree silently grew amongst the toadstools behind them. Its roots and branches protruded into the room. The roots had twisted out of the ground and spread themselves greedily across the surface of the floor, and then vanished back into the ground. The trunk had unusual blue shimmering leaves.

The branches stretched up into the ceiling and beyond. A few of the branches were hanging over Ben and Lisa's head.

The size of the tree had altered the shape and appearance of the room, it had transformed into an outside space. The smell of soil and undergrowth grew as birdsong and a gentle breeze played with the leaves of the tree. A bright sky emerged in the distance.

"Me?" Ben snapped back.

Lisa was now on her feet, staring right at Ben. "You take me to the library, because Mom thinks that you're so responsible. A responsible idiot!"

"When we get home, I'll tell Mom you said she's an idiot."

"You," she poked with her forefinger at the space around his chest, "not Mom. You - you're the idiot."

"STOP IT!" Mrs Marquel's sharp voice seized their attention.

They spun around expecting to see her but instead were shocked as their eyes encountered the tree. Confused and still not sure where the voice came from, Ben took a few tentative steps towards the tree. Lisa closed in tightly beside him, still clutching the now crumpled gift box.

21

"Where are you going?" she whispered.

"Trying to get out of here."

"Let's go the other way."

"The only exit was there." He nodded in the direction of the tree.

"Really?"

"Yes, silly."

"I'm not silly. Idiot."

"Still arguing?" the voice sang. "Will you ever learn?"

Ben stood still and tried not to let his voice sound scared but more enquiring. "Mrs.... Mrs ... Mac?"

"Yes, it is me."

Lisa clutched at Ben's arm and asked, "Is she the tree?"

"It gets worse by the minute," he mumbled.

"I'm not the tree," she said. "Come closer."

They couldn't stop themselves. Her melodic tones drew them closer. Eventually, they saw a hollow in the middle of the tree trunk. In it was a small, seated figure. They both stopped in bewilderment as they recognised the figure - a miniature-sized Mrs Marquel.

"Did... did...Ben do that to you? Squash you to that size?"

Ben wasn't impressed. It was typical of Lisa to want to get him into even more trouble. Mrs Marquel laughed - a loud hearty laugh that didn't belong to her now-tiny frame. She shook her head in amusement, waved her right hand as though she was shooing a fly away and stood up. The scarf draped around her shoulders cascaded to the floor of the hollow; it shimmered, shades of blue like the leaves against the dark bark. Her garments flowed naturally around her. She looked quite regal, until her unkempt hair came into full view.

"I'm not as young as I used to be. Why run after you when I know the outcome? In my younger days, I would have run you ragged, and not be out of breath. It would be a matter of fun for me," she chortled, as some of her memories became vivid.

Ben believed he could beat anyone in a race, Mrs Marquel included, and now that she was so small, he thought he would take advantage of this. He spoke boldly. "If I grabbed you and threatened to squash you, would you let us go?"

"No, you wouldn't. And no, you cannot," she announced, as if it were a suggestion that was unheard of. "Enter if you dare! And you did." She placed her hands on her hips. "You cannot leave here until you complete what you HAVE to do. It would have been easier if you two were not so, so cantankerous."

"What?" they both asked.

"Argumentative!"

"We're not," Lisa said indignantly, now that she understood what cantankerous meant, "Ben likes to say the opposite to what I say. And I didn't want to enter..."

Ben was about to plead his innocence, but Mrs Marquel interrupted abruptly.

"Stop, there you go again."

They fell silent.

Mrs Marquel adjusted her shawl so that the ends dangled out of the hollow. She mumbled to herself as she did so. This appeared to keep their attention for a little while.

"Now," she said with a crumpled smile, "to the matter at hand." Mrs Marquel may have been small, but her presence was still quite imposing.

"Don't be afraid, you both have a lot of courage, if you put aside the bickering."

Ben and Lisa were taken aback to be given a compliment.

"Lisa, I see you still have your gift, although the box looks a bit worn." She furrowed her brow.

Lisa looked at the gift box in her hands. She felt embarrassed and fumbled, trying to put the ripped pieces back in place. Mrs Marquel ignored this and gave Lisa instructions on how to open it. Ben realised that the gift held some kind of importance; he scanned the area for his box.

Lisa eventually opened her box and found inside a blue and purple striped pocket-sized book with an outline of a gemstone in gold on the cover.

"Take the book out carefully. There is something precious embedded there." Then she addressed Ben. "Forget looking for your box. You..." she threw her hands in the air, "unceremoniously flung yours to the ground. So, nothing for you at this point. You will have to prove yourself later." She wagged her finger at him with a mischievous grin. Ben looked away disgruntled.

Lisa gazed at the cover and read the title aloud. "The Kingdom of Sanguel by Arabella M. What is this book about?"

Mrs Marquel grinned.

"It is a story that will guide you. A book more suited for your age group."

Ben felt pleased that he wasn't the one receiving the sharp edge of Mrs Marquel's tongue.

"What does the M stand for?" Lisa asked, tracing her finger over the bold lettering on the small book.

25

"Menacing." Ben mumbled quite uninterested. Mrs Marquel ignored him because Lisa yelled and looked up at her.

"Arabella Marquel. You're Arabella Marquel." She stared at the book, and then at the little woman in the tree, who by now was laughing and jumping up and down. "Yes, yes, that will do for now." She almost tangled herself in her shawl.

Ben couldn't work this spectacle out. An imp-like woman, jumping up and down in the hollow of a tree - his sister forgetting that they needed to get away from this mad woman. Instead, she was marvelling at this name on a book! He was definitely confused now and irritated.

"Who cares? Arabella, Clarabella, Rockerfella - snot!"

Immediately the mood changed and Mrs Marquel stopped jumping and laughing. She extended her neck towards Ben, as far as it could supernaturally go (as though a giraffe had taken over her body). Her face enlarged beyond its normal size, so that it was a couple of inches away from Ben's face. Both children wanted to run, if this were possible, but the sheer terror that gripped them glued their feet firmly to the ground.

Mrs Marquel opened her mouth in slow motion and her voice followed suit,

"I c...a... r...e and y...o...u WILL c...a...r...e!" As soon as she released the last word, her head slowly began to reduce in size. Her neck retracted until it was back on her miniature body. Her garments floated lightly with the gentle breeze.

This announcement whirled in the air for a while. It had a trance like quality and they were now ready to listen to what Mrs Marquel had to say.

"Let's start again. Forget the nonsense of the past and concentrate on now." She took on the regal, commanding tone again. "My name is Arabella, and you will refer to me from now on as Arabella. If you refer to me as Mrs M, Mrs Marquel or even Mrs Mac...," she stared directly at Ben and then Lisa, "I cannot assist you. The name Arabella MUST be used." She shuffled forward as if to tell them a secret,

"My name means to oblige, or the obliging one." She smiled proudly and stroked her shawl. The colours shimmered. "I am here to help you progress." She paused, deep in thought, and then continued. "Though heavens knows why you two argumentative beings were chosen to complete this task."

Another short silence.

27

"After which, you can go home and not until then." She turned around and picked up her miniature version of the book.

"Lisa turn to the back of your book." Arabella used her book to illustrate what Lisa needed to do. "Peel the last cover over like this."

Lisa held the book carefully in front of her with her left hand, peeled back the last page with her right-hand thumb and index finger. In the inset of the book was a small silver key. Lisa lifted it out and held it in her hand not sure what to do with it.

"You must get to the crossroads and use the key. The book has the details of all you need to know. Now go quickly. Tia and Rafe will be waiting for you."

"But where are we going?" Ben asked tentatively, not wanting to upset Arabella and scared that they would never see their home again.

"Do as I say and then you will return home..." Arabella informed them that they had to journey to the kingdom of Sanguel.

Lisa and Ben were a lot happier knowing they had two other people to travel with them. They were not certain of all the details, because Arabella would sometimes speak in riddles and not give them all the answers to their questions. Arabella made sure she impressed upon them three important points. Firstly, to keep the book safe, as this was their ultimate guide. Secondly, meet the others at the crossroads. Thirdly, work together and only then they could return home.

Arabella stepped backwards deep into the hollow. When they thought she had disappeared her voice trailed, sternly.

"Call me. You will find me. Stay on the path. Stay on the path." Twigs and shimmering blue leaves that covered the tree hollow eventually changed to green.

Ben took a deep breath, and looked out on the woodland area with radiant blue skies.

"Let's get going. The others are waiting."

Lisa was surprised at Ben's new attitude. "You sound happy."

"With Mrs M gone, the quicker we do this the quicker we get home."

Lisa agreed with that. She packed her scruffy box into her rucksack, put her glasses on and walked slowly as she flipped through the book.

Ben was in a hurry. "Come on, keep up."

Instead of following the path Arabella had pointed out to them, they veered off onto an adjacent dirt track.

Chapter 3

The Journey

Rafe and Tia were already on their way to the crossroads. They were on a grey cobbled path. It stood out from the dirt tracks that crossed it at various intervals. They were trying to make sense of what Arabella had told them.

"All I asked was what time will we get home and she said, '*What's a second when you have hours? What's a minute when you have days*?' I really didn't understand what she meant."

"That's Mrs Mac," Tia said, "she hardly ever gives a straight answer and she does things out of the ordinary. Once when our class was in the reading room, waiting for the storyteller to arrive, she told us a story. It was so good. She did voices and everything. We were disappointed when the storyteller arrived - but guess what - the storyteller had been waiting outside the whole time. Mrs Mac didn't even apologise. She looked at the time and said, '*If only I had more time,*' you know, in that strange voice, just like the narrator today." Tia mimicked Mrs Marquel's voice. "Her voice is so different when she's Arabella."

"I think she was the narrator."

"I think so too...," Tia paused for a moment, deep in thought.

Rafe waited for her to share her thoughts.

"This is weird. One minute we're in the library, next minute here - wherever 'here' is." Tia viewed the sparse woods and beautiful weather.

"I don't really know how I agreed to this."

"Did we have a choice?" Tia asked, knowing the answer.

Rafe gave his take on it. "Not really, no other options. It's a bit like my dad saying you can either wash up or dry up. Well, if you don't want to do either, there's no real choice. It becomes a responsibility or you're drawn into it." He shoved his hands in his jacket pockets.

"That's what makes it scarish. We have to do something we don't really understand..."

Rafe started laughing. "Tia. Scarish? Really."

"Yep. It's like being a bit scared but not totally scared, a bit exciting."

Rafe shook his head. Tia smiled, extremely pleased with her word. Then a sense of foreboding engulfed her. "What if we don't get back?"

Rafe tried to be positive. Although he had some reservations, he didn't want them to show. "We'll be fine. Nothing can go wrong. We'll look out for each other."

"But what if... if it all goes wrong?"

"Remember, if we need help we call Arabella."

"Ray, I'm not a baby any more. Tell me the truth. What do you really think?"

Rafe stopped walking and turned his cousin towards him. He looked at her so she knew she had his full attention. "I really don't know. I felt a bit nervous at first, but what I do know is that I'll make sure you're alright."

"I know you will, but..." She felt tears prick at her eyes. She did everything to try to hold them back.

"But what?"

"I thought my mom and dad would always be with me. They're not here. That went wrong."

"Are you feeling a lot scarish now?" he asked. Tia produced a weak smile. She appreciated his attempt at the use of her word.

"Kind of," she shrugged.

"Remember, your dad will be back, he works away that's all." His voice was gentle. "We can't bring your mom back. But, she would want the best for you." He hugged her and she gripped him tightly permitting a few tears to flow. Tia didn't want her cousin to think she was going to be a burden to him on this journey.

Rafe's parents had told him they needed to allow Tia time to grieve for her mother. Her father leaving to work in another country would also prompt more fears and feelings that she may not be able to deal with all at once. Most of all, they needed to give her the time to express how she felt.

They stood quietly. Tia held on to Rafe. The birds continued to sing, a light wind tickled the leaves on the trees.

Then Tia released him.

"I'm fine now. Really. The feeling came and now it's gone." She turned away from him and wiped her tears. Rafe smiled a warm, *'you'll-be-okay'* smile. Deep down he hoped she would be fine. Now he needed to give her something to take her mind off it,

"Did that book indicate where the crossroads is?"

Tia pulled the book out of her waist bag. "I don't think it does." She flipped through the pages.

33

"Check the map."

"The map doesn't say how many metres. It shows the crossroads with yellow shading around it, some trees, a black and white pole, like a pelican crossing post - it has a yellow top."

"I suppose we need to look for those markers then."

Tia started to feel a little more cheerful. "Let's jog it. It'll be quicker."

"Wait a minute." Rafe took off his jacket. Tia put the book away and patted her waist bag. She took her jacket off, tied it around her waist and wiped her brow, with the bottom of her t-shirt as Rafe had done. They both laughed.

"Do you think the others have made it to the crossroads yet?" Rafe asked,

Tia chuckled. "I doubt it. Lisa said they argue all the time – so, they're probably arguing right now."

Rafe shook his head, "No way. Arguing shouldn't stop you from walking?"

"Oh yes it can," Tia giggled.

*

Lisa had taken off her jacket and placed it in her rucksack. Ben had finally convinced Lisa to put his jacket in too and, of course, an argument developed because

34

Ben had left his rucksack behind in the library. Ben wasn't happy that Lisa had the book which contained the information they needed.

"Give me a look."

"No. I've looked at it and we need to follow the path until we get to a crossroads with yellow grass," Lisa said, promptly, not knowing if it was grass, sand or a yellow blob on the map. What she did know was that Ben wasn't going to have the book because he always had some type of accident with them. (Their mom had to pay several fines over the years for Ben's lack of care of the library's property.)

"How do you know what's in the book? We spent most of the time listening to Mrs Mac."

"Arabella. Stupid!"

"Arabella when we need her. Yeah, she is obliging," said Ben, sarcastically. "Obliging when she scowls at us. Obliging when she puts the books back that I want to read, obliging when she hushes and shushes."

Lisa joined in. "She's truly obliging!"

They both laughed for a while.

Ben decided to take advantage of the good mood he believed he had built. "She told us to follow the path." He turned to Lisa. "Are we on the right path? Does the book show where we are?"

"That's for me to know and you to find out." She patted the book in her hand smugly.

"Look Lisa, you're too young to be making decisions for us. I'm the eldest and I have a better grasp of things than you do. Let me see. You're just holding it." He tried to pull the book away, but Lisa anticipated this, moved it out of his reach and ran ahead.

"You better make sure you're right, 'cos if you're wrong when we meet the others, Tia and Raff I'll tell them you're dumb, and WE'LL complete the task without YOU."

Lisa put her glasses away.

"Who cares? You still have to follow me. And it's Rafe you nitwit." She waved the book at him and laughed with glee. "Come on, to the crossroads." With that, she ran on ahead, looking over her shoulder to see Ben jogging behind.

Ben knew he could catch up with Lisa. He was a good sprinter. He didn't like the idea of Lisa being in control of anything because she often made a mess of things. Not that he was much better, but he didn't like being the one without the method of control. He began to work out how he was going to get the book.

*

It didn't take Rafe and Tia long to reach the crossroads. At first, the yellow soil added splashes of colour to the brown and green vegetation. The tell-tale signs of the grey cobbles kept them on track as they weaved between the trees.

Eventually they found an area that was completely yellow. Tia thought it looked like a beach. They came to a clearing shaded by two giant oak trees. They were grateful for the shade, stopping for a brief moment to admire the sheer size and impressive nature of the trees. The yellow soil had taken full advantage of this area. The cobbles had disappeared.

"Are we in the right place?"

"I can't see the crossroads. But the book indicates that this is the place; the tree, the soil looks like mustard sand." Rafe mused, "The post must be somewhere."

Rafe and Tia were startled to see the soil start to bounce, as though it were on a pulsating drum skin. A low hum filled the air. Disbelief and fear took over as they felt the vibration creep up their legs, taking over their bodies and shaking them like rag dolls. To run would be impossible. Rafe and Tia eventually took surfer positions to keep their balance. The yellow soil moved together into small mounds, revealing a stony crossroad.

The tremor ceased.

"I'm glad that's over," Tia said.

Rafe pointed to a bulging mound of soil at the centre of the intersection. "I don't think so."

"It looks like a balloon being…"

"Come over here Tia, don't get too close. You don't know what it's going to do."

The bulging area rumbled low in the ground. A small opening spat out soil. Rafe grabbed hold of Tia. The mound grew larger. They took a few steps backwards. The rumble gushed loudly into the air. They covered their ears. The bulge exploded; showering clumps of soil as two thick tree roots emerged, intertwined and shot upwards. Tia and Rafe, their ears covered, clamped their eyes shut to avoid the shooting debris. Rafe hunched over Tia. Tia, glad for the protection, nestled under Rafe's arm. A strong wind spun and howled through the air about them looking for a place to rest. Tia and Rafe prayed for it to stop.

*

"Are you sure you know where we're going? I think we should have met the others by now," Ben said. "Look, there are signs of a road over there." He pointed to a path that had grey cobbles. Willow trees bowed gracefully along its way.

"Should we be over there?"

"Ermm?" Lisa shrugged, and looked completely confused.

"You mean you don't know?" Ben remarked sarcastically.

"Let me think..."

"That'll be a first."

Lisa ignored him, trying her best not to show her uncertainty, but Ben knew he had unsettled her enough for her to doubt where they were. He stopped walking and pointed to another area behind some trees,

"That looks like another path. This could be the crossroads."

Lisa turned her back towards him and started leafing through the book, but in her panic, she kept missing the page with the map. Ben was eyeing her every move, although he was trying to show he was uninterested.

"What does it say?"

He inched towards her.

"I'm... well the book looks different. I can't find the page..."

Ben tried to peer over Lisa's shoulder. "Let's have a look,"

Lisa blocked his view as best as she could, her back and elbows nudging him out of the way, as he moved left and right behind her.

"Just rip the book in half," Ben suggested.

"No. Why?"

"Because we can both have a part and share the task equally."

Lisa didn't like the idea of ripping the book, but she had become confused about where their position was on the map. She knew Ben would be good at map reading (although she didn't want to admit this), but to share half of the responsibility sounded like a good idea.

"Ok. Sounds fair, you take the map."

"Just the map?"

"Yes."

"OK." Ben still wanted the whole book in his grasp.

It was the first time they had both agreed on such a major decision. Lisa eventually found the double pages that had the map. Ben held onto the pages and Lisa held onto the book – they pulled. The pages didn't budge.

"I thought you were strong?" Lisa sneered

"You're not gripping it properly!" Ben tried to yank the book away.

"No. Just pull."

The pages began to feel like butter in their hands. A strong gust of wind threw Lisa and Ben to the ground. The book, still open, took to the air like a bird in flight, releasing pages as it flew.

*

Tia and Rafe slowly opened their eyes once the commotion had ceased.

Tia peeked out from under Rafe's arm. In front of them stood a twenty-foot wooden pole (it really looked like a tree stripped bare of its branches and leaves), it was fourteen inches thick, grainy, with small, wiry nodules. It stood firm in the ground as though it had been there for years. A steady wind started to gather pace.

"What is this?" Tia asked, not expecting Rafe to know the answer. She began to step towards it.

"Hold on Tia, something else is happening."

The yellow soil around them shot towards the pole. Rafe grabbed Tia and once again arched over her to protect her as much as he could from the pellets. The wind roared about them. They shielded their faces as the wind swept the soil into a swirling sea of yellow mush. The soil bound together in streams of clay, and rushed up the exposed tree roots eagerly. Once covered, the rest of the soil dispersed into the air, the wind subsided and the soil rained lightly to the ground.

Rafe released Tia and they both stared in astonishment at the structure.

"This is amazing!" he gasped. "Wow. Mrs M said it may be a little unsettled when we got here, but I didn't expect this."

The yellow soil had created a perfect cylinder around the rooted structure. It was now a bright yellow post.

"Wondermush."

Rafe laughed, "I suppose that's wonderful."

Tia nodded not taking her eyes off the shining pole. "The post in the book had black and white stripes, like a pelican crossing."

"I hope we won't be attacked by black and white paint," Rafe said jovially, and gave a quick glance around, hoping it wasn't really going to happen.

"It's happening." Tia pointed to the middle of the post.

Black paint oozed from inside of the post creating a black ringed section, then a white section, replicating up the post. This was a more pleasant affair and a lot less boisterous, apart from an annoying hiss as each section was completed. A metallic smell lingered in the air.

Tia took out the book, thumbed through the pages until she got to the section she was looking for, "The bottom and top section will remain yellow."

"Will we be able to approach?" Rafe enquired. When Tia started to giggle, he thought the metallic smell had gone to her head.

"What's so funny?"

She eventually pointed to his hair, but Rafe thought she was pointing to something behind him. Still mystified, he waited for her to calm down from her full-on laughter.

"Ray, Ray, I'm gonna call you Mega Dandruff man."

"What?"

"Your hair, it's got so much yellow stuff in it."

Rafe brushed over his hair, and some of the yellow soil fell out. He still didn't understand why Tia found it so amusing until he shook his head. The soil flew out in all directions. Tia took a few steps towards the post.

"OK, D man, you need to shake a bit harder to get the rest out."

43

Rafe did so, but couldn't see any more falling soil.

"Has it all gone?"

"No not yet. Just a bit more at the back," she smirked. "Close your eyes Ray, so the last bit doesn't hurt your eyes. Shake to the left, then the right, now forwards."

She couldn't see any more soil in his hair, but she found his actions hilarious. She left Rafe head banging and ran towards the post. Rafe heard Tia's swift exit by the crunching of the grainy soil under foot, and knew he'd been had.

"Ha, ha, very funny, little Miss T."

Tia was in good spirits, smiled sweetly and waved. It had been a long time since she had played a prank on Rafe. He always got the better of her. Now that she was living with her cousin, it was easier for her to understand how to prank him back. Rafe was impressed with Tia's new found skills and now knew he had to raise his pranking game.

Rafe joined Tia at the post. Tia was examining it. It was cool and smooth to touch.

"Look. It's solid." She leaned against it.

A number of small key holes drew Rafe's attention. He noticed there was one in each of the black and white sections.

"I get it," he said, as though he had previously had a conversation with Tia about the key holes. "She said the key should be used at the crossroads."

Tia didn't have to hear anymore. Excited and slightly nervous, she unzipped her waist bag and searched between tissues, clear lip balm, hair bands and a small nail kit, amongst other items. Rafe always marvelled at how so many items squeezed into that small space.

"Here goes," Tia said, as she pulled the silver key out. It didn't fit the slot. She tried another; the key went in and she giggled with expectancy, but it wouldn't turn. Her fingers slipped off the key.

"Tia. Take your time. And try not to force the turning." Tia wiped her fingers on her t-shirt. "That's really easy for you to say." She tried again. This time it opened. "Yeah. Fanthabulouso!" She jumped up and down. Rafe congratulated her.

Tia peered inside the small compartment and caught a glimpse of something shining on the inside. She reached inside fearlessly. Gliding past other items, her fingers carefully pulled out a chain.

"Look at this, it's just fanthabulouso." The silver chain had a pendant on it; it was the shape of a droplet of water, the outer shape midnight blue and the inner section glittered with encrusted diamonds.

"It's the shape of the pendant on the front of the book." Tia balanced the pendant on the cover. Sure enough, it was the same shape. She held it out to Rafe, "Clip it on for me."

Once the pendant was around her neck, it automatically clipped securely together and took on new life as the colours bounced in the sunlight.

"Whoow this is beautiful. It makes me feel a bit strange, a bit tingly. Great!"

Rafe took this as his cue to open his section. He zipped his key out of his inner jacket pocket (this was awkward to do as he still had his jacket tied around his waist.) Tia hurried him on, she was excited to see what Rafe would find, although she hadn't completely removed everything from her compartment.

Rafe found his chamber on the second go.

"Yours opened so easily."

"I took my time." He smiled smugly. "Or, I was fortunate – you know what they say, 'fortune favours the brave'."

Tia rolled her eyes. "Hurry up. I want to know what you've got."

"You're so impatient, Tia!"

Tia tiptoed and strained her neck to see into Rafe's chamber but it was no good. Rafe looked down at Tia with his hand still in the chamber. He could see her eagerness. He looked back in the chamber and then slowly started to grimace and panic.

"Some-things- got- me!" he yelled.

Tia screamed, "Pull your hand out!" She dropped the book, got her hands around his waist and pulled hard. They both fell to the ground. Rafe howled with laughter, Tia was not amused. She slapped him on the shoulder as she stood up.

"Your face...," he laughed. "It was really worth it."

Tia ignored him.

"Don't be upset; take what you dish out." He got up and dusted himself off.

"Alright, you got me. But I really thought something had your hand."

"Tia, if that were true, you'd know about it. I'd scream so hard and loud you'd think I'm Auntie Sandra with a spider in her sight!"

Tia started laughing as she pictured the scene.

"Come on. Let's see what I've got." The chamber was deeper than Rafe had expected. He pulled out an empty lightweight rucksack. It was black with a main zip and two smaller side zips.

"A container with ice cold water." He took a satisfying gulp, placing the container on top of the rucksack lying on the ground. "A torch, a pendant - the shape's different to yours, a book like yours." He shoved the book in his back pocket. "Another torch…, I think." He examined the item.

Tia had read something in the book about the pendant and she wanted to try it out, she pressed her forefinger against the pendant. Immediately, she disappeared.

"Tia. Tia!" Rafe yelled frantically.

Tia giggled.

"Where are you?"

"Right here."

Rafe felt a tug at his waist and he jumped sideways.

"Put your pendant on."

Rafe scrambled for his silver pendant. It was rectangular with two curved edges. Blue and white crystals covered the water droplet shape engraved within the pendant. He put it around his neck and the clasps sprung together. "I can't see you," he said, anxiously.

"Wait a minute. Now who's being impatient?"

"I'm not being impatient, this is just so weird."

Then Tia reappeared beside him with a bright yellow glow around her.

"Are you alright? You look a bit hazy."

"It makes us invisible," Tia yelled with joy. "I'm still invisible until I press this again."

"But I can see you. You're not invisible."

"It's a cloaking device - I read it in the book. I have the invisibility glow that only someone wearing the device can see."

"So, I'm invisible too?"

"No, Einstein, not until you press your pendant."

"Less of the Albert jokes, madam."

"If you press yours, you'll vanish too; then I'll be able to see your haze."

"How long can we stay like that?"

"One press invisible, twice visible again. Isn't it great?" Tia pressed her pendant repeatedly. "Now you see me... now you don't"

Rafe pulled his book out. He didn't intend to press the pendant until he knew how it worked and what it might do to him. He turned to the page that had a list of do's and don'ts. As he started to read, the words began to fade.

Chapter 4

Ben

Lisa and Ben sprang to their feet and tried to grab at the floating pages. They jumped repeatedly, grabbing the air above them as the pages, just out of their reach, danced in the air. The book had been ushered into a tree quite a distance away from where they were. After a few minutes of jumping, they were both out of breath. They watched dumb-founded as the pages gently glided to the floor and scattered about them.

"Can you believe it? All the jumping and grabbing and they landed with no help from us," Lisa moaned. "And the book landed in that tree over there."
Ben eyed the situation - the book versus gathering the pages.

"Well," said Ben with a wicked grin, "we need to get it down." He knew Lisa didn't like climbing trees.

"WE? - How do you suggest WE do that?"

"Well, Miss Sherlock. WE need to climb."

"It's not funny Ben. At school, Mrs Poole shouts too much when we do that obstacle course. She doesn't make it fun and then when we really want to go fast she says, '*slow down someone is going to get hurt.*' No one's going to get hurt." She viewed the tree.

"That story has nothing to do with climbing the tree," Ben laughed. He was going to take full advantage of the situation. "It's important when climbing to avoid spider webs. That tree looks quite big. It may have some enormous spiders in there."

It was working.

"Let's pick up these pages first." Lisa began to pick up the pages, and was astonished to find that they only had writing on one side. She tried to show Ben her discovery, but he had already made a dash for the tree. Lisa felt some relief she didn't have to battle with Ben to climb the tree, and if it meant Ben got the book down at this point, that was fine by her.

The tree was a great height. The nodules and crevices at its lower trunk made it ideal to get a good foothold for a climber. The branches spread out like arms displaying its fine growth and its dense leaves.

51

Ben was enjoying the distance he had put between himself and Lisa. He had noted where the book was in the upper region and advanced quickly.

Lisa now stood at the base of the tree. She placed her rucksack on the ground and put the pages she had collected in her jeans pocket. She actually admired Ben's progress, but wasn't going to let him know and she didn't want to get her hands or clothes dirty just in case she got into trouble when she got home.

Lisa scanned the area and realised she was standing on a track that went as far as the eye could see from the north to the south. She wondered if they were close to the crossroads. She hoped the book held those pages. As puzzling as she found the map reading, she had made up her mind to retrieve the book when Ben came down. She would annoy him until he gave in. That normally worked, even with her parents. However, in an instant, she changed her mind. She saw something coming from the north. She couldn't quite work out what it was, but it had a large plume of dust around it. It had the appearance of something metallic, but then again, it looked like a herd of charging horses. The strange thing was she couldn't hear anything. It was like watching a film with the volume turned down. She decided she wasn't going to be on the ground as the *thing* approached. It would be better to look at it from above than face-to-face.

Lisa leaped around the tree to one of the bowed branches and scrambled upwards. She grabbed onto any branch or surface that looked like it would hold her and moved along as quickly as possible. This wasn't as easy as she had thought, and a couple of times her feet and hands failed to reach their intended target. Her fear propelled her upwards.

Ben, in the meantime, was glad to see the book in his eye line. The last time he had looked down, Lisa stood at the bottom of the tree. To his surprise, he heard the crunching of branches coming up the tree at speed. He could hear her voice but wasn't sure what she was saying because she was breathing so heavily.

He was quite impressed that a reluctant climber could gain so much ground to challenge for the book. However, he had the prize firmly in his sight.

He extended his arm and grabbed the book from the branch. He quickly tucked it into his back pocket and decided to descend as quickly as he could just to teach Lisa a lesson. He would laugh at her when he was on the ground and she was stuck in the tree.

53

Lisa was on the opposite side of the tree to Ben. As they drew parallel to each other, pointing downwards, Lisa attempted to alert Ben. "Som – thin - comin."

Ben couldn't understand what she was saying. All he knew was that he wasn't about to be beaten by her, or tricked into handing over the book. He descended rapidly by missing a couple of branches at a time, arms and legs moving in synchronised motion. He had done this a number of times with friends when racing each other around tricky Xplorers camps. He was pleased with his expert descent.

Lisa's face filled with horror as Ben looked upward towards her. Mistaking this for Lisa being irritated because he had outwitted her, Ben began to laugh. "Catch me if you can," he chanted. Losing his concentration, his hands slipped, forcing his legs out of harmony with the rest of his body. The branches and twigs parted company with his feet and hands, plunging him into an uncontrolled descent. His laughter turned to a howl for help. He was falling into the path of the on-coming, silent, dust-spurting contraption.

As it arrived beneath him, the roof snapped opened. Ben fell in.

He and the contraption were gone in an instant.

Chapter 5

Change of Plan

Rafe and Tia heard a deafening cry. They shoved all the items in their rucksacks and sprinted towards the shouts.

Lisa had fortunately clung to a branch in front of her as dust and warm air engulfed her. She coughed and squinted as the dust subsided. Tears automatically washed her eyes. She rubbed her eyes free of dirt and peered down at the spot where Ben should have landed. There was no sign of him.

Lisa lowered herself to the branch below. She straddled it and pushed her back against the main trunk of the tree to feel safe and view the ground beneath.

"Ben," Lisa yelled desperately. "Ben." She anticipated that perhaps he had rolled out of view. She wandered if he was playing a trick on her and the *'thing'* hadn't passed by. She wiped her hands on her blue top, disliking the smudge it left behind.

55

"Ben, stop playing around," she shouted. Her voice swam out into the air only to receive a reply from the birds. Whatever she saw surely must have taken him? Swallowed him? Eaten him whole?

Lisa felt that Ben could be a right pain but she didn't want anything awful to happen to him. Now she was all alone in a place she didn't want to be. All she wanted to do was go home.

She brushed away her tears and thought about what Arabella had said - *'Keep the book safe. Meet the others at the crossroads. Work together.'* This all seemed impossible to achieve now.

"I can't see anyone," Tia said.

"I know, but I'm certain the shouts came from over here."

They ran across the dirt track.

"Look, there's something under that tree."

"It looks like Lisa's bag. LISA…," Tia called.

Lisa immediately recognised Tia's voice and was overjoyed.

"Tia. Tia. I'm here." Lisa swung her legs over the branch to face the direction where she heard Tia's voice, but only saw Rafe. She smiled at him, gave a frantic wave and began to climb down the tree. She pushed leaves and twigs out of her way, and a couple of times she almost missed her footing, but composed herself and continued.

"Are you alright?" Rafe asked.

Lisa jumped off the last branch. She tried to make it look effortless, but stumbled to the ground as her heel caught the edge of a protruding root. Her pale face flushed with embarrassment. Rafe went to her rescue. Tia giggled at Lisa's not-so-flattering-descent.

"And what's so funny?" Lisa said, indignantly. She looked around for Tia and was puzzled that she couldn't see her. Therefore, she assumed Tia was hiding behind the tree.

"Come out Tia."

"She's right there." Rafe nodded his head in Tia's direction, forgetting that Tia was still only visible to his eyes. Lisa looked. When she didn't see Tia, she turned to Rafe, one hand on her hip. "This isn't funny."

Rafe held his hands up as though surrendering, "We came to see if someone was in danger. We heard a cry for help!"

Lisa felt close to tears again, but managed to hold them at bay. "It was Ben."

"What?" Tia and Rafe said in unison.

"What happened?" Rafe asked.

57

"It was so quick. I don't know who it was or what it was."

"Oh Lisa - that's terrible," Tia said and put her arm around Lisa's shoulders. Lisa screamed and lashed out at whatever it was that had touched her and jumped towards Rafe.

"Something touched me!"

"Owch," Tia yelled as she hit the ground. "I must still be invisible."

"Invisible? Tia?" Lisa was confused.

"It's OK," Rafe said, patting Lisa on her shoulder as she clung to him. "Tia has a necklace on that makes her invisible." As Rafe said this, Tia appeared. Lisa almost jumped up into the tree with fright.

"It's this." Tia proudly displayed her pendant. Lisa moved in to take a closer look. Rafe breathed out in relief as Lisa released him.

"Wow, that's beautiful. Look at the colours. It's like a freshwater pool – if I could I'd jump in."

"Well, when you press it, it makes you invisible," Tia said, excitedly, "although it didn't respond to my double click."

"You've been playing with it too much," Rafe scoffed.

Tia ignored him. "It's called a cloaking device – like in the book."

58

"The book?"

"Yes, the one from Mrs M, I mean, Mrs Marquel. Didn't you get one?" Rafe asked. He thought Lisa might still be in a state of shock following Ben's disappearance and Tia's invisibility act.

"I know who you mean. I haven't got it. Ben has it." The moment she said it, she wasn't sure how to explain the situation to the others. She didn't want Rafe to know how childish they'd been.

"So, what happened to Ben?" Rafe coaxed.

Lisa went over to her rucksack, in search of anything to avoid eye contact. She rustled around in it as she tried to explain what had happened. Her garbled speech was not helping, so Rafe probed a bit further,

"Why were you both in the tree?"

"Like I said - we were in the tree, hiding, 'cos – cos - something was coming and Ben lost his balance - and fell. I think the thing took him." She straightened up and stared into the distance.

"Don't worry," Tia rubbed her friend's arm, as so many people had done to her, to comfort her when her mother had died.

Lisa regretted her actions now and felt responsible for Ben's fall.

"Ben has the book. I'm sure he'll keep it safe. Although I'm not sure what condition it'll be in." She forced a smile. Rafe suspected there was more to this story, especially after witnessing Lisa and Ben's behaviour at the Land of Sanguel event, but he thought it was pointless pursuing this as Lisa looked so upset. They paused awkwardly for a moment.

Tia broke the silence.

"You need to get your special items at the crossroads." Tia linked onto Lisa's arm eagerly. "More importantly, your pendant."

"Have you got a key?" Rafe asked.

"Yes. It's in my - ermm - bag. Or my pocket, I think." She began to search for it with Tia's help. Rafe stood back unimpressed. He tried to hurry them on.

"We really need to get a move on." He looked up at the sky. "It's getting dark and we need to look for Ben and find shelter."

"Found it." Lisa held the key up as though she ought to receive a prize for her efforts.

They wasted no time heading back to the crossroads. Tia told Lisa about the yellow soil and the post's creation, with dramatic effect. Rafe listened until they got to the post.

At this point, he helped Lisa to open her chamber. Lisa proudly put on her pendant. It was the same shape and colour as Tia's.

"Do you think we could get Ben's things?" Lisa asked. She would want nothing better than to show up with Ben's belongings. She decided she would let him beg for his pendant or even make him do many things for her before he could receive them. Her dreams were soon shattered.

"Have you got his key?" Rafe asked.

"No." Lisa felt deflated.

"What about the box in your bag? Has that got Ben's key?" Tia asked hopefully.

"No, that's my box. Ben threw his away."

"Why?" Rafe and Tia echoed.

"Don't look so surprised. That's just like Ben to do something like that."

The other two couldn't comprehend what Lisa meant.

"Ben really wanted to go home and thought by giving the box back - well, throwing the box at Mrs M… we could go home. The rest is history," she said, as she packed her items into her rucksack.

"We may have difficulty working together. He won't have what he needs," Rafe said, "and you seem to be saying he did it deliberately?" Rafe wasn't happy with the situation. He took the book out of his bag and then flicked through the pages.

"Mrs Marquel said we should meet at the crossroads. We didn't." He looked at Tia and Lisa. They both nodded in acknowledgment. "There are now empty pages." He raised his eyebrow as he leafed through his book, "I'm sure there were words here before."

"It was all in there." Tia handed him her book. Rafe flicked through her book and shook his head. "Perhaps not meeting means we lost out on information…. Or that something else happened…," he said, slowly, hoping to find the answer. "We really need to try and find Ben. Possibly an apology to Arabella may sort things out." He looked at them hoping for their agreement.

Lisa took a little while to respond. She had a strange knowing feeling that ripping the book may have had a consequence, perhaps the cause of the missing information, but she wasn't willing at this stage to admit this. "I think you could be right. Let's find Ben," Rafe said, "Come on then. We'll follow the track where he went missing."

"Ray, I'll follow the map, if it's still there." Rafe handed the book to Tia and placed his in his rucksack.

Lisa couldn't believe how easily Rafe handed the book to Tia. She knew the struggle she would have had with Ben.

Tia was happy to set out to look for Ben. She didn't like the thought of him being on his own, or that something had taken him away. She thought Lisa was putting on a brave face without him. Rafe wished he could return home with Tia, and leave behind the two lunatics he had just met. This task was becoming more complicated than it first seemed.

Tia managed to find pages of the map. She browsed over it and said, "Look, if we follow that dirt track," she glanced at Lisa, "you know, where we met you. It leads to some houses or a village. Houses mean people - we may find help, or Ben."

"Let's see." Rafe looked over the page.

"It's just past the woods," Tia pointed.

"You two know your maps," Lisa observed.

"I used to wonder why my parents always took out guide books when we went on holiday. Then they showed me how it helps to get around and find places."

"Oh." Lisa was surprised at Tia's explanation, as she never wanted to look at maps on holidays. She wanted sweets, adventure or to do as she pleased. Her parents and sometimes Ben, when he was in the mood, took charge of those things.

They set off towards the village.

"Ray used to be part of the Xplorers club."

"Oh," Lisa smirked.

"Why the look Lisa?" Rafe raised an eyebrow. "All guys want to be part of the Xplorers in junior school. When you get into senior school it changes into something else."

"It's just that Ben belongs to that club."

"Isn't he past it?" Rafe said, doubtfully.

"Oh...Yes...he stopped a few months ago." Lisa decided it was best not to ridicule the Xplorers. She didn't want to upset Rafe. "All that stuff will be useful now, I suppose."

"We'll see," Rafe said.

"We could call Arabella?" Tia said.

"No, no, not yet," Lisa said, hastily. "I'm not sure if we can call her too often. She wasn't that obliging to Ben, so let's wait 'til we find him."

Rafe and Tia weren't sure what to make of Lisa's request, but decided to respect her wishes.

*

Tia and Lisa walked slightly ahead of Rafe.

64

"Your cousin's quite serious."

"Not always. I think he's more serious 'cos of the situation and he joined the Barrades." Tia whispered.

"The what?"

"Barrades. Like the Xplorers but... more high-tech for boys fourteen and over who are thinking about going into the Army."

"Oh." Lisa didn't know this group existed.

"Even Uncle Dan – his dad, said Rafe'd be a great army man."

"A soldier!"

"Yes. Anything like that would suit him when he fully grows up." They both looked back at Rafe, amused and filled with admiration that he knew what he wanted to do.

"Please don't tell him I told you."

"Why not?"

"He doesn't like anyone knowing that's all."

"OK."

Rafe was busy trying to spot a place for them to rest for the night. The night had drawn in a lot quicker than they had expected. With it came a slight drop in temperature; they had already put on their jackets and shared Lisa's jelly babies and Rafe's snack bar.

"We need to rest," Rafe said.

"I'm not tired yet," Lisa said. "I feel as though I want to keep going, at least until we find Ben."

"Not even thirsty?" Rafe remarked, especially as he had noticed how much Lisa had been talking.

"Well, I hadn't really thought about it. It all seems to be going quickly."

"We'll need to get off this track, just in case that thing comes back. We don't want to be caught sleeping if it comes by at night," Rafe urged.

Lisa and Tia didn't need to be told twice. They followed Rafe off the track into the woods. The undergrowth started to increase in height in places; they had to push through tall grass and bushes. Rafe and Tia weren't fazed by this excursion. Lisa was a little tentative at first, especially pushing through the bushes. However, once she saw their bravery she took courage even though she was a little scared of the shadows.

"This will work." Rafe was standing in front of what he thought to be a tree with a deep crevice. However, it was two trees twisted together, creating a crevice at the base which would provide shelter and a warm place to sleep. As Tia and Lisa walked towards Rafe, he looked startled. He placed his fingers against his lips indicating immediate silence. They hurried quietly towards him.

"Quickly, someone's coming. Get in there." He pointed to the crevice. They moved into it as deeply as they could. There wasn't enough room for Rafe.

Tia grabbed hold of his rucksack while Rafe pulled himself up onto the first branch of the tree and climbed onto the next branch. The leaves helped to camouflage his presence. He managed to wedge his body in a safe spot. He was a good climber but found the leaves very sticky, especially as they brushed against his hair and face. Rafe leaned forward slightly to get a better view of the area. He could feel the give in the intertwined trunks and decided not to move any further just in case it attracted any attention or gave way.

Rafe noticed their position was up on a rise. Trees and dense foliage marked each side of the trail beneath him. The moonlight bounced shadows from the over-hanging trees along the worn trail.

The noise Rafe had heard was definitely heading their way. Whatever, or whoever, was coming their way, had horses. He heard the sound of hooves steadily strike the ground as they approached. An occasional clinking sound resonated in the air. Rafe was bewildered at what could possibly be coming out of the darkness.

Chapter 6

Entourage

Rafe peered through leaf-clad branches of nearby trees and caught sight of two figures emerging purposefully out of the darkness onto the track that ran before him. They wore dark, all-in-one garments, trouser legs tucked into calf length black boots, hands gloved and hoods pulled forwards obscuring their faces. A gold stripe ran around the hoods and the edge of the cuffs.

They both marched with one hand resting on a leather belt around their waist. Just below their hands, attached to the belt, was a 35-centimetre-long wooden baton, which resembled a miniature baseball bat. A cloth pouch of similar length to the wooden baton hung on the opposite side of the belt, its content concealed. Rafe eyed them carefully and tried to take in every detail.

Behind them followed a cluster of hooded figures, with similar garments but without the gold stripes, belts or

69

batons. Instead, some of them had their arms wrapped around containers that looked like large clear mixing bowls with handles and lids. The figures, of varying heights, shuffled along with their hooded heads slightly bowed.

Rafe didn't know what to make of it, but he was in awe of his next sighting. Behind the cluster, he saw two beautiful black horses; they strode along pulling a cart, its contents covered. Their handlers, also hooded, walked alongside the horses gently holding their reins. The horses needed little guidance. They knew the destination.

Eight figures marched behind the cart. They were dressed like the two figures at the front of the convoy, but were much taller and broader than the others in the cluster. They walked with an authoritative stride – each matched the other. Their low murmurs filtered into the night air, disturbed by the occasional intentional tapping together of the clear bowls from the middle of the convoy.

It was obvious they were not happy with this continuous disruption. They immediately dispersed in an orderly fashion; two took up positions alongside the cart, two went into the middle of the cluster and the others marched alongside the cluster of figures. Their boots stomped the soil. The cluster responded by straightening up, positioning themselves in an orderly manner, tightly gripping onto the bowls in front of them. The horses' hooves were firm as the convoy quickened their pace. The creaking of the cartwheels increased and flowed into the rhythm of the march.

As they went by, Rafe held his breath. They were not aware of him although he sat above them, and he certainly didn't want to be seen. A strong breeze rustled the trees around them, parting the branches above their heads. Shards of moonlight shone through for a brief moment, allowing Rafe to get a better view of the figures at the back of the cart. They both tilted their hooded heads upwards as though they had heard him. The dark, oval void that met Rafe's eyes startled him. He stepped backwards in disbelief at the absence of faces. He missed his footing and started falling backwards. He grabbed at the branches beside him, and for a brief moment, he breathed out in relief as they tried to support his weight, but the tension on the branches was too much. Rafe groaned in dismay as they snapped, and he fell to the ground.

The convoy travelled onwards unaware of Rafe's predicament.

Fortunately, Rafe had a soft landing. He scrambled on all fours to view where the convoy had gone. They were almost out of sight.

"Ray?" Tia's voice was low and hesitant. "Ray, are you okay?"

"Yes. Hold on." Rafe returned and crouched down in front of Tia and Lisa.   Packed closely together, neither dare move as they saw the horror on Rafe's face. Rafe was not sure how to proceed, as he kept thinking about the facial void. He didn't want to frighten them. Although he knew he could eventually tell Tia, he wasn't sure how Lisa was going to react. He quickly gathered his thoughts, which seemed to take forever for the two waiting to hear his account, and hastily described what he had seen, leaving out the lack of facial features.

"You stay here. I'll come back and let you know what's going on." Rafe signalled for his rucksack. Tia clung on to it.

"Hold on, is it safe to come out?" Tia whispered.

"I'm not sure, but I should think you'll be fine if you hide a little longer in there."

"I'm cramped."

"If you want to get out of there, do it quietly," he whispered, and looked directly at Lisa. "Very quietly. Stay

low and close to this tree, just in case they come back."
Rafe took his rucksack from Tia's outstretched hand.

Lisa and Tia both moved forwards at the same time and wedged themselves in the entrance of the crevice. They both giggled at this. Tia wiggled herself free. This gave Lisa enough room to free herself too.

"It's a pity we didn't get a glimpse of them," Lisa started, then lowered her voice as she dusted herself off. "We heard something, didn't we? I think I saw shadows and heard strange tinkling noises. What was that tinkling noise?"

Rafe looked at them as though they hadn't heard a word of what he had just told them. "It was the large bowls I told you about."

"Strange objects. What would you use them for?" Tia asked.

Lisa shrugged.

"We'll only know if I follow them," Rafe responded.

"Do you think they could be the ones who took Ben?" Tia asked.

Lisa brightened at the chance of finding Ben.

"We don't know unless I find out," Rafe said and turned to go.

"Wait for us, Ray. We're coming too."

73

"No, you're not. They'll see you coming a mile off," Rafe said, pointing at Tia's bold flowered jacket.

"No worries," she said, as she swiftly pulled the jacket off and turned it inside out to reveal a dark blue interior. "Reversible!" She smiled, as she put it back on and grabbed her rucksack.

"Nice." Lisa approved.

Rafe realised he couldn't avoid the faceless issue. He needed to prepare them. "The things that went by, they didn't... didn't..."

"Come on Ray, what?"

"It was... it was... difficult to see their faces."

"OK. That's it?" Lisa asked rolling her eyes in dismay.

"Yes." Rafe was not expecting that response. He wasn't convinced that they fully understood what he meant, but he didn't want to force the issue.

"It's difficult to see anything with trees, branches, leaves, and...," he continued. They looked at him as though he was a little crazy. "Never mind, let's get moving." Rafe gripped the straps of his rucksack. He decided they'd find out soon enough, but questioned whether he had got it wrong. A *haunting void*? *What had he really seen?* Either way he wanted to know what was going on.

74

"Come on. Be careful, we're on a slope. They were below us, so be careful not to slip – keep our distance at ALL times," Rafe said, impatiently and headed in the direction where the figures had disappeared. "Keep close to the trees to avoid being seen." He looked around to make sure Tia and Lisa were behind him. "Be as quiet as possible. And use your eyes and ears."

"Anything else?" Lisa asked sarcastically and nudged Tia with her elbow. Tia glanced at Lisa to say 'please avoid those witty comments', but it was too late. Rafe had heard her. He grunted over his shoulder,

"Yes. Be quiet!"

If they had waited a minute longer, they would have noticed that one of the trees had a circle of glowing, blue leaves.

Chapter 7

Twisted Trees

It didn't take them long to arrive at the place where the figures had congregated. Once Rafe heard movements in the woods ahead, he slowed down and ushered Tia and Lisa closely behind him. As they weaved between the trees, they instinctively crouched down and moved towards a formation of rocks. An amalgamation of ferns around the rocks made their position even better. They peered over the stony screen.

The gradual slope below them had areas of barren soil, scanty vegetation and dried leaves. The slope levelled off into a large area where the figures were busily working in the foreground of a hilly terrain.

"You didn't tell us there were horses!" Lisa exclaimed.

Rafe batted his forefinger furiously against his lips for Lisa to keep quiet (or at least lower her voice). She looked away to avoid his annoyed stare hoping for support from

Tia. Tia, who was crouched between them, shrugged helplessly and concentrated on the activity across the way.

The cart had been detached from the horses, and emptied of its contents. The figures were all busy in uniform and disciplined activities. They had assembled two long wooden tables in front of the hillside. On the first table were numerous butterfly nets and three rows of containers, including the ones carried by the figures. On the other table was a row of empty wooden barrels. Each had a different coloured lid - gold, blue, white, green and red. More barrels were set up underneath and behind this table.

The horses were under a gazebo, each with a brown blanket covering their body and tail. Their handlers placed black, square pads on their bridle to shield their eyes. They snorted and settled as the handlers stroked and patted them.

"Look," Lisa whispered. "They look like glass mixing bowls with lids."

Rafe nodded, but he was more interested to see past the hoods of the many figures and yet intrigued with their well-organised actions. "It's like a military operation."

It was clear however, that the figures with the gold stripes were in charge. Five of them didn't move once they had taken up position in the clearing, facing the entourage.

They stood erect, their legs slightly apart with gloved hands holding batons behind their backs. The other five circled the activities, stopping every so often at key points, using their batons as pointers, then they would move on to make sure everything was correct.

"Bet they're catching butterflies." Lisa's voice rose with excitement. Rafe shushed her.

"No way. Butterflies in the dark? Can that be right?"

"No Tia, I think Lisa's a little excited. Moths come out at night. That's more realistic. Lots of them, lo…ts of them." He repeated as he saw the revulsion on Lisa's face.

"Yuk. I'd prefer not to see that." Lisa slumped around, her back against the rock.

Tia giggled, "It wouldn't be all that bad. Keep watching."

"No thanks."

"Don't you want to see what they're really going to do?"

"Nope. I can't see Ben, and I'm certainly not going to watch them catch moths!"

Rafe chuckled. "Moths are harmless. They just flutter around and make a nuisance of themselves."

"No. Rafe you've made me think about loads of moths. Yuk. Yuk. Yuk!" Lisa shook her head feverishly. Tia nudged Rafe and moved close to his ear,

"You shouldn't tease her, she's not like me. Go easy." Rafe rolled his eyes and continued to look at the scene ahead of them. Tia nudged him again.

"I didn't say it to creep her out. It's just that, moths ...."

Tia realised that Rafe was only going to make the situation worse so she covered his mouth with her hand.

The figures who were standing guard all turned around at the same time and marched past the short clearing to a set of trees. The trees ran five rows deep and eight rows across. They grew in pairs a few metres apart, each pair twisted together to form one tree, which grew to eight feet before the branches protruded from their ebony coloured trunks. The branches sprayed outwards in an umbrella fashion. The leaves were fern-like and rubbery in texture. The under-leaves grew spores that, when fully matured, would be released into the night air by specific vibrations. If the spores didn't release, birds would eat them during the dawn.

Once under the twisted trees the guards spaced themselves out equally across the area and began to open their pouches.

The figures that had completed the unpacking picked up a net in one hand and a container in the other, their thumbs poised on a lever which would open and close the lid. They moved out into the open space and created a semi-circle facing the twisted trees. The others positioned themselves behind the tables or in front of the barrels.

The other five senior figures stood guard around the tables and in the middle of the semi-circle.

All remained motionless, until the figures under the trees removed a golden baton from their pouches and held them above their heads. A deafening silence fell over the area. It was as though the sky was holding the air back until the golden batons rotated in the air. With every twirl, the batons began to open up like a capsule accompanied by a humming noise, which increased in intensity.

The batons continued to spin without assistance.

The air resumed its movement.

Rafe and Tia looked on in amazement as the under leaves of the twisted trees started to emit a dim glimmer of light, then flickers of green, red, blue and white appeared. Last of all a faint gold glimmer could be seen. Tia and Rafe were both lost for words. Tia tapped Lisa's shoulder, but Lisa shrugged her off. Tia tugged at her shoulder with vigour. Lisa turned slightly and caught a glimpse of multicoloured lights between the gaps in the rock and fern leaves. She quickly turned around and caught the magnificent view. The backdrop of the night sky hosted a rainbow of circular colours dancing on the tree leaves. The colours were coming from budding spores as they bulged into golf ball size.

The gold batons, now held low, emanated a swishing sound, it grew louder, but it was not overpowering, more hypnotic in its rhythm.

One gold baton rose back into the air and instructed hundreds of spores to detach from their leaves. They drifted upwards at first and then shot towards the ground. Immediately, six figures ran forward and briskly swept up as many spores as they could into their nets before they hit and seeped into the ground. They flicked the levers on the containers. The lids flew open the spores swiped in, and lids clamped shut. Another gold baton lifted into the air and more spores rained down, six more figures ran forward and so it continued.

Rafe, Lisa and Tia gasped at the whole scene - the colours, the sounds, and the skilful action of the figures, placing the filled containers on the table and retrieving an empty one. The figures attending to the tables carried filled containers to the barrels and emptied the spores by hand into the correct coloured barrel. As the barrel content increased, they could see ripples of light shining through the grooves of the barrel.

Another set of figures carried the filled barrels and placed them in front of the cart, an empty one put in its place on the table.

The horses remained calm. If a spore came close to their heads, the handlers would brush it away or pull away spores caught on their manes and brush the mane free.

Rafe was so taken with it all that he didn't hear Lisa and Tia's conversation.

"….so, if I push it, I'm invisible? You're sure they won't see me?"

Tia smiled excitedly. "Yes. I'm sure. We tried it."

"Well, I'll go quickly, get one and come back."

Tia made sure Rafe couldn't hear her. She turned her back to him and mouthed her words, "I'm coming."

"Let's go."

Both pushed their pendants and ran towards the frenzied scene. By the time Rafe turned his attention back to Lisa and Tia, they were halfway to their destination. The only things that marked they had been there were the crushed undergrowth and their rucksacks. Rafe's heart shot into his mouth. He wanted to stand and shout for them at the top of his voice. Instead, his eyes searched frantically for them. He wanted to run out and find them. Then, he caught sight of a glowing figure heading towards him, and it was then that he realised they had used their pendants. Relief swept over him, and then he became annoyed. He couldn't understand why they would put themselves in danger.

Rafe watched as the uncharacteristic yellow spore came towards him.

"Whoow. This is great," Lisa giggled with joy. "We couldn't resist it. They are so, so, lovely and pretty." She hadn't noticed Rafe's annoyance rising; she was so preoccupied admiring her merchandise. She tried to give it to Rafe, as though he had asked for it, but realised she couldn't pull it off her hand; it was very sticky. In fact, it was stuck to her left palm. She tried to shake it off while she wiped her other sticky fingers on the side of her jeans – it wobbled but remained attached. She turned her hand upside down hoping it would release and fall to the ground – but it didn't.

Rafe said nothing. He had one eye on her and the other on the scene ahead. He was still anxious that Tia hadn't returned.

"Oh no, no, no," Lisa tugged and pulled again, and again. Finally, the spore burst, yellow slime seeped over

83

her palm and dripped onto the ground, giving off an over-powering lemon smell. The odour created a bitter taste at the back of her throat, "Uggh." She wiped it onto the plants and moss beside her,

"This is worse than gum," she complained.

"Where is Tia?"

"She wanted a gold one. She'll be here in a bit," Lisa rambled on. "She's invisible too. She'll be fine," accompanying her statement with a smile, to which Rafe returned a fake one. Before he had a chance to berate Lisa, they heard a commotion. They jerked their heads over the rocks to see two figures holding Tia. She was clearly visible with gold slime dripping from her hands. Rafe scrambled to his feet to go to her rescue, but Lisa grabbed his feet to stop him from doing anything too hasty. Instead of holding him back, she caught Rafe off balance; he fell and hit his head against the rock. Lisa panicked.

"Rafe, Rafe?"

No response.

Lisa threw herself down beside him and tried to shake him awake. "Rafe. Rafe?"

When he didn't move, Lisa sobbed.

Chapter 8

Whatever Next?

The moon shone high in the night sky.

The sound of owls now punctuated the silent air. A large grey owl flew over the quiet scene. It swooped low then high into the night sky, its wings gliding through the air. Meanwhile, a girl with a water canister in her hand, kneeling beside a body, prayed that she hadn't killed her friend's beloved cousin.

Rafe felt a cold substance flow over his brow. He shook his head in panic. It pulsated. He raised his hands to his head to try to stem the throbbing. It didn't work.

"Thank goodness you're alive." Lisa breathed out and closed the canister.

Rafe took a while to focus. He tried to sit up, but dizziness got the better of him and he flopped back down and closed his eyes.

Lisa shook his arm. "Oh, please wake up, don't die please. Please don't die."

"No one's dying," he groaned. "My head..."

"Thank goodness. You're alright."

Lisa helped Rafe to sit up and gave him water. He took a sip and leant against the rock next to him. He was trying to recollect what had happened but it all seemed like a dream.

"Where am I?"

"We're in the woods, somewhere." Lisa knew she had to tell Rafe that Tia was missing but she didn't know how. "I'm Lisa.... remember."

"Yes, Lisa."

"Yes. That's it. I'm Lisa."

"You already said that. My head feels like bricks were dumped on it."

"You hit it ... when you fell."

"I've got a sticky patch." Rafe felt the wound on the side of his forehead. He noticed blood on his fingers.

"It doesn't look bad, healing already. Not much blood," Lisa said, brightly.

"I wish my brain knew that."

"I put some water on it to clean it. I did first aid once, and they said always keep wounds clean. They heal better, you see... I lost more blood cutting my finger once on a ..."

"Do you ever stop talking?"

"Thanks." Lisa felt indignant.

"Sorry. I've been told I can be harsh. Tia ...." He looked around him and started to get up, using the rock as an aid. "Where is Tia?"

"I'm sorry Rafe, really, really, sorry." Lisa scrambled to her feet as words tumbled out. "Tia wanted to come. I couldn't say no. I thought the necklace, pendant - thing, would protect us - keep her safe. It all happened so quickly. She reappeared and they must have seen her... She'll be fine. She's really clever. She always gets herself out of trouble at school. That's why so many people like her. She'll be fine... she'll...,"

Lisa's chatter had brought the frantic scene back to Rafe's mind. The throbbing in his head was aggravated by the questions nagging at him. *Why would Tia do something so foolish? Who had taken her? Was she hurt? Scared?* The more Lisa spoke the more irritated he got. He steadied himself on the rock, holding his forehead with one hand,

"You don't know if she's fine!" he snapped.

"Well, I think Ben must be OK and Tia's got more sense, so she should be."

"You seem to have a knack of getting rid of people. All that arguing you do - and chatter, is nothing but trouble," Rafe raised his voice. His head throbbed even harder.

"I don't mean to." Lisa looked away, not knowing what to do.

"I don't want anything to happen to Tia. I'm here to protect her." Rafe stopped. He felt as though he had let her down, but letting out his frustrations on Lisa wasn't going to change the situation. He had promised to keep Tia safe and now he didn't know where she was. He bowed his head in despair.

Lisa's voice was small. "I'm upset with myself." She really was concerned about Tia. She believed Ben was annoying someone somewhere else. (This reassured her he was safe). At this stage, she wasn't going to admit to Rafe that she was the cause of his fall. She didn't want to be left alone in these woods.

They both fell into a thoughtful, anxious, silence.

"Arabella, where are you? Arabella, I need to know where Tia is. Arabella!" Rafe was bellowing at the top of his lungs. He really didn't care about the pain in his head, his heart was in far more pain.

"Rafe, I don't want to sound negative. But do you think Arabella is..."

"Do you think she is what?" Arabella's voice swam above their heads.

Their eyes darted from tree to tree until they saw silvery blue leaves against the dark bark of a tree to the left of where they were sitting. Perched inside a hollow was Arabella in her long flowing garments. Rafe was relieved and couldn't wait to tell her what had happened. "They've taken Tia."

"First things first, you both must be hungry..."

"Did you hear what I said?" Rafe was desperate. "I can't eat until I know she's safe."

"Well, I must say you are both in a predicament. A right pickle, with Ben gone, now Tia and a wound." She said this as though it was a natural everyday occurrence.

Rafe continued. "Where is she? Is she safe? How can I find her?"

Arabella put her right hand up as though she were stopping his words like traffic. It had the desired effect and Rafe stopped. His head started to pulsate again.

"She is OK. They'll not harm her." She chose not to say, *'They'll take care of her for as long as they need her'.*

Lisa was still worried. "So, where is she?"

"She is in the Kingdom of Sanguel."

"Where?" Lisa asked.

"Your map - the book?"

"We have the map," Rafe recollected, reaching into his pocket, but he couldn't find his book.

"Your book, Lisa?" Arabella asked.

"Oh," Lisa said, hastily. "Ben has mine... I mean ours." She dared not say she only had a few pages.

"Tia has the other," Rafe said. A sense of relief helped put his feet in motion as he went over to Tia's rucksack to make sure.

Lisa shifted from side to side.

Arabella shook her head. She stood up and paced the small space – deep in thought. Her blue shawl dragged behind her. "It's best if you wait till morning." She paused, scratching at her messy hair and dislodging a few hairpins. She arranged them back in place as though creating a masterpiece.

Neither of them said anything, as Arabella began to pace the hollow again.

"You must eat. This has been far more difficult than it needed to be." Arabella magically extended her shawl out of the hollow and down to the ground. When she pulled it up again there were nutritious bars and hot drinks in flasks on the ground for both of them. "These bars will fill you up. There are enough for you to take with you and share, if you so desire." She peered at Lisa and then Rafe. "The fruits of the woods are also good, all edible; some an acquired taste." Her bright smile faded quickly as she began pacing the hollow almost tangling herself in her shawl. Lisa wanted to laugh but thought better of it.

Rafe was reassured that Tia had her book, but he had to find his. Lisa helped herself to the food. She ripped open a bar and watched Arabella who seemed lost in thought. Lisa was the first to speak, her mouth full of the delicious bar. It tasted of a chicken dinner all rolled into one.

"Where's Ben?"

"You and Ben really need to learn to listen to each other. He would be with you now if you had not decided to rip the book in two."

Rafe looked at Lisa in disgust. He now knew she hadn't told them the whole story. Lisa could feel his stare burning into the side of her face as he chewed on his bar. She refused to give any eye contact. The situation was embarrassing enough.

Arabella continued: "Because of that vandalism, you have released some of the information. Out it went." She sprawled her arms into the air in a dramatic fashion, as though she had just released them. Looking into the sky and then at Lisa, she said, "I had to scoop words, words."

Lisa focused on chewing.

91

"Do you know why I had to do that?"

Lisa shook her head.

"So that they wouldn't get into the wrong hands." Arabella held her arms behind her back. "So now you have what you have!"

Rafe listened carefully. He remembered how the words had vanished from the page as he was reading about the pendant.

"Now I see," he muttered.

"Speak up. I can't hear you."

Rafe cleared his throat. "I now see why the words disappeared."

"Yes. A smudge is not so bad, but a severe separation, divide, split, rip, brings about muddle and trouble." Her messy hair wobbled, her eyes squinted.

"Tears, despair." Arabella lifted her head, no tears in sight, eyebrows narrowed. "I can't always help you. This has weakened me. So, remember, you must work together. You went off the path and now you have to face the consequences of your actions."

"I'm so sorry." Lisa moved swiftly and stood directly under the hollow, looked back at Rafe, tears impending, then up at Arabella. "I don't think Rafe and Tia should be punished for Ben's stupidity."

"My dear Lisa. What one of you does will affect the rest," she leant forwards, glaring at Lisa. "You don't understand what you need to do, because neither of you read the book in its entirety. Henceforth, the map is the only useful part at this point. The story may well be re-written - and as for being punished, you don't understand the meaning of the word, but you will meet children who do. You have brought about problems that did NOT exist because you're too selfish. This must change." Arabella straightened up, her voice much lighter. "Remember, the pendants will help for a certain length of time."

"How long for?" Rafe asked, half knowing he may not get a straight answer. He was not disappointed.

"How deep is the ocean? Everything has changed because of the ripped book. Use it stupidly and it will not serve you well." She glanced in Lisa's direction. "You need sleep. Start in the morning, and don't leave those bars and drinks lying around. Take them with you." She smiled her little crooked smile, as though she had told them a joke. Lisa began to pick the bars up and put them in her rucksack to avoid another scolding.

Rafe found his book and torch in his rucksack. He found the page with the map. "Head to the village..." His finger traced the path they were travelling.

93

Arabella confirmed they were heading in the right direction.

"Remember, keep on the path. Do NOT divert. This journey has already taking longer than it should. The village needs you. Now sleep. You will be safe here." Arabella yawned. Her voice began to fade. Seeing this, Rafe quickly asked her a vital question.

"What were those things that took Tia?"

"You will soon find out – something to ponder. Keep your focus. Don't leave any signs of being here. Check the zipper on your rucksacks." She chuckled and stepped back into the hollow. The blue leaves shimmered, covered the hollow and disappeared.

Rafe sighed. "I was hoping she would answer me."

"She didn't even tell me anything about Ben. Nothing." Lisa began to get upset. This time Rafe felt sorry for her. "Don't worry. I think Ben's just fine. If he were in danger she would have told us."

"Really?" Lisa sniffed back the tears. "Mrs Mac is not normally helpful, at least not to me or Ben."

"She talks in riddles. It can be…well…awkward, but if you get through all of that, she is helpful. I'm sure there are clues in what she said."

"Ben must be alright. Adults say no news is good news. So, I think I'll rely on that."

"Let's do as she says, sleep and start off in the morning. We'll find them." Rafe put a reassuring arm around Lisa's shoulders. "Oh, check the zippers"

Rafe turned his rucksack over and started to chuckle. "I bet she meant inside." He looked over at Lisa. She had checked the zipper on her school rucksack.

"I think she meant the bags we got at the crossroads," Rafe said.

Lisa pulled the small bag out of her rucksack. Some of the bars fell out as she did this. Rafe raised an eyebrow.

"Some of these are for you." She handed a few to Rafe. "I wasn't going to eat them all. I just wanted to do what she said before she got annoyed."

"I believe you," Rafe teased.

"No, really."

"I'm joking Lisa. It's fine." He diverted his attention to what he had just pulled out of a small zipper compartment. "This is what she meant. It's not the zipper, but the pocket of the zipper that has a ..." He rolled out a paper thin, full sized sleeping bag. "Wow, this is like something out of those Sci-Fi films."

They laid their sleeping bags side by side under the tree where Arabella had appeared. Lisa didn't waste any time in getting inside her sleeping bag. Rafe demonstrated how to roll her jacket into a pillow and placed it under her head.

Lisa yawned. "It's really cosy and warm."

Rafe clambered into his, dragged the rucksacks beside them and finished his hot drink. "I forgot to ask why we had two torches."

"What?"

"Never mind."

"Does your head feel any better?"

"Much better." He touched the dried wound. "It feels like it's almost healed."

"That's a good sign. Tomorrow will be better when we're all together." Lisa yawned.

"I hope so." Rafe stared into the night sky. He was now certain that this journey was going to be more difficult than he had first thought. They had to find Tia and Ben.

Chapter 9

Insiders/Outsiders

The next morning the sun spread its warm rays across the sky. Butterflies danced about their heads, brushing the tips of their nose and skipping on their foreheads. Lisa opened her eyes and smiled. She gained amusement from Rafe, who still had his eyes closed, wanting more sleep, thrashing the air to get rid of whatever was touching his face.

They had breakfast from what Arabella had provided for them the night before. Rafe placed Tia's rucksack in his. He was optimistic they would find her.

Once back on track they started talking about the previous night's events.

"Those lights were fantastic. Although when I was close to them, they made me feel, kind of, ill. All I could see was splodges of mixed colours floating in my sight." Lisa shuddered. "I've never seen anything like them before. It was pretty and fantastic all at once."

"Yeah, 'til it slimed all over your hand," Rafe laughed.

Lisa joined in with the laughter. "Oh yeah. Now that was yukkie. It was so sticky. I don't know how they got them in the barrels without getting them stuck on their hands."

"They wore gloves."

"I didn't even notice!"

"I told you before."

"I forgot with all the excitement. I wonder if that's why they had hoods. I had a bit in my hair," Lisa pointed to the spot, "It's still a bit sticky."

"Germs. Geeerrrrrmsssss," Rafe teased.

Lisa gave him a friendly push and pretended to wipe her hand on her sticky spot then on Rafe. He laughed and moved away as though it was the plague.

Eventually, the track came to an abrupt end. In front of them were high, dense hedgerows, grown as far as they could see, left and right. Dried leaves dominated its spread. The trees that loomed above it also had very few green leaves.

They walked along the hedgerow for a while, until they came to a section that had dried out. There were glimpses of a bronzed surface beneath the faded greenery.

"Lisa, come here. Look at this."

Rafe pulled at an area of tangled leaves and twigs, until his fingers touched the bronzed surface. Lisa leaned in and looked at the colours marbling in the sunlight.

"It's like the pillars at the Library," Rafe said.

"Really?"

"Take a good look. It seems to run behind the hedgerow."

Lisa stood back a bit to get a better view as Rafe pulled away more of the parched twigs.

"It definitely is. And, you know, that main wall in the reading room."

Lisa shrugged, "I look at the books not the walls."

Rafe stepped back and shielded his eyes to get a better look at the height of the wall. "It looks like more than four metres ..."

"How does this help us?" Lisa asked.

"I'm wondering if we could get over it, because it could mark the return to the library."

Lisa began to get excited. "Wouldn't that be great? Only that Ben would have got back before me." This made her feel deflated.

Rafe was hopeful, "Who cares about who got here first. As long as we're all safe and can return home." He slipped his book out of his pocket. "No, it's not the library. The village is behind this wall."

They heard a steady rumble, and saw a dust cloud seeping through the sparse vegetation to the left of them. Birds screeched and fluttered in the vicinity. They heard men's voices mixed in with the clamour. Lisa froze to the spot. Rafe grabbed her arm and pulled her behind a tree. He tried to peer around it to see the cause of the disturbance but the rising dust watered his eyes.

Fortunately, they had both covered their mouth and nose to avoid a coughing fit.

The voices came again, much clearer.

"Nothing found?"

"No."

"We'll try again later. The games are due to start soon."

"We'll send it out after that."

Rafe and Lisa heard rumbling and a booming clang of metal. Birds took to the sky again. A restful peace descended.

"Are you OK?" Rafe whispered.

Lisa nodded, but her eyes were wide with terror.

"It sounds like the thing that took Ben."

"Let's find out."

Seeing Lisa's reluctance, Rafe pointed to their pendant. "This will help." Rafe pressed his pendant. Lisa did the same without hesitation.

"Stay close."

Lisa didn't need to be told. She moved in behind Rafe as they cautiously headed to where the voices had come from. They wound their way into a clearing with grey soil underfoot. The wall showed itself in its splendour. Two grey pillars of equivalent height anchored double metal doors. Inset in the larger doors were two smaller doors. These doors had an overlay of metal stripes running in a criss-cross fashion.

Lisa was scared. "Hope we're not entering the land of the giants."

"Either way, this is the easiest way to get in."

"Do we have to?"

Rafe was undeterred. "Come on." He stretched forwards and hammered on one of the small doors. Lisa was about to turn and run. Rafe grabbed her back. "They can't see us," he urged.

A man with long dark hair poked his head out of the entrance. Seeing no one, he closed the door with a bang. It happened so quickly they remained outside.

"We may have to wait until someone else turns up and…" Lisa's sentence was cut short as they heard metal being scraped across the width of the large doors. The right door clunked as it opened. Rafe and Lisa jumped aside as the longhaired man appeared again, this time on horseback. He galloped off down a track.

Rafe seized the opportunity to dash through the rapidly closing door, pulling Lisa with him. Two extremely tall men slammed shut the screaming doors. They shoved a metal bolt across the middle of them. Both wore dark blue tunics and trousers. They wore bronzed breastplates over the tunics, with swords harnessed to their backs, and on their heads were white, cotton turbans.

The guards marched towards Lisa and Rafe who panicked, not knowing which way to run. Instead of seizing them, the men marched past and disappeared down one of the three archways set in the stone walls, which marked the perimeter of a courtyard.

Lisa shuddered. "That was close."

Rafe chuckled. The realisation that they were invisible dawned on him.

"Invisible!" He touched his pendant. "This is really going to take some time to get used to."

They stood facing the metal doors where the bronzed wall was much easier to see. Behind them was a dry fountain that marked the centre of the courtyard. The fountain had a circular platform where a statue once stood. Only the remains of half-crumbled feet were on show, no inscription or plaque. Dried leaves and grit surrounded the base.

To the right, against the bronzed wall, were withered vines. They dangled in the sunlight, begging for water from the bronzed statue of a robed man carrying a yoke with buckets dangling from chains on either side of his body. The buckets were in a tilted pose to demonstrate the pouring of water. However, there was an absence of water and there were crudely chiselled holes in the bottom of the buckets.

Along the length of outer wall ran dried brambles of varying height until the bronzed wall converged with the stone wall.

Lisa was the first to interrupt their silent viewing, "How tall were they? I was right…giants!"

"I'm not so sure. Anyway, let's not get side-tracked. We need to go through one of those archways." He looked at the wide archway to his immediate left and then craned his neck to view the one over his left shoulder, having to turn in the process.

"Let's avoid going where there's noise," Lisa said.

"I think we should investigate anything with noise, like where those guards went. There are some rumblings over there." Rafe jerked his head towards the archway furthest away, past the fountain.

"Why?"

"Because this must be the village of Sanguel and we need to find Tia and Ben or have you forgotten?"

"Let's toss for it. Heads I choose, tails you choose." Lisa searched in her pockets for a coin.

"Nah. Forget that. So far your decisions haven't been the best."

Lisa looked forlorn.

"Don't get all mardy," Rafe said and tapped Lisa on the shoulder to get her attention. "We may as well take each path and see where they lead. I can only imagine that the one the horse and the rider came from was that one." Rafe nodded towards the horse dung on the ground of the wide archway.

"That's what that smell is." Lisa screwed up her face. "It's getting stronger the more I look at it."

Rafe chuckled. "Then don't look at it."

"Let's go through there." Lisa pointed over Rafe's shoulder, while placing her other hand over her nose.

"Why?"

"Because."

Rafe wouldn't relent. "We'll go through the archway the guards went through."

"Why?"

"Because you ask a lot of questions, and we have so few answers." Rafe started moving towards the archway.

"That's not helpful," Lisa huffed. "We could get caught."

"We don't know how long this invisibility lasts for, so let's just take advantage of it," Rafe said, without looking behind him. Lisa reluctantly sped up.

*

They came to a stone wall perimeter that stood two metres high and eventually reached a solid wooden gate.

"Cooking." Lisa sniffed the air.

"Not too loud. I'm not sure if we can be heard – even if we can't be seen."

Lisa lowered her voice and peeked through a gap between the wall and the gate. "Can't see a thing."

Rafe decided to push the gate. It yielded enough of a gap for them to slip through. They were awe-struck. Log cabins stretched out before them. They weaved their way between them. Some cabins were single-storey. They clustered together with unlit open fires at the centre of their limited space. The two-storey cabins had patches of grass around them with various vegetables patches. Chickens clucked about the area indiscriminately. The wood and deep soil smell reminded Rafe of camping. They crept around the outside of the cabins and peeked through some of the windows.

"Well, we seem to be alone... It's like a ghost town," Rafe said.

"Why can I smell food? Can you smell it?"

"Yes. There's smoke coming out of that chimney over there."

"Let's take a look." Lisa moved swiftly to one of the larger cabins. Rafe was surprised at her boldness.

"Look Rafe, there's hardly any furniture...,"

Rafe raised an eyebrow. "Table and chairs..."

"Whoow a real fire place and... "

Three rapturous shouts of 'hurray' startled them. They automatically followed the sound of the masses. They jogged between the stone wall and the back of the cabins. As they progressed, the smell of food got stronger and the sound of a merry crowd grew louder.

Double gates were opened wide to reveal a vast field in front of them. A hive of activity was taking place with the villagers setting up tables and chairs in long rows. They carried baskets and platters of food, in arms or on heads, to tables already set up with coloured cloths and utensils. There was an area designated for cooking food, where they were roasting chickens and pigs on open fires. Some of the tables had fruits of all kinds and freshly baked bread.

Small children and dogs ran around, chasing each other, getting into trouble and running off again. Some of the older children sat in trees avoiding work. Small, unlit lanterns were hooked on poles around this area and multi-coloured bunting swayed in the euphoric atmosphere.

"Doesn't this look like the event at the library, but more festive? The people even seem familiar..." Rafe wasn't really looking for an answer because the evidence was in front of them.

The smell of the food was delicious and overwhelming.

"I'm hungry," Lisa groaned.

"I don't think anyone would appreciate seeing their food drifting in the air," said Rafe.

"I'd eat it so quickly they wouldn't have time to see it was missing," Lisa laughed, but as she looked down her laughter stopped abruptly. "We're visible again."

107

"Really?"

"Yes. Tia told me that when we're visible we can see our shadows." Lisa pointed at their shadows stretched out in front of them. She began to panic. "What are we going to do?"

"We need to get out of sight until we find out if these people are friendly."

They headed to a nearby tree for cover. Rafe eyed the crowd. "We don't look much different to them… jeans and tops." He shifted his position to get a better view. "Tunic tops and trousers. We should be fine."

"But some of the women have those long skirts and shawls and those head thingys," Lisa said.

"Wraps."

"Wraps?"

"They're called headwraps. Don't worry. Some of the girls are wearing jeans." Rafe observed some of the children in the nearby trees. They were causing mischief, throwing twigs on unsuspecting villagers settling on the slope below them. Rafe and Lisa had a chuckle as they weaved through the gathering of villagers up towards the trees.

An obstacle course set on velvet grass was the main feature of the gathering. To the far left of it were two large grey marquees. Between the marquees and the obstacle course were five rows of benches with a small raised platform in front of them.

To the far right of this entertainment area, back up the slope, were the tables ready for dining. Some of the villagers sat on chairs scattered about this area, chatting and laughing, waiting for the event to begin.

Lisa and Rafe stood near the top of the mound amongst the villagers looking across at the obstacle course. Lisa was rummaging in her bag for a food bar. As Rafe drank water from his canister, he noticed a dry moat separated the main land from an area of land opposite. An elegant white house embedded in the hillside graced the area. A metal water wheel rose just behind the house. The rhythmic churning of the wheel produced relaxing sounds.

A substantial grassy ridge spread outwards from the house and flowed around the hillside. The dry moat surrounded the hillside like protective arms, encasing the house and water wheel.

"Did you see that? Did you see that?" Rafe jumped for joy, but Lisa hadn't seen what he had just observed. She was too busy eating and drinking.

"The thing...hooded figure... it entered the house!" Rafe was oblivious to Lisa's lack of attention. He was staring at the entrance to the property. "Tia could be in there. Ben too!"

"What? They're here?"

"Lisa. Are you listening?"

"Yes. What?" Lisa wiped her mouth with her sleeve.

"I saw one of those figure things go into the house on the hill."

"In there?" She pointed to the house with her water canister. "Let's go."

"Go? We don't even know how to get over there. We need a better view." He scanned the area quickly. "Up here." Rafe secured his rucksack on his back and began to climb the tree.

Lisa shook her head in despair. She reluctantly put away her water and watched Rafe's movements. Not wanting a repeat of Ben's saga, she followed carefully. A couple of times her rucksack dragged thin branches along, but it didn't hamper her progress. Once they were secure in the tree, they could see a lot more of the area and the proceedings.

"I wonder what the celebration is all about," Lisa said.

"It looks like some sort of event or competition. The main thing is that house. We need to get in there to find Tia and Ben."

The door of the white house opened. It was a grand door with an emblem of a waterfall jewelled with crystal glass and blue shaded gems. Three guards adorned in the same apparel as those on the gates came out. Two carried a carved wooden chair the other carried a folded gazebo. The chair had the elegance of a throne with a woven red tapestry cushion. They positioned it at the front of the house, providing a superior view of the activities. The gazebo secured over the chair provided shade not only for the person who would occupy the seat but also for the two figures now stood to attention each side of the chair. The third guard returned to the house.

"It looks like the king is coming," Rafe mused.

"Or queen!" Lisa said.

"But where is the hooded figure?"

"Are you sure?" Lisa looked at Rafe.

Rafe ignored her; he knew what he saw.

Two bells situated in the tower of the house rang out. They ushered in the end of conversations and the villagers' preparations. The ground in front of Lisa and Rafe swelled with people.

The front door of the house opened again. A tall man with humble demeanour appeared at the door, his dark hair swept back into a single long plait. He was modestly dressed; brown slacks and a cream cotton tunic, which hovered above his knees. The sleeves hung over the palms of his hands. This was in stark contrast to the regal apparel of his guards.

He made his way to the chair and stood patiently in front of it. Everyone stopped what they were doing, even those who were tending to cattle or crops in the surrounding fields made their way to the mound.

The man smiled a wide welcoming smile and played with the colourful beads plaited into his goatee.

"Cheesy or what?" Rafe scoffed, as he felt an instant dislike of this stranger.

"Truly cheesy," Lisa affirmed as they watched the smile linger until everyone settled down.

The man remained standing. The bells stopped ringing.

There was a short silence and only the echo of the bells lingered in the air.

The sound of dhol drumming came from within the two marquees. The drummers, male and female, dressed in light blue tunics and trousers, led the procession of proud boys and girls between the ages of seven and fifteen out of the marquees to the line of benches. They were dressed in white t-shirts and black shorts, each with a number on the backs of the t-shirts. When they got to the benches, the crowd jumped to their feet, cheered and waved.

Lisa let out a shriek and almost lost her balance. Rafe had to grab Lisa to stabilise her on the branch.

"Calm down, you could break something." Rafe was relieved she hadn't fallen.

"It's Ben."

"Where?"

"Behind the tall kid playing that drum thing," Lisa pointed. "He's number ten."

"He looks much bigger than I remembered."

"Please don't tell him that, he'll get too big-headed." Lisa was comforted that Ben looked like he was enjoying himself. It was then time for Rafe to feel jubilant, as the last person to walk out of the second marquee was Tia. She didn't wave at the crowd but looked at them as if she was searching. Rafe waved to try to get her attention, but Tia didn't see them.

The frenzied crowd started chanting "Battle, Battle."

Rafe and Lisa looked at each other in disbelief. *Was there going to be a fight?*

'LET THE GAMES BEGIN.'

Chapter 10

Let the Games Begin

A woman dressed in loose fitting, yellow tunic and trousers, made her way between the rows of competitors to the platform. She raised her megaphone and addressed the excited crowd.

"Welcome all of you to our prestigious games. We will cheer on all competitors and celebrate our most determined." She grinned at the rows of elated participants. "We must also thank our exceptional leader, Evelyn, for his wise counsel as founder of these games. Without him we would be a lost village and Kingdom." She bowed towards the man sat under the gazebo. The crowd stood and cheered loudly. He smiled, stood and clapped towards the crowd in the most gracious manner. Rafe pretended to push his forefingers towards his opened mouth as though he was going to make himself sick. Lisa giggled.

114

Once the crowd settled down, the woman continued: "This year we have a new circuit to challenge the most athletic and skilful. We wish you all the best. Garford will now tell us all about our new course."

The crowd applauded as the woman stepped down from the platform. Garford, a young athletic looking man dressed in navy blue shorts and white t-shirt took to the platform. He had no need for the megaphone. He had a miniature horn attached next to his lips by a small metal strap. It ran from the horn along his cheekbone to the side of his head just above his ear. This strap then arched over his head to a small black box secured to his neck with a slim leather belt. This invention amplified his voice so all could hear him clearly.

"Thank you, Wilma, for your great introduction – as always." He blew her a kiss. "Before I proceed, this wonderful – comfortable - invention which enables you to hear me from such a distance is another one of our esteemed leader's magnificent creations."

Again, the crowd stood enthusiastically and cheered ferociously. Again, Evelyn stood and half bowed to the crowd as though he were not worthy of their praise.

Garford addressed the participants with great showmanship. "We hope you are all ready. Remember the

115

first part of the course is, as usual, for the timed trials: the straightforward running track, hurdle and low tunnel. No problem - but the new circuit is not so easy. Now, keep your ears and eyes fully alert as I talk you through your new course." He jogged his way from the platform to the starting line and began to explain the circuit as he strode along it. The spectators also listened intently, relishing the anticipation of the competition.

The course started with the children having to run and jump over three low hurdles. They had to balance on a long narrow beam that ran in an N shape, head up a ramp through a tunnel, which reduced in height so that they had to crawl out at the other end. Once through, they had to pack a pile of bricks into a cart and pull it through another tunnel. This tunnel was unstable under foot, deliberately done to unbalance the cart and the participant. They could only exit the tunnel if all the bricks were still on the cart, and disqualification would take place if bricks were missing.

The next stage was to unpack the bricks onto a heavy cotton sheet. Meanwhile another set of team members would assemble a tower from planks of wood. The teams would finally raise a victory flag and descend via a slide from the tower platform to the finish line.

"But first," Garford announced, "we have timed trials. Boys first then girls."

Cheers went up.

"Come on seven-yearers. Let's see what you've got - to the starting line." He swung his arms in the air like propellers and then pointed them to the bold white line. The seven-year olds jumped up and ran to the start line. The officials in black t-shirts and shorts got them ready.

"This is really exciting," Lisa declared. "I want to go down, sit in the crowd and get something to eat."

Rafe put his hand on her arm. "I think it's best to stay here until we see where Ben and Tia are taken to, then go down and get them."

"But the smell of the food is making me feel really hungry," Lisa moaned.

"Stop looking in that direction. Have another bar."

"But it's...,"

Rafe became stern. "Lisa. The way you do things without thinking has gotten us into more trouble than we need, or have you forgotten?" He paused.

Lisa opened her mouth to protest, but Rafe continued. "One more thing. Who knows how different this situation could be? So, for now, let's just be patient."

117

As Rafe said this, a horn blew loudly, the crowd roared - the games had begun.

Rafe and Lisa became more engrossed as they watched Tia and Ben race. Tia took a little while to get out of the tunnel but when she did, she sprinted and caught up with her opponent, passed her with a few paces to spare, and won. Tia didn't celebrate by jumping up and down. Her plaits fell forwards as she leant forwards to take deep breaths. Ben on the other hand jumped and punched the air when he won.

"He's such a show off. I'm sure I could have won," Lisa said, folding her arms, as though he had just beaten her.

Rafe was amused at her response - but quickly became pre-occupied with the participants returning to the marquees.

"Come on Lisa, let's Bangdashee."

"What?"

"Hasn't Tia taught you that one?" He wasn't expecting an answer. "Let's get moving – Bangdashee, Bangdashee." He laughed. Lisa followed and hoped they could grab something to eat on the way. She had no such luck. Rafe went in the opposite direction of the food tables. He moved quickly through the crowd. No one paid them any attention.

Rafe and Lisa worked their way round to the back of the marquee occupied by the females. Rafe was surprised when Lisa pushed herself in front of him. "I'll look in. You be look-out."

On seeing Rafe's raised eyebrow, Lisa explained her actions, "You don't know what they're doing in there. They may be changing or doing things girls do."

Rafe stood back slightly embarrassed; the thought hadn't crossed his mind. His only concern at this point was Tia.

Lisa peeked inside. There were a number of partitioned areas with female officials walking between them. Some carried bottles of water or sliced fruit and others carried sports kits. They hadn't noticed Lisa's head protruding through the flap.

Lisa popped her head back out to speak to Rafe. "I'll have to go in and bring her out."

"OK. But be…"

"I know. Safe. You do sound like a grown up," she smiled.

"Safe and sensible," Rafe cautioned.

Lisa took off her rucksack and gave it to Rafe. He put his hand firmly on her shoulder and smiled confidently at her. Lisa pressed her pendant. Nothing happened. She tried again." I can't feel the tingle." She pressed it again. Nothing happened.

Lisa was determined. "I'll find her without it."

"Are you sure?"

"Yes. There are so many people moving about in there, I doubt if they'll notice me." Lisa took a deep breath and slipped inside.

Within a few moments, she was back with Tia in tow. Tia almost knocked Rafe over when she jumped on him in excitement. Rafe dropped the rucksack. Lisa was pleased that she had reunited them. She picked up her rucksack and dusted it off without complaining.

Rafe was elated. "Are you OK?"

"Course I am. I'm in team orange." She pointed to the orange t-shirt she was now wearing. "It's great. I think the green team is slightly stronger because the guys are bigger, but we have a good chance of winning."

"Well done Tia. Whose team is Ben in?" Lisa asked.

"The orange team. We're together. He's fine and he's already made some friends."

"Ben?" Lisa shook her head. "Unbelievable."

"I'm glad you're both together 'cos it makes it easier for all of us to get away," Rafe said.

"No, we can't," Tia said forcefully. This shocked Lisa and Rafe. She continued without waiting for their response. "If we win this, we help to get water for the village – the whole kingdom - and we get a special ceremony at the big house. I mean Hill House."

Rafe looked at her as though she'd been put in a trance. "What are you talking about?"

"Don't worry. It's all fine. We'll tell you all about it later." Tia's words tumbled out of her mouth at great speed.

Rafe tried to protest, but Tia wasn't going to concede. "No. No. Ray. I have to do this. We can talk about it later in the celebrations. Everyone is friendly, don't be worried, watch the finals, got to go…"

With that, she dashed back through the opening. It closed behind her, just as they heard a woman's voice call out, "Orange team, assemble quickly."

Rafe and Lisa looked at each other bewildered at what Tia had said.

"Well," Rafe began as he blinked and looked at the marquee half expecting Tia to return. She didn't.

"You think I talk fast," Lisa said, not sure what to say.

"No. I said you talk a lot. A lot. Tia talks quickly when she's excited," Rafe said and went into a thoughtful silence.

"After all that worry," he mumbled.

"What?" Lisa hoisted her bag over her shoulder.

Rafe didn't hear what Lisa was saying, he was still deeply worried about Tia. He knew that under normal circumstances she would be a bit more reserved – rely on him a bit more, but this was not normal circumstances.

"Rafe. Rafe." Lisa pulled at his arm, "We can't do anything now, let's see if we can get some food before my stomach drops out. I've done too much walking today, enough to last me a lifetime."

Rafe reluctantly followed Lisa. He had an unsettling feeling about the whole proceedings. He needed answers - who were the hooded figures? Why did the village need water? How were Tia and Ben going to help them get water?

"Food, Rafe, food. Wake up."

"I'm coming."

*

"They are really friendly." Lisa licked her lips after finishing a chicken drumstick and tumbler of apple juice, while stood behind the crowd watching the last event. "That nice woman must have seen how hungry I was."

122

"It was those puppy eyes you gave her. Using your glasses had the full effect - and now no glasses?" Rafe mused.

"Works all the time. I put them away. Don't want my messy fingers on them. I only really need them for reading." She chuckled.

"You could have eaten one of the bars Arabella gave us."

"That's for emergencies only."

Rafe laughed and gave Lisa a side hug. "Who's becoming responsible?"

Lisa smiled, she was beginning to like the compliments she was getting from Rafe and didn't want him to be too concerned about Tia.

"You shouldn't worry so much about Tia."

"I have to."

"She can look after herself."

Rafe turned to Lisa. "Did you know her mom died?"

"No." Lisa replied softly, shocked by this revelation.

"I don't think she's told anyone. I know how it affected me... she was my favourite aunt, so it must have been worse for her... Anyway, since then Tia's lived with us and I've always made sure she's been OK. She was bullied at her last school for being a loner. She was grieving and never fought back. Since coming to our school, she's really tried to make friends. She likes to do things she did with her mom, like go to the events at the library. Sort of a comfort thing - like wearing the waist bag her mom made."

The news saddened Lisa, as Rafe spoke. "I can see why she wants to help out, but at the same time I don't want her to put herself in danger. She likes helping other people. Sometimes I think that's why she said yes to Mrs M."

"You're like her cousin bodyguard."

"I'm not sure if I'd say that, but I know I want her to be happy again. Well, more happy than sad."

Riotous cheers and shouts went up from the crowd in front of them. This prompted Rafe to move forward to get a better view. Lisa followed, full of admiration for Rafe's dedication to Tia.

They made their way through the crowd boldly, feeling more comfortable in their surroundings.

The orange team were just behind the green team. They were hoisting planks of wood to the tower. Tia and another girl of similar age were climbing up the other side of the tower followed by Ben and two other boys. Once on the tower, Tia and the girl fitted the two wheels to the lowering mechanism to wind down the slide. The boys assembled the platform with fervour.

The crowd yelled and shouted with excitement. The competitors thrived on the atmosphere and tried their hardest to complete the task quickly.

The green team had all their members on the platform in their tower and were having difficulty raising their flag - some of the ropes had tangled around the flagpole. This gave room for the orange team to assemble all their team-mates on the platform and start to hoist their flag.

The orange team flag began to rise just behind the green flag. The orange team got poised to go down the slide. As soon as the flag was flying high, they began to descend. The teams were neck and neck. One of the green team members fell as she jumped from the slide; the orange team took advantage, dashing victoriously to the finish line.

Cheers went up.

Members of the green and orange team went back to assist the girl who was now hobbling along the course. They lifted her off her feet and carried her across the finish line.

The crowd roared and the bells rang out for the teams. Those sat on the benches ran to celebrate with the winners.

"Such team work," Garford yelled and jumped with excitement. "This is what our competition is all about."

Evelyn stood up and applauded with purpose, his head aloft and a wily smile. The victors had certainly guaranteed him a set of healthy, strong children.

Chapter 11

Celebrations

The winners and runners-up gathered at the place where a ten-metre wooden bridge rose from the bed of the dry moat, only used for such ceremonies. Garford and Wilma, who were now wearing their ceremonial attire - elaborate embroidered blue gown and trouser suit - led the children across to present them to Evelyn accompanied by trumpeters. It was a grand affair.

Evelyn, also dressed in a decorated long silk vest with gold and silver beading, greeted each child with a handshake and placed a medal around their neck. He paused for a short while as he gazed at Tia's necklace. "You have a beautiful necklace." He spoke gently.

"Thank you," she said as she waved at the cheering crowd.

"I haven't seen one like this in years. It is enchanting," he smiled, not releasing her hand. "Where did you get it?"

127

This time Tia caught his intense stare, which betrayed his kind words. A chill ran down her body. "My... mother," she stammered and pulled her hand away.

"Where is your mother?" he asked looking out onto the crowd.

"She's dead." Tears instantly began to fill her eyes. She wiped them quickly, took her medal from his hand and stepped back in line with the other children who were marvelling at their medals and waving to their families across the moat.

Evelyn smiled at the crowd, but he was unsettled as he greeted the remaining children, he would speak to his guards the moment he got an opportunity.

Evelyn strode over to Wilma and Garford. "We have had a most pleasing result."

They both nodded and smiled like Siamese cats. Wilma handed him a golden megaphone. Evelyn put it to his lips,

"These children have made us all proud. Parents and loved ones, they have done well to gain such a prestigious position at Hill House. Now, let the celebrations begin!"

Garford came forward with a black pouch. Evelyn dug his hand into it and thrust his hand in the air releasing coloured strips of paper. As he did so, a band started to

128

play. Drums, flutes and tambourines got the celebrations underway.

The competition officials ushered the children back across the bridge to the clamouring crowd and the bridge lowered.

A large table laden with food was set up in front of Hill House for Evelyn and his entourage, which included Garford and Wilma. Waiters escorted them to their table and tended to their every need.

Evelyn probed Garford and Wilma about Tia.

*

The evening sun dimmed and the gold and silver lanterns were turned on to light the celebration areas.

Tia recounted to Rafe and Lisa how, on the night that she was taken, she had felt ill and couldn't see. She didn't remember anything else apart from waking up the next day knowing she had to take part in the games. She recalled that she was in an empty dormitory and Wilma had taken care of her. Rafe tried to get more out of her, but Tia couldn't remember anything else. They decided to go and find Ben to plan their next steps.

Everyone was having a great time, groups and individuals were dancing around tables, chatting and laughing. They finally caught up with Ben, sat on a table with another boy successfully devouring a plate of food. Tia and Rafe settled down around the table, accepting food from the servers who carried platters of delicious food - except Lisa who stood unimpressed over Ben.

"Well, well. Benjamin Rosen." She poked him in the shoulder. "Filling your face, as usual."

"Hi," Ben managed to say with his mouth full.

Lisa placed her hands on her hips. "Nice to see you Lisa. Glad to see that you're alright. I'm so sorry I left you on your own." She put one hand on her chest, widened her eyes in fake horror. "I thought something awful had happened to you, but it's great to see that you came to find me. You're a wonderful sister and you're far more mature than I am," she prompted with a false, sweet grin.

Rafe and Tia found this highly amusing, as Ben continued to eat.

Eventually Ben cleared his mouth with a slurp from his cup. "I'm fine. Thanks for asking. But I was so hungry."

"Seems like extreme hunger runs in the family," Rafe whispered to Tia.

Lisa snatched a cake from Ben's plate.

"Get your own."

"You've got too much."

"Give it back."

Lisa licked the top of the cake. Ben still tried to snatch it back. She bit out a chunk and handed it back to him. As Ben stood to get ready to knock it from her hand, Rafe stepped in.

"Ok, that's enough." Rafe didn't like the direction this little antic was taking.

Ben sat down. Rafe was much bigger than he was.

Lisa took this to her advantage and ducked behind Rafe, silently mocking Ben from behind Rafe's back. Tia pulled her onto the bench beside her.

"Give it up," Rafe said.

Lisa laughed. "It's OK. We do this all the time."

"I know that's what Mrs M didn't like – remember?"

Lisa settled down and composed herself as she remembered the warning she received from Arabella.

"Who's your friend?" Rafe asked.

"Oh. Sorry this is Alamo," Ben said.

Alamo greeted all of them. He was dark in complexion with short, curly black hair. He wore a short-sleeved top with dungarees.

"Eat." He smiled and pointed to the plates of food in the middle of the table. "This food is not just for us."

While they enjoyed the festivities, Ben filled them in on what happened to him.

"So, what was that contraption thing?" Tia asked.

Ben shrugged, diving into his cake plate. Alamo explained cheerfully that it was a great invention by Evelyn called Silent Horses. They were made of metal and would lead the way to the village and pick up anyone who was lost in the woods. They all thought it a bit strange, but Alamo was optimistic and told them that people travelled from different kingdoms and sometimes individuals got lost and this was a way of keeping them safe.

The conversation moved on to the subject of the hooded figure. Rafe mentioned that he observed one of them enter the house. Alamo's explanation took on a more serious tone. He lowered his voice and the others leaned in to hear above the celebrations.

"They are the Defenders and they have the honoured responsibility of protecting us. The ones with the regal stripes – gold or blue - are not to be messed with. They are responsible for the collection of lights for Hill House. I'm also told that they benefit the village in ways I don't really understand, by collecting the water."

"Why are their faces covered?" Rafe asked

"They look scarish, but their...."

"Yes," Lisa butted in, "really scarish," selecting Tia's word.

"What?" Alamo asked, not sure what the word scarish meant.

"Ignore that, tell us more," Ben said, as he tried to kick Lisa under the table to keep her quiet and whispered, "Cut those silly words out. It's not helping."
Tia heard what he had said and felt sorry for getting Lisa into unwanted trouble.

"It's my fault. It just means they're a bit scary looking," Tia said.

Alamo continued, "Oh, they have to dress like that, because the lights are so bright it can cause sickness and temporary blindness when up close. And if you hold them with your bare hands, the outer coating disintegrates into a liquid form and it can be difficult to get it off... so I'm told."

"Yuk," Lisa said.

Alamo looked at Lisa, as if waiting for her to explain what had happened. Lisa said nothing. It was Rafe who informed the rest of them of what they had seen, feeling he could trust Alamo with that piece of information.

"Do they burst in Hill House?" Tia asked. She imagined Hill House filled with gooey residue.

Alamo found it funny. "I don't think so but they need to be collected frequently. I'm not sure why Hill House uses them. We have lanterns, candles and in some place electric lanterns powered by the water wheel."

Rafe looked at the house standing out against the night sky, and the table of dignitaries surrounded by fairy lights. "Have you been inside Hill House?"

"No, but I hope to. Well, I will now that I'm on the winning side." He kissed the medal still hung around his neck and spoke proudly, "My brother and sister went there some time ago. It's a great opportunity to help the rest of the village - supply water or whatever task I may be given. It will help us all."

"Are your brother and sister there?" Tia looked excitedly at Alamo.

"Yes. I haven't seen them for such a long time."

The group fell silent in response to Alamo's apparent sadness. The merriment continued around them as this small group sat in an awkward silence.

"I'm sure you'll see them again." Tia tried to make it better. "Just like how we found each other."

They all agreed. Tia continued. "I can't wait to help out. It's great to know we can be of some use to the village."

"That's right," Ben said, "I was told that all the children want to compete to help their families and the rest of the village. It's exciting."

"Some of the girls in the tent said we can make jewellery, but the real honour is to help supply water to the village. I really don't mind which one." Tia smiled then yawned. "Sorry about that. I'm feeling quite tired now."

"Where are you staying?" Alamo asked.

They looked at each other. None of them had considered this. Alamo thought he had the remedy. "You'll need to sleep somewhere tonight. So, stay with us. I'll ask my parents." He didn't wait for an answer. He went off to find his parents in the festive crowd.

Meanwhile, Evelyn had sent his guards out to find out if there were any more strangers in the village.

Chapter 12

Suspicions

Adults danced into the evening, taking the place of their young children who were now falling asleep on the grass, benches or in arms that cared for them. With Alamo gone, the small group spoke more freely.

"I'll tell you what's weird." Ben leaned in, the others followed suit, "When I was in that contraption, Ara…, I mean Mrs M appeared."

They all brightened up.

"What did she say?"

"She was as helpful as a chocolate oven." Ben shook his head. "She said things in her jumbled way." Ben avoided telling them how he had bumped his head trying to look out of a narrow-slit posing as a window and how he had become quite upset, to the point of tears. "She told me that the rest of you were on the way, and I needed to compete and win in the games." He rubbed crumbs off his

136

medal, polished it against his top. "She also said that when I get to the stables where the silent horses are kept, I should speak to Mr Peri, Alamo's father and tell him I was there for the competition. So, you see I was destined to win," he boasted.

"So... I'm to be commended for pushing you out of the tree?" Lisa smiled.

"No, no," Ben said, wagging his finger. "That was all me. I sensed I needed to depart before you messed things up."

"See. You knew I didn't push you!"

"Before you two start trying to score points, just remember that the book got ripped in your little squabble," Rafe said, sharply.

They both looked sheepish.

Rafe continued. "We were told that it has altered what we know, because some of the information in the book has vanished and our invisibility doesn't work as it should."

"Invisibility... what's all that about?" Ben asked eagerly.

"We all got various items from the crossroads. Have you got your key?" Tia asked.

"Key..." Ben sighed as the realisation dawned on him. Rafe and Tia were looking at him expecting him to reveal his key, while Lisa smirked wondering how he was going to get out of this.

"I'm such an idiot. I confess." He raised his hands and looked at Lisa, "It's my fault. I threw my gift at Mrs M's feet - before I knew she was Arabella," he added hastily, "so I doubt I'll get my things."

"Perhaps we should call her?" Tia offered.

"If it's not an emergency, she's not coming out for me," Ben said, dismayed.

Rafe didn't want to labour the point so he changed their focus. "I know the maps in the book are still relevant. Have you got your book?"

"Yes. It's in my socks."

They all looked under the table as Ben pulled up his trouser leg to reveal the small book held to his ankle by a piece of string. This even impressed Lisa. Tia revealed that her book was safely in her waist bag under her t-shirt.

"I thought you were looking a little podgy, but I thought you had too much to eat," Rafe laughed. Tia gave him a friendly push.

"The thing I didn't like was when that man, Evelyn, noticed my necklace," Tia said, amongst the laughter.

Rafe was not happy. "Who?"

"Evelyn," she replied.

"I thought he was a she," said Ben. "You know, the only Evelyn I know is this old woman who ran the shop around the corner from the library."

They all ignored Ben.

"What did he say?" Rafe was irritated that Evelyn had noticed Tia and the necklace.

"He asked where I got it from and I told him Mom gave it me. He asked me to point her out. Well I couldn't."

Lisa was upset now, and hugged Tia. "He's a mean, nasty man."

"We need to be careful of him. I didn't get a good vibe when he came on the stage," Rafe said.

"Everyone thinks he's wonderful," Ben said. "They keep saying he's done so much for them. He helped the village develop a water source and some of them now have electricity as a result. They want to supply more homes with it."

"What's all this about water?" said Rafe. "It doesn't make sense. There's a lot of greenery but the moat is dry, the fountains are dry…"

"There must be a water shortage," Lisa said.

"But, there's a water wheel," Tia added.

Rafe scratched his head. "Is this what Mrs Mac sent us here for?"

Alamo was back with a happy demeanour. "My parents are happy to have you all stay for the night. We can go now if you wish."

Everyone was happy to get a goodnight's sleep with a friendly family.

"Let me just finish these cakes," said Ben, as he hurriedly piled a few more on his plate. They all laughed at him.

*

Tired, merry people returned to their homes. Sleeping children slumped over the arms of their parents. Those who were still awake gladly accepted piggybacks from their fathers or older siblings.

Alamo's home was one of the large cabins with a split-level. A pot-bellied man dressed in worn out dungarees and an orange woven shirt warmly welcomed them. His wife had dark hair and kind brown eyes. Her dress swept close to the grey slabbed flooring. The whitewashed walls displayed three tapestries depicting the scenery of the woods, village and fields.

A large fireplace enhanced the room; its embers emitted contented warmth to the space that served as a dining room, kitchen and living area. Electric lanterns hung on the walls. The space also accommodated a staircase; next to it ran a narrow passageway, which led to a small room and cupboard.

The smell of cinnamon and vanilla lingered in the air as Mrs Peri had baked for the celebrations. A large untouched cake, left in reserve for family and friends, sat in the middle of the dining table. Hot chocolate simmered on the stove. The children politely refused to consume anything else. They had eaten enough for one night.

Upstairs, there were three bedrooms and a bathroom. Mrs Peri led the girls to their bedroom and Alamo led the boys to the other. Both rooms had two single beds with quilted bedding and a chest of drawers. The wooden flooring had colourful woven rugs situated in front of each bed. There were drapes hanging from the ceiling, behind which was a rail to hang clothing. The windows were obscured by shutters, a glimpse of moonlight crept through the slats, providing a comfortable and peaceful atmosphere.

Alamo opted to sleep on the floor, taking some spare bedding from the cupboard.

Soon they were all fast asleep, except Rafe. The thought that Evelyn only used children to help the village played on his mind. He struggled to work out why or how

141

this helped to supply water to their families. Rafe had also overheard the conversation of other villagers proudly stating that their child was going to compete at the next games. Rafe decided he couldn't risk Tia being on her own, or anywhere near that man. At that moment, he felt the need to check she was alright. He slipped out of the room, and made his way quietly across the landing to where Lisa and Tia were sleeping. As he moved across the stairway, he heard voices downstairs. He couldn't hear what they were saying, so he pressed his pendant, but nothing happened - no tingle rising through his body. He took a few tentative steps then crouched down to get a better view. He sensed an eerie presence. He could only see the back of a man sat on a chair with something grey and feathered perched on his cloaked shoulder.

"Thank you for looking after our guests. I'm happy that you will take good care of them." The man stood up with a flutter of wings resonating up the stairs. He moved out of view towards the front door.

Rafe sensed the words held a menacing tone - whoever had visited the Peri's wasn't happy that they were there. Rafe decided they had to leave first thing in the morning before the Peri's awoke.

Chapter 13

Gone

The next morning, cockerels called into the bright morning sky. The smell of bacon and eggs filled Lisa's nostrils. She looked over at Tia's bed. It was empty, her bedding folded neatly and placed at the bottom of the bed. Lisa rubbed her eyes; she couldn't believe Tia hadn't woken her. She sprang out of bed and got dressed.

By the time Lisa reached downstairs, she saw Mrs Peri lifting the eggs on to a metal tray, which she placed in the oven. Lisa greeted Mrs Peri. Mrs Peri looked over her shoulder. "Good morning. I hope you slept well." She placed slices of bacon into the frying pan.

"Very well, thank you." Lisa stood beside the dining table, yawned, and stretched "Where are the others?"

"Please sit. I hope you are hungry."

Lisa pulled out one of the six chairs that surrounded the table. Only four places were set for breakfast. In the middle

143

of the table was freshly baked bread, which already had chunks pulled out of it. A jug half filled with orange juice sat next to four cups.

"Everything smells lovely," Lisa said. There was no response from Mrs Peri; she was busying herself with the breakfast.

Lisa continued: "It feels very homely."

Still no response. Mrs Peri was deep in thought. Lisa felt a little awkward and decided to survey the room instead. A sideboard filled the wall next to the stove, which housed plates and cutlery. Opposite the dining table was the fireplace and along the wall was a run of clothes hooks; a multi-coloured shawl hung next to a black shawl. The front door ran adjacent, next to it a large window with green drapes on either side. Underneath the window was a wooden bench with comfortable cushions and a small bookcase nestled in the corner.

"Morning Rafe," Lisa said cheerily. She was happy to talk to someone.

"Good morning Mrs Peri, Lisa." He ruffled her hair.

"Hey." Lisa laughed and shook her hair back into place.

"Did you sleep well?" Mrs Peri asked as she placed the bacon on the metal tray.

"Like a log," Rafe said and rubbed his head, oblivious to the idea of leaving before the Peri's awoke. Lisa patted the chair next to her, shuffled closer to Rafe and lowered her voice as she eyed the back of Mrs Peri. "She doesn't seem to be listening."

Rafe yawned. "She's busy."

"I know that, but…"

"Have you been talking too much?" Rafe chuckled.

Lisa leant back in her chair and folded her arms. "No."

"Don't get upset, I was only teasing."

Lisa continued to sulk. Rafe decided to change the subject, "Is Tia still sleeping because Ben and Alamo are already up."

"That's what I was trying to say…," Lisa began. The door flew open, a blast of sunlight and a cool breeze ushered Mr Peri in. He took off his cap and placed it on a hook beside the black shawl. His demeanour was cheerful, his voice bounced off the walls as he spoke, far louder than he had the night before. His bald patch gleamed with sweat.

"Good morning. Good morning. Good sleep?" He strode over to his wife and pecked her on the cheek.

"Yes," they both answered in unison.

"Good, good, good, I see. Time to eat, I see." He rubbed his hands together.

"Sit down, I'll serve this now," she said

Mr Peri quickly washed his hands, dried them on a cloth that hung below the basin. He sat at the table as Mrs Peri set a plate down with two freshly fried eggs. He wasted no time, pulled off a chunk of bread and jammed it into the runny eggs, gobbling it down in no time.

Mrs Peri gave Rafe and Lisa a fried egg each and offered them bacon, which Lisa refused. Rafe had three rashers and Mr Peri had the rest. Mr Peri poured himself coffee from a jug Mrs Peri had just placed on the table.

"Help yourselves to juice," he said. "Nothing like a good night's sleep, nothing like it." He slurped his coffee, the steam curling around his moustache and drifting into his nostrils. He breathed out satisfied.

Mrs Peri sat down and poured coffee into her cup.

"Where are the others?" Rafe asked. Mrs Peri avoided eye contact and hurried back to the stove, cup in hand. Mr Peri took a short while to answer as he shovelled down his eggs. Lisa and Rafe chewed as they waited for his reply.

"All gone," he beamed, looking at his wife proudly, as he placed a piece of bacon on a lump of bread and devoured it. Mrs Peri glanced nervously at Lisa and Rafe as she sipped her coffee.

"So, where are they?" Rafe asked again, feeling his appetite begin to drain away from him.

"Winners can't delay, no delay, their inevitable and invaluable tasks."

"What?"

Mr Peri noticed Rafe's anxiety. "They are all fine. I presented them to Evelyn myself." He gave a satisfied grin.

Rafe wanted to shout out, '*No*' but did all he could to control himself. He concentrated on the plate in front of him and managed to say, "How could you do that?"

Mr Peri was oblivious, "It's expected of me."

Rafe's eyebrows narrowed. "Did you say goodbye to your son?"

"Well, well." Mr Peri was certainly confused by this question.

Rafe sprang to his feet, his chair scraped the floor, cutlery slammed to the table. "Did you?"

This shocked Lisa. She looked to Rafe then to Mr Peri as though it was a tennis match.

"But of course, of course I did...," Mr Peri started. His wife put her hand on his shoulder to calm him.

"But you didn't allow us the chance to do the same... did you?"

"But you were sleeping, sleeping I tell you."

"That doesn't matter...,"

"Now listen. Sit down and eat your breakfast. It was an order that had to be carried out." Mr Peri's voice was firm and resolute.

"And why didn't you let us know about this?"

"Because orders come through at any time, any time, you cannot stop that, no one can. An order is an order!"

It dawned on Rafe that the person who came to the cabin that night was Evelyn. Who else could give out orders that had to be followed, he thought. The situation was worse than he had initially considered. He wanted to kick himself for sleeping too long.

"Take us to them."

"It's too late to ...," Mr Peri began. Rafe wanted to charge upstairs and grab his belongings. He felt he had let Tia down again.

Mrs Peri spoke calmly with deep concern. "They should be able to say goodbye."

Her husband looked bewildered and scratched his head as though he were looking for another option. "But I've done as was expected of me. I cannot make the trip a second time... I mean, a second time means the long way."

"Omar, you must take them up there once you've finished eating," Mrs Peri said, quite forcefully. She got another egg from the stove, placed it on his plate with some bread. Mr Peri's face brightened. Mrs Peri smiled reassuringly at the children and filled Mr Peri's cup. "You can't deny them the chance to say goodbye."

Rafe and Lisa glanced at each other, seeing the turnaround in Mr Peri's demeanour. Rafe sat down with a sigh of relief, although he was still anxious about Tia. Mr Peri swallowed his food and looked across the table. "Okay, okay, eat up, eat up and I'll see what I can do." He winked at his wife, who smiled weakly and returned to the stove.

Rafe and Lisa ate quickly as they listened to Mr Peri going on about how proud he was of his children, and how he and his wife had benefited from their children's commitment to them and the village by serving at Hill House. Whilst Mr Peri was clearly very happy about this, Mrs Peri said nothing and sipped her coffee. Mr Peri told them he was the athlete in the family, although Rafe and Lisa saw no signs of this supposed athleticism, unless he was entering a man versus food competition, which Mr Peri would most certainly win.

Rafe and Lisa wasted no time in gathering their belongings. Lisa felt sorry for Rafe and knew that his outburst was about losing Tia. With the bedroom door closed, she decided to call upon Arabella.

"Please Arabella, don't do it for me, come for Rafe, he's really sad, upset about Tia. I'm even getting a bit worried about Ben." She paced in front of the chest of drawers. "Arabella, Arabella." She was about to give up when she saw a blue leaf at the side of the chest of drawers. Lisa quickly called Rafe, without attracting attention from the adults downstairs. By the time they got back to the room, they could see Arabella's head just above the chest of drawers, as though she were stuck. Before they could say anything, she began to speak, "Listen carefully. As soon as you are out of here, get rid of the old goat, he's hopeless. He will do more harm than good. Use the map to get yourselves inside Hill House."

"The goat's taking us now." Lisa couldn't stop herself from giggling. Rafe didn't feel in the mood for laughter and nudged Lisa.

"I doubt if he'll get you inside, he's all about himself. His reputation is all that matters to him. His wife is much kinder."

"What matters is Tia may be with that Evelyn creep and he's already asked about the necklace and...,"

"I understand your fears Rafe. Rest assured that she is safe for now. The good people in Sanguel don't normally ask questions of strangers. They are welcoming and are used to travellers coming and going. Evelyn's creations have brought him much admiration and popularity, but he is not to be trusted. Tia is a lot stronger than you give her credit for, give her a chance." Arabella's voice began to crack.

"What do you mean – for now?" Lisa asked, but Arabella didn't answer. She was gone.

"Isn't that just typical?" Lisa stamped her feet in annoyance.

"I'm with you on that."

"Who were you talking to?" Mrs Peri's voice jolted them around as she stood outside the open doorway.

"No one," said Lisa. She tried to sound confident, but her actions demonstrated otherwise. She didn't know what to do with her hands.

"Actually, we were admiring the chest," Rafe said calmly, wondering how long Mrs Peri had been standing there.

Chapter 14

Hill House

"It was nice of Mrs Peri to pack sandwiches for us," Lisa told Mr Peri.

"Yes, yes," he said and patted his bulging jacket pocket. "She's a wonderful wife, a little too sensitive sometimes." He pulled his cap into his face to block the sunlight from his eyes, while enjoying the cool morning air.

They walked through the village where daily chores had already begun, passing the competition site where some of the villagers were dismantling the obstacle course. Others tended crops in the adjacent fields.

"Where's the bridge?" Rafe asked.

Mr Peri chuckled, even though he heard Rafe's disappointment, "No, only winners, winners, go through that entrance. We have to go around the back. Hope you're both up for the walk. Try to keep up with me." He sped off in front of them. This impressed Rafe and Lisa, but it was short-lived as he started to breathe heavily,

153

having to stop on a number of occasions to drink from his hip flask and wipe his brow.

The stony, gravelly terrain exhibited sparse vegetation, and the few trees provided minimal shade. The side of the hill was always in full view, and Mr Peri kept saying: *'We're almost there'* – and they still hadn't reached their destination.

They came to a craggy area of land pinned in by hillside.

"Watch your footing," Mr Peri puffed. They stopped in front of a two-wire fence, which ran as far as the eye could see - on one side the craggy area on the other flourishing shrubbery shaded by the hillside.

"Wait here," he told them.

They watched him climb clumsily over the wires. Rafe and Lisa held back their chuckles as Mr Peri's trailing leg got caught on the top wire. He was suspended on one leg for a short time as he worked out that he wasn't moving forward.

"Do you need some help?" Rafe called.

"Not-at-all, a bit of exercise does one good," he said, not looking back at them. He swung his leg off the wire, which propelled his body into a half twist and stumble.

154

Unbelievably he regained his balance and sauntered ahead.

Rafe smiled at Lisa. "What's he got in that flask, water or whisky?"

Lisa giggled

"I suspect both, but the contents are not in equal amount. We know which one is more potent," Rafe laughed.

"What's potent?"

Rafe looked at Lisa, and realised she wasn't being funny she really wanted to know the answer. He thought for a moment of playing a trick on her, by telling her the wrong meaning, but changed his mind. Tia was the only one he played those types of tricks on, because she could take the joke. He wasn't sure how Lisa would react.

"Stronger...intoxicating."

"Yep, he certainly has it potently," she laughed.

Now Rafe laughed but didn't correct her; he thought he'd leave it to her parents - a joke to be told at family get-togethers.

Mr Peri stood at a door embedded in the rocky hillside. Creepers surrounding the door frame. He pressed a grey button situated in the middle of the door and took off his cap, wiped his brow with the back of his hand and wiped his hand on his trousers. He put his cap back on.

Rafe and Lisa took refuge under one of the few trees in the area, a short distance from the wire fence. Mr Peri waved at them and gave them the thumbs up, as if he had it all under control.

"I don't think Arabella likes him," Lisa said, as she took her water canister out of her rucksack. Rafe did the same and rested against the tree.

"I think it's more his stupidity than like or dislike," Rafe said, as he glanced over at Mr Peri, who was shifting from one foot to the other as if it were a cold day. "She did say we must get away from him and get inside Hill House."

"Perhaps there's another way in. I'll have a quick look at the map before he comes back. See if there is another entrance."

"Lisa, you're going to look at the map?" Rafe mocked playfully.

Lisa unzipped her rucksack. "Ha ha, I'm learning."

"I thought Ben had your book?"

"Yes, but I got it back. Not that difficult if you know how." She smiled up at Rafe then buried her head in her bag.

"You're certainly full of surprises," Rafe chuckled.

"I put it in my bag last night, cos I got juice on my jacket. I was saving it from a sticky end. Goodness knows I've been in enough trouble with this book. I didn't want the few pages to stick together." She unzipped another compartment and began taking out the contents. "I can't seem to find it." A cold sweat swept over Lisa. "I really haven't got it!"

"Are you sure?"

"Yes." She hurriedly threw some of her items back in the bag. "What are we going to do?"

"Don't let him see that anything is wrong," Rafe encouraged, putting on a fake smile. "He'll start asking questions."

Lisa glanced at Mr Peri. He was watching them. She waved and smiled at him taking her time to place the rest of her belongings back in the bag.

"It could have fallen out at the Peri's."

She stood up and faced Rafe, with her back turned to Mr Peri. "I can't see how. I was so careful." She re-traced her steps to Rafe as Rafe kept a watchful eye on Mr Peri.

"I think I saw Mrs Peri in my room before we left."

"We have a big problem," Rafe sighed. "We can't leave the book in someone else's hands, that's if Mrs Peri has it. We need to get into that house."

Lisa shrugged in despair. "We can't get rid of Mr Peri as Arabella said. I've really messed this up again."

"Your book could be under the bed, not found, let's not panic, let's think about this." Rafe put his canister away. "We need to get it back…there is a way of doing this. One of us could go in there and the other goes back with Mr Peri, gets the book and waits for the rest to return."

Lisa screwed her face up, "I'm not sure what's in there. Mrs Peri's fine, but to walk all the way back with that nitwit – it would be like dragging me to a football match - screaming."

"Well, when you put it like that, I'll go to Hill House. You're with the nitwit," Rafe smirked.

Before Lisa could protest, Rafe said, "The door's open!" They couldn't see who Mr Peri was talking to, but by the upward tilt of his head they assumed the person to be quite tall, or that Mr Peri had really lost his mind and was talking to the greenery dangling from a ridge above the doorway. Within a few minutes, the door slammed in his face. The bang resonated in the peaceful air.

Mr Peri didn't move.

"What just happened?" Lisa asked.

"Looks like it could be bad news."

"No way."

Mr Peri turned, moved his cap closer to his eyes and walked away from the door shaking his head.

Rafe took a deep breath, "Looks like plan B."

"B?"

"The football match."

"Oh no."

Mr Peri walked back deep in thought. He didn't try to climb over the wires as he had done previously. Instead, he walked along the wires until he came to a waist high metal gate. It automatically opened as he approached it. Lisa and Rafe watched him keenly, as he stomped towards them.

"Well, well, well," he started, putting his thoughts into words. "It seems like we cannot enter today." He paused and looked at both of them, as if they were going to walk away obediently with no questions asked. Neither of them moved.

"Why not?" Lisa asked.

"What was said?" Rafe added.

"Hold on, hold on, hold on." His voice rose each time he said 'on', "It's not so straightforward."

Rafe shook his head. "Not straightforward?"

"Yes, yes, yes," Mr Peri mumbled, lost in thought again.

"All we want to do is see Tia and Ben." Rafe was getting agitated. Lisa's annoyance grew as Mr Peri delayed and struggled to give them a clear answer.

"My son's there as well and he's fine. I have two children…"

"We know - two of your children are already there…" Lisa began to try to hurry him along.

"And how prestigious it is. It's an honour," Rafe finished.

"So, you get it." Mr Peri smiled, pushed his cap backwards and mopped his brow with the back of his hand. He didn't realise they were not in agreement with him, but were really saying *what's that got to do with us'.*

"Now, all you two have to do is to compete." With that, he began to walk back to the village.

"What?" Rafe and Lisa said, in unison, and marched after him.

"I agreed that you would both compete. It's such an honour, as you know. Such an honour."

"We can't just go in?" Rafe pointed back to the door, almost tripping over the gravel, "We have to? No - YOU agreed that WE should compete?"

"Yep, yep, yep. I thought we already cleared that part up. You will compete."

"I can't see the point." Rafe was now frustrated with Mr Peri's proud yet irritating stance.

"It's an honour to provide help for others and if you can't see that, I don't see what you are doing here." His voice started to fill with an icy tone. He didn't look at them or slow his pace. "You'll have plenty of time to prepare, plenty."

"When is the next competition?" Lisa asked, not wanting to know the answer.

"Six months."

This filled both of them with horror. Staying in this place for six months wasn't what they had bargained for.

"So, what do you expect us to do now?" Rafe tramped alongside Mr Peri, Lisa lagging behind.

Mr Peri saw this as pure anxiety and used it to his full advantage,

"Prepare, that's all you'll have to do. Not to worry. No, don't worry. We'll get you ready. Evelyn will like that. Now, let's get moving, eat your sandwiches on the way, we need to get back before it gets dark. The woods at night aren't good, not good at all." He pulled out his sandwiches and started chomping on them as he went.

Rafe slipped back to walk with Lisa and tugged her back to slow her pace slightly so they could talk.

"It's not right, whatever he has said or agreed," Rafe exclaimed.

"We were told not to trust him and to get rid of him, now look."

"We don't need him to get into that place. Let's just go back, get the book and we'll head out on our own."

"But the woods -,"

"The woods nothing, we were out there and you weren't scared before. Don't listen to him."

"I really don't want to compete. I hate races and climbing. Climbing is the worst thing ever. Ever!"

"You're beginning to sound like Mr Peri."

Lisa frowned not knowing what Rafe meant.

"Repeating your words." He gave a half smile, as he glanced at Mr Peri striding on proudly, muttering to himself. "We are not waiting around to compete in anything. And as for the mention of that Evelyn creep, we are not doing anything for him."

"So, what are we going to do?"

"As I said, go back, get the book. Get out of there!" Rafe was adamant.

Chapter 15

Mrs Peri

By the time they got back to the village, it was dusk. They were convinced Mr Peri took a different route home so they wouldn't remember how to get back to the side entrance at Hill House.

The yellow glow of lanterns and lights from the cabins lit up the village. The villagers were getting ready for their evening meal. Those with smaller cabins cooked outside on open fires. Others with the large cabins cooked within their homes. Smells of food and laughter created a comforting and homely feeling. Smoke rose and danced way above the flames. Villagers greeted the trio as they passed by and offered bowls of soup. Mr Peri refused for all three of them, stating his wife would have their meal ready. Rafe and Lisa didn't like him speaking on their behalf. They would have gladly accepted a morsel, as they had no way of knowing whether Mrs Peri had indeed done as he had said.

When they entered the cabin, Mrs Peri wasn't surprised to see them. In fact, she had a pot of meat stew ready for them. She greeted them warmly, yet asked nothing of the day, nor did she enquire what they had done. Instead, she gave them just enough time to wash their hands and eat their meal - there was no time for them to search for Lisa's book.

Mr Peri enjoyed eating with his fingers whenever possible. He licked his fingers with great satisfaction after dipping each piece of bread in his bowl of stew. Three loud bangs on the cabin door disrupted the unsettled but cordial meal. Mr Peri burped loudly as he got up from the table and wiped his hands on a cloth that his wife had provided for him.

A small man stood at the door. Excited and out of breath, he managed a polite wave to the diners as he informed Mr Peri there was an emergency council meeting. The man hovered impatiently at the door, as Mr Peri grabbed a piece of bread from his unfinished meal. With his mouth full, he told his wife not to wait up for him, as he grabbed his cap and jacket. The small man slammed the door behind them.

Lisa and Rafe finished their meal, but before clearing away, Mrs Peri ushered them into the back room.

"Please. Be seated," she said, urgently and turned on a silver lantern hanging beside the door. A waistcoat hung on a run of four hooks on the door.

"We have been fortunate to get electricity in some parts, powered by the water," she said, in a nervous tone.

A round table with two wooden chairs and four unusual metal chairs sat around it. Mrs Peri sat closest to the door. Lisa sat next to her, then Rafe. He found the metal chair surprisingly comfortable. Behind Rafe was a large cupboard with engraved scenery on the doors, a window with closed shutters situated beside the cupboard. Underneath was a large metal chest. The adjacent wall had floor to ceiling bookshelves. Engraved wooden mugs were scattered amongst the dusty books. Tapestry, which adorned the remaining walls, brightened the cramped room.

Mrs Peri nimbly made her way to the bookshelves, as Rafe and Lisa viewed the room and wondered what was going on. Mrs Peri rummaged amongst the books disrupting particles of dust. Finally, she pulled out Lisa's book. The astonishment on their faces was clear to see, as

Mrs Peri proceeded to explain how the book had come to be in her possession.

"I took the book out of your bag." She sat down, laid the book delicately on the table in front of her and placed her hands on the top of it. Her slender fingers gripped it like a crab. "I have to be honest - I knew the book didn't belong in this house. As you can see, many of our books have not been read for a long time." She averted her gaze from them in embarrassment. "I've never seen such a book. It was so soft, so magical. The name on the book caught my eye."

Rafe and Lisa dared not interrupt her. They wanted to know more.

"I knew you would be back, if only to retrieve it." She lowered her voice, as though someone was trying to listen in on her conversation. "When I saw the maps, I knew, then, that you must be here to help us."

Rafe was shocked at her statement. "Help do what?"

"You are here for us," Mrs Peri said, this time with an expectancy that they were going to say yes.

Rafe was unsure what to say, as far as he was concerned they always seemed to be off track and he somehow felt that, perhaps, this was another diversion.

"My concern is Tia. We were supposed to meet Lisa and her brother and, well, it hasn't worked out as expected…,"

"It's true, "Lisa interrupted. "If Ben hadn't fallen out of the tree, we could have been home by now. We shouldn't really be here."

Mrs Peri lowered her head, tears pricked her eyes; a few escaped and ran down her cheeks. She quickly wiped them away. Lisa placed a caring hand on her shoulder.

"I'm sorry," Rafe said, "we're of no help to you."

"I don't want to burden…" She sniffed, then straightened up, not wanting to make the two youngsters feel any worse. "It's just that I recognised the name, and some of the maps have scenes from our cupboard." She lowered her voice again, "Arabella Marquelleth."

This grabbed their attention. Rafe turned to view the cupboard then got up to take a closer look. Intrigued by this link, but not wanting to give anything away about Arabella, he asked. "Who is this – Marquelleth?"

"I don't know her personally. Her name is whispered amongst the villagers, but we can never say her name aloud. Evelyn has banned it."

On hearing this Rafe felt a sense of injustice, "His name keeps cropping up and I …" He stopped himself from saying any more. He wasn't sure what Mrs Peri would make of his thoughts on Evelyn, especially that everyone seemed to idolise him.

"What were you going to say?" Lisa probed, unwittingly.

"Nothing," Rafe said, giving her a quick glare, which she recognised and so took a deep breath and went across to look at the cupboard with him.

"Sorry," Lisa murmured. She remembered how Mr Peri flipped today and she really didn't know if Rafe was trying to avoid the same thing with Mrs Peri.

Mrs Peri paused as they observed the cupboard.

"Is this a magical cupboard?" Lisa asked.

Mrs Peri gave a weary smile, "No. If only. It would solve many of our problems. A long time ago, special people made pieces of furniture at Hill House. These crafts people were highly skilled, some of noble birth. They carved scenes of their lineage or stories of the woods and the beasts that exist there."

Rafe and Lisa looked more closely at the carvings and listened keenly.

"Each piece of furniture tells a story. Eventually, the crafts people were no more and the stories no longer told. The Marquelleth family, in some form, have always been the rulers of the land."

"Rulers!" Lisa looked back at Mrs Peri.

Rafe straightened up, thoughts flying through his mind.

"Yes. Evelyn is part of this family and claims to be disappointed at the gradual letting go of these crafts people, blaming some of his family for destroying this creativity. You see, he is intelligent and skilful. He has creations, inventions - like these chairs." She stood up and demonstrated the simple collapse mechanism of her chair as though it were a magic trick. "You are honoured when you are given any of his inventions."

Rafe nodded in approval. "That's why they applauded him at the games."

"Yes, he has created so many things, and when the water dried up, because of the disappearance of the crafts people, he gave us a new water source."

"How could the water source be linked with the crafts people?" Rafe was confused.

They all sat down. Mrs Peri continued. "Evelyn told us that the loss of the crafts people destroyed the water source that we previously had, and that our children would be the answer to the shortage."

Rafe and Lisa looked on in disbelief, but said nothing.

"It's more complicated. It divided the various towns and villages around. Fights broke out over which child should go. Anyway, let's not worry about that now, it was a long time ago. Evelyn defended the rights of the people when other factions of the nobility opposed him. The story has been altered over time." She hesitated for a moment and then took a deep breath. "I must tell you what I know for sure."

Mrs Peri started talking with an intensity they hadn't heard in her tone before. "Evan, my eldest son has been working at Hill House with our daughter Meela for many years." Her voice trembled slightly. She composed herself and went on. "One night, he returned. He didn't look well." She refrained from any descriptions that would cause her further upset. "He said they needed help. The work wasn't what they had expected and they were not being treated well."

"But everyone wants to work at Hill House," Lisa interjected.

"Evelyn introduced the games to find the fittest and strongest children to help obtain water, and in return, the families are rewarded for their children's services. He built the water wheel not long after the children started work at Hill House. Water, which had been in such short supply, was now plentiful. Evan said their treatment was good, at first, but it got progressively worse. He hadn't seen Meela for some time. This was distressing to hear."

Rafe was disgusted at the thought of children working at Evelyn's suggestion. "Why were the adults not given the option?"

"Adults farmed the land and provided other heavy work. It's been like this for as long as I can remember. No one questions it anymore… it's our way of life. However, now I feel guilty that we were able to live very well for many years until Evan told us the truth. How could we live like this, at the cost of our children's suffering? Not only mine but others' as well. Those people, without children, how we used to pity them. They have the smallest cabins and resources." Mrs Peri rocked gently to ease the pain she was feeling.

"Why did you let Alamo go?" As the words came out of Lisa's mouth, she regretted them, "I'm sorry." She bowed her head. Mrs Peri didn't take any offence to this question.

"I didn't want him to go. I've always tried to stop him, but he vowed that when he became fifteen, he would find his brother and sister. Alamo didn't have the same athleticism as Evan or speed as Meela, but he makes up for it with clear thinking, wit and now strength." It was clear, from the pride in her voice, that she loved her children and admired their courage. "My husband has always encouraged him. He takes great pride in his children. He is overwhelmed with the prestigious place we now hold in the community, because of them. He thinks they have helped the villagers and us beyond which we couldn't do ourselves."

"He's very patriotic, I presume." Rafe wanted to say 'idiotic', after seeing the man in action that afternoon, but didn't believe calling him an idiot would help the situation.

"Yes. He invests all his spare time in council matters for the benefit of the villagers. Working in the stables with the horses is wonderful, but that awful contraption Evelyn created makes me shudder every time I visit the stables. Omar will not have a bad word said against Evelyn. He was delighted when Evelyn visited us to check if you were alright. He ordered that Ben and Tia should leave early and not to disturb you both."

A blanket of fear fell over Rafe and Lisa.

Chapter 16

Plan B

Rafe's mind was spinning. He felt he had let Tia down and not managed to keep them all together as Arabella had instructed. Her words *'work together'* echoed in his head. He had to find a way to rescue them and Evelyn seemed to be so many steps ahead of them. Rafe's attention jolted back to what Mrs Peri was saying.

"There is a map in here, like the one Evan had." She flicked past the empty pages. Neither Rafe nor Lisa were prepared to answer questions about those pages. Fortunately, Mrs Peri didn't ask. She focused on pursuing her optimistic search. She turned the book towards them. "Here it is." It was a map of the area surrounding Hill House.

Rafe's confidence started to rise, as he anticipated rescuing the others. "There must be entrances and exit points."

"I'm sorry. I'm not sure where they all are. I was busy tending to Evan's wounds. But I remember… here." She pointed to a hilly area. "There's an entrance to the mines."

"Mines?" Lisa quizzed.

Mrs Peri nodded slowly, not wanting to say any more.

"Are you saying that the children work in mines?" Rafe staggered his speech, hoping Mrs Peri was going to stop him and say it wasn't true.

She didn't.

Rafe felt sick. He glanced over at Lisa. She looked horrified. "That means Tia and Ben could…" Her voice trailed off, she was close to tears.

Children working in mines?

Rafe was desperate for a solution. "Could your husband help?"

"I think it's best not to let him know. I'm not so sure how helpful he would be," Mrs Peri said, firmly. "He wasn't very cooperative when Evan came back. He escorted him back to Hill House."

Lisa and Rafe looked on in horror at what she was saying.

"He felt ashamed that Evan had left his post. He didn't want anyone to see guards enter this house. It would have been a shameful, undignified thing." Mrs Peri paused and sniffed, took a delicate, woven fabric from her skirt pocket and dabbed her nose. "Anyway... that was then. Now it's different. I respect Evelyn, but I don't trust him. So, I have a plan." Mrs Peri got up, opened the large chest and began to unpack the material that filled it. Before she reached the bottom of the chest - through excitement or impatience - she yanked out two dark all-in-one garments. Mrs Peri held them up in front of her with great satisfaction, as though she had just rescued them from the depths of the ocean.

"These are used by the Gatherers – they collect the lights used in the mines. Stand up. Stand up," she ordered. Rafe and Lisa jumped up and glanced at each other to see if either of them understood what was going on. Mrs Peri put each hooded garment against them to see if they would fit. She swapped them around.

"Put them on."

Lisa appeared horrified. She wasn't going to take her clothes off in front of them. Mrs Peri saw Lisa's mortification and quickly added, "Over your own clothes, of course. Evan left his and Alamo found one in the stables."

Once they put them on, it became clear to Rafe what they could do dressed as Gatherers. He was back in rescue mode again.

175

Lisa's garment fit her height, but it had far too much room around her body, which made her look like a crumpled shirt. Rafe's hands vanished under the cuffs.

"Not to worry. They can be altered."

They both laughed at each other. This was a much-needed distraction. Rafe shook his long sleeves and watched as they flopped around in front of him trying to catch Lisa. Lisa twisted her body from left to right, so that the extra material rippled around her body. Mrs Peri smiled, as it reminded her of when her children were young. Her eyes darted over the garments. She went over to the cupboard. Rafe shuffled out of the way. Mrs Peri took out a sewing box decorated with carvings. Once opened it smelled of cedar wood. She took out scissors and pins on a multicoloured pin cushion in the shape of a butterfly. Mrs Peri went to work pinning the excess material. "I can get this finished by tomorrow, which means you can join them!" she said, triumphantly.

"Join who?" Lisa asked, keeping as still as possible. She didn't want to get stuck by pins, as she had seen Rafe grimace once or twice.

"Those who collect the lights," Mrs Peri said.

"It's our way of finding the others," Rafe smiled. "Get into Hill House."

It finally dawned on Lisa. "A disguise."

"We'll need gloves." Rafe gave a light-hearted wink at Lisa.

"Don't remind me."

Mrs Peri mumbled something with pins between her lips and looked in the sewing box. She pulled out a tape measure and small square pieces of fabric and eventually a pair of gloves, which she handed to Lisa.

"They fit," Lisa exclaimed. "I'm glad I don't have to feel the sticky, runny stuff."

"What's the sticky, runny thing?" Mrs Peri asked, taking the final pin from her lips and placing it back in the pin cushion.

"Lisa caught a spore or light and it broke like a sticky egg."

Lisa looked slightly embarrassed, remembering the night's antics.

"I didn't realise they could break, I was told they provided special light in the mines. Where did you see them?"

"Before we got to the village, they were catching them," Lisa said, as she took her gloves off.

"That's good," Mrs Peri said. "That means when you join them you'll know what to do." She sighed happily. "I'll make sure I get you gloves by tomorrow – now that I know how important they are - and belts."

"The ones with stripes had on belts. We haven't got stripes," Rafe said

"From what I have been told the ones with stripes are called Defenders and the others are called Gatherers. You're both far too kind to be part of the Defenders. No belts then."

"They certainly had a lot of authority," Rafe said, as he remembered how they controlled the events of the night. "Tia said they didn't harm her."

Mrs Peri said nothing. She knew that Evan didn't have anything good to say about them. Rafe continued: "Their faces weren't visible when I saw them."

"Oh, I forgot…pull your hood up and forward."

Rafe and Lisa followed her instructions. "Now, just reach on the inside of the hood…on the left."

They both switched from reaching into the opposite side of their hoods and had a chuckle.

"There is a gauze, a thin mesh of material. Pull it around your face."

Lisa found it awkward at first, but managed it.

"It's unbelievable. I can still see through it." Rafe moved his head in all directions.

"See Rafe, they did have faces, they were just covered."

"Not all of them Lisa. I would bet on that."

"You just wanted to scare us," Lisa mocked.

"I'm sure the Defenders were different." Rafe was convinced about what he had seen and no one was going to change his mind.

"Well," Mrs Peri began, "I've been told the Gatherers go out once a week at night to catch the lights, but most recently they have had to go out every couple of nights. Something has happened - I'm not sure what. So, let's use this opportunity. I've also been reassured that they don't check numbers, they just want obedient workers. I have a plan to allow you to blend in with them in the woods before they get to the twisted trees. Then it's up to you."

"I'm sure that's where we first spotted them," Rafe said. Lisa nodded in confirmation, remembering the strange looking trees.

"Be careful, now step out of those suits. I'll make you a bedtime drink and go over how you get there tomorrow night. And remember don't say a word to my husband." Mrs Peri left the room. They could hear her moving about in the kitchen.

179

Rafe closed the door and spoke quietly. "What do you think? Does she seem genuine?" He stepped out of his garment.

"Yes. She's doing a lot to help us."

"We have to trust her. If we get in trouble, we'll call Mrs M or use our pendants."

"Our secret weapons," Lisa grinned, as she pulled her arms out of the sleeves. "It's interesting that her name is Marquel and Evelyn is related to the Marquelleth family." Lisa sat down to remove the final part of her garment from around her ankles and accidentally caught a couple of protruding pins. She sucked at the grazes on her hand.

"Now I see why she wanted our help, to get her kingdom back from that Evelyn creep." Rafe thought for a moment. "Perhaps her name is Marquelleth. Marquel could be the shortened version."

"But why wouldn't she tell us that in the beginning?"

"And therein lies the answer," Rafe said.

"What?"

"If she had told you and Ben what it was, '*I need help to get rid of an evil person who has stolen my kingdom and release the children working in mines*' would you have said yes? Never mind the name thing."

"If she said they needed water, I would."

"Come on Lisa, even if water wasn't involved, I know I'd have second thoughts. It's because of Tia why I'm here."

"You're right," Lisa conceded. "I just wanted a good book to read and go home. I'm too young to be thinking like a grown up."

Rafe laughed, and placed his folded garment on the table. Lisa did the same. They ambled into the kitchen thinking about their mission.

Once Lisa and Rafe had gone to bed, Mrs Peri sat in the small room, hastily completing the alterations before her husband got back. She felt guilty about the parts of the story she had left out. She didn't want to scare them unnecessarily. She knew they would eventually find out.

Chapter 17

Infiltrate

"Arabella, Arabella?" Lisa called.

There was no response. It was late afternoon and Lisa had been trying to contact Arabella for most of the day.

"Arabella will you come now, we need your help!" Lisa lost her calm. She hoped to get some advice before going on the night's event, but no blue leaves appeared.

"It's not fair, you turn up when you want to and ignore us when you don't. Whatever happened to obliging?"

Rafe entered the room, as Lisa got angrier. She kicked at the chest where Arabella had last appeared.

"Shush. I could hear you outside," Rafe said.

"She should be helping us now. Where is she?"

Rafe led Lisa away from the chest of drawers and sat her down on the bed. "Let's try to rely on what we do know."

"Like what?" Lisa said, despondently.

182

"Well," Rafe sat beside her, "We can trust each other to find Ben and Tia - even Alamo."

Lisa slowly nodded her head in agreement.

"We've seen the Gatherers and Defenders. We know what they do, so we've got that advantage."

Lisa still looked glum.

"Don't we?" Rafe put his arms around her shoulders.

"Yes. But I messed things up."

"Forget about that, we've seen Tia and Ben and they are doing well. In fact, they were more determined to help the villagers than we were."

Lisa agreed.

"If Evelyn hadn't got involved, we may have had a different plan. We may have decided to compete in the games."

"No Rafe. One thing I'm sure of, I wouldn't have. I even hate climbing trees!"

This gave them a brief source of amusement.

"Lisa, I've tried to get Arabella to show up."

Lisa looked at him expectantly.

"It's not good news. She hasn't. I've even tried walking around invisibly, spinning, kneeling, in hope that I could see her, or conjure her up."

"You must have looked really silly," Lisa joked.

"I felt silly," Rafe laughed, "I felt like I was five, playing let's pretend. Anyway, the point is, she didn't come for me either, so don't be too hard on yourself." A seriousness crept into his tone. "What did hit me was, we must stick together and find the others; this may help us complete our purpose here and then we can return home."

Lisa felt reassured by this. "I wish you were my big brother."

"You must be missing Ben."

"Just a little…. But don't tell him I told you."

"I'll think about it. It may just stop you two from arguing so much…" Rafe jumped off the bed, as Lisa launched a friendly push.

"You've got to be quick to catch me," He laughed and dodged her grasp.

Mr Peri's voice boomed up the stairs. "Time to eat. Time to eat."

"Coming," they both called back.

*

"That was a lovely, lovely meal." Mr Peri rubbed his wife's arm to show appreciation. "And seeing as we have guests and they'll be with us for a bit longer, they'll chip in with the household chores, now that my youngest son is busy making us proud." He stretched his large arms upwards, intertwined his fingers and rested his palms behind the folds of his neck.

"I don't think they need to start tonight." His wife winked at Rafe and Lisa.

Lisa was grateful. She hated housework. Mr Peri noticed the frown on Lisa's face and laughed heartily.

"It's fine. You have plenty of time to see how this household works. Rafe, you're tall and strong. You need to get as much rest as possible to compete in the upcoming games. I went to a meeting last night. Top secret – we are looking at moving the games forward by a few months. Comes from the top," he said, smugly leaning backwards, the chair creaked under his weight.

"I'm not so sure I want to compete," Rafe said, mischievously goading Mr Peri.

"Oh. No, no, no." Mr Peri remonstrated. He moved his hands in the air as though he were trying to stop a train. "You will enjoy it. I'll show you what you need to do, I'll produce another winner." He turned to Lisa. "You'll need a bit more time. I would start you off with housework, build stamina…"

"I think that's enough talk for one night," Mrs Peri interrupted. "They need a good night's sleep before they can even begin to think about those things, Omar."

Rafe and Lisa took this as their cue to leave the table immediately.

"Thanks, that was a lovely meal. Good night," Rafe said.

"Go, go, go. Get some rest. In the morning, we will talk about it," Mr Peri said, as though it was his suggestion for them to go to bed.

As they went up the stairs, Lisa released her annoyance. "He's got a cheek. Housework!"

"Ignore him. Let's get some rest and concentrate on what we need to do tonight."

"I wonder if he's ever lifted a plate, apart from lifting to lick it. Yuk!"

Rafe burst into laughter. "When you get going, you're something else."

Lisa continued to imitate the licking of the plate with much hilarity. It was good for them to try to relax. They had a dangerous task ahead of them.

*

Mrs Peri paced the dining room floor. She peered outside a few times to make sure her neighbours had gone inside their cabins. She wore a long black shawl that covered her head as well as the rest of her dark clothing. Mr Peri was asleep upstairs; they dared not disturb him, although his snoring could have disturbed most of the village.

Rafe and Lisa hurriedly got ready in the back room. They dragged their blue outfits over their jeans and tops. They both secured their books in the secret panel Mrs Peri had sewn into the black tops she provided for them, along with the correct footwear.

"I could hardly sleep, knowing what we had to do," Lisa whispered as she tied her laces.

"Me too," Rafe said, as he pulled on his gloves. "They fit perfectly." He admired them as he flexed his fingers. "Can't wait."

Lisa looked at him as if he were going crazy.

"What?" Rafe asked, oblivious to Lisa's apprehension.

Lisa shook her head and picked up her gloves, "How can you be excited?"

"My adrenaline is on the up, I like this – it's all positive. We're going to do something about our situation instead of it happening to us. You've forgotten your torch." Rafe handed it to her.

Lisa opened her zip and pushed it into her pocket. "Did you find out what the other torch was?"

"I think it's some type of weapon. It flicks out so quickly, it's quite firm, and it leaves a nasty indent on anything you whack."

"How do you know that?"

"I was swinging it around and it hit the side of the dresser. I hope no one spots the damage."

"Rafe…? I'm surprised at you." Lisa pulled her gloves on and fitted the edge firmly under the sleeves. She made sure that nothing could leak into any part of her.

"I had to find out what it could do."

Mrs Peri entered the room. "Good," she said, pleased with the alterations she had made. "Just pull your hoods over your heads for now. Come quickly." She turned the lantern off.

They followed her into the darkened dining area. Lisa held on to Rafe's arm, not wanting to bump into any of the furniture. Mrs Peri peeked out of the front door to make sure the coast was clear, then ushered them quietly outside.

The dimly lit electric lights created a calming feel across the village. The chilly night air carried the smoky aroma from the dying embers of the cooking fires, which crackled lazily. Dogs lay at front doors or by the faded fires, almost asleep. They cocked their ears as the trio passed, but none moved to investigate their presence.

Mrs Peri led them to the courtyard against the dry-stone walls. The guards were deep in conversation, their backs to the trio. Mrs Peri put her finger to her lips and pointed to the statue holding the buckets, then to the corner filled with dried brambles.

"There is an entrance in the corner," she whispered. "Keep close to the wall. I'll go first, then you, (she pointed to Lisa) and you." Rafe nodded.

The shadows from the walls and dried vines obscured her movements. Once she was out of sight, Lisa followed. She moved against the wall slowly, keeping an eye on the guards. Mrs Peri pulled her into a narrow nook. It was Rafe's turn - he was half way along the wall when the guards stopped talking.

The moonlight bounced off the metal doors and caught Rafe's silhouette for a brief moment. Rafe held his breath.

A guard caught a glimpse of him from the corner of his eye and turned. Rafe froze.

"Who's there?" The guard shouted and strode towards Rafe his hand on the handle of his sword.

Rafe pushed at his pendant, but the gloves kept hitting the wrong point. As the guards closed in on Rafe, his legs sprang into action and he darted into the nook. He squeezed himself past Mrs Peri and Lisa who pushed down on a lever and sealed the entrance. They could still hear the startled voice of the guard.

"There was someone here."

"Are you sure?"

"Yes."

They hacked away at some of the brambles and banged at the secret entrance, but only felt the cold hard stone.

"You must be seeing things."

The trio didn't wait around to hear any more. Lisa and Rafe's hearts pounded as they followed Mrs Peri in single file along a narrow passageway, with walls on both sides and the glimmer of sky above. It ran for ten metres then came to a dead end. A hint of dampness rose in the air. Mrs Peri reached into a ragged hole just above her head and pulled out a small lantern. She pressed a button on its base and it lit up. The flame glowed blue, illuminating flowing movements in the dark end wall. Lisa and Rafe looked on in amazement as Mrs Peri swept the dark area aside to reveal a tunnel.

She jerked her head around. "Cloth, not stone." She smiled and descended into the archway. The damp slope levelled off into lumpy soil under foot. They finally took a sharp right and pushed through a bushy area concealing the entrance into the woods.

Mrs Peri turned off the lantern.

Lisa hugged Rafe. "Thank goodness you're OK."

"I thought they had got me, I really did."

Mrs Peri was glad Rafe was fine but wasted no time. She strode on at pace. They had to run to catch up with her. She headed in a relatively straight line into dense wood, weaving past trees and bushes. She stopped a few metres in front of a dirt track.

"Hide here." Mrs Peri tucked them behind a close circle of trees and foliage. She whispered further information, "Remember, they will pass along there." She pointed to the track. "Don't speak to anyone, just follow what they do. Avoid the attention of the Defenders."

"Avoid the striped ones," Lisa said aloud.

"Yes." Mrs Peri had a hint of agitation in her tone. She didn't want to be interrupted. "Do not run past the twisted trees. Stay in the opening to catch the lights. Trust no one, until you meet with Alamo and your family. I will keep your bags safe."

"Thank you for all your help," Rafe said.

Mrs Peri placed the lantern on the ground. "I will set the disturbance now." She took a handful of grey seeds from her skirt pocket.

"I hope this works," Lisa mumbled.

"Don't worry it will. Horses hate it under their hooves. Now, cover your faces." Mrs Peri moved quickly through the bushes onto the dirt track and scattered the grey seeds. The moon obliged, hiding behind clouds as she quickly completed her task.

Rafe and Lisa tried to secure the gauze across their faces, but their gloved hands were like icy fingers trying to handle silk. They were grateful for Mrs Peri's return, as she assisted them to secure the gauze properly.

With a quick embrace, she picked up the lantern and weaved through the bushes, merging in with the darkened foliage.

Chapter 18

Gatherers and Defenders

The moonlight hit the tops of the trees. The shadows it cast below provided perfect camouflage for Rafe and Lisa.

"It's unbelievable how much you can see," Lisa whispered as she viewed the vegetation along the track.

"Hmm."

"Even into the trees."

"Hmm."

"I feel comfortable in this." Lisa stretched her arms out in front of her, flexing her hands. Rafe pulled his hood further forward to make it feel more secure. He kept a watchful eye for the entourage.

"I'm nervous." She waited for Rafe to respond, she couldn't tell by his body language if he was listening. His frame was still and his head positioned in the direction of the anticipated convoy.

"Are you raising an eyebrow at me?"

Rafe chuckled. "No."

"Are you OK?"

"I'm fine. Try and listen for them." He pulled Lisa closer to the tree. "Keep vigilant. If anything goes wrong, use your necklace and return to Mrs Peri."

"OK, but we'll be fine, won't we?"

"Yes."

"Mr Peri said the woods were…" Lisa heard the call of an owl. She started to imagine that there were things lurking in the dark and began to get scared. She moved closer to Rafe.

"Stop worrying. That idiot said those things to scare us, just so we'd stay with him."

The dull thud of horses' hooves and squeaking wheels alerted them to the coming entourage.

Their hearts began to race.

Two Defenders came into view, followed by a group of Gatherers with Defenders dispersed among them. The horses and cart creaked along with their handlers and two Defenders at the back of the convoy. Rafe gave Lisa the thumbs up sign. She nodded, and they both crept closer to the track.

The horses jerked their heads upwards. The handlers gripped the reins in response, but the horses shunted backwards and snorted heavily. Their handlers tried to get control of them but the horses reared up onto their back legs, the cart flung some of its contents out and screeched loudly. The other items rattled and jolted about in the cart. Three Defenders and two Gatherers ran to steady the cart and its contents. The horses stomped and neighed. The handlers tried their best to settle them. Two Defenders stood guard as the commotion continued; the remaining Defenders and Gatherers ran to the edge of the track and grabbed branches from the bushes. They were only a few metres away from Rafe and Lisa, who quickly joined in. With a handful of branches, they also dashed onto the track to help sweep the ground free of the seeds. With the increasing dust and commotion, not even the guarding Defenders spotted their arrival.

The horses eventually settled down and the Gatherers turned their attention to the dislodged contents, placing them back under the cover of the cart. Once everything was back in place, the convoy continued, although the wheels of the cart had an extra screech and scrape as they turned.

*

Eventually, the convoy arrived at the clearing. The Gatherers made their way to the back of the cart. One of the Defenders had already unhooked the back flap in readiness. The gazebo and blankets were the first items taken from the cart. Rafe and Lisa filed in line with the rest of the group. Rafe assisted three other Gatherers to lift out a long wooden table. As they put it in place, Rafe quickly scanned the area and realised they were at the same spot where they had watched the Gatherers. He shook the unfortunate memory of Tia being taken from his head and concentrated on what he needed to do.

Once in front of the open cart, Lisa froze. She saw arms and hands grab items, and when she looked up, their lack of faces made her shudder. A Defender shoved a pile of nets towards her. Her hands automatically went up to scoop them, but instead they landed on the floor. She tried to pick them up, but stumbled forward and ended up on the ground. The Defender leant down, so their hoods were almost touching. Lisa thought she was going to get some help or advice, but instead the voice that met her ear was not pleasant; it was low and fierce.

"Pick these up or pay the penalty!"

The gloves made Lisa's hands feel clumsy - she snatched at the nets and shook dried leaves free from them. She tried to stand with confidence, but trembled as she did this. She managed to hold the nets firmly in her arms. A shove in the back by a brutal palm got her moving.

Lisa staggered forward, and then regained a suitable pace. She wished she knew where Rafe was. All she saw before her was dark figures of all heights, their movements swift and effective, much quicker now that she was amongst them. She placed the nets with the others on the table. Lisa quickly headed back to the cart not wanting to have the same encounter again, as she saw the Defender hovering menacingly in her vicinity.

The moon provided enough light for them to complete their tasks. Once the Defenders started to make their way to the twisted trees, the Gatherers took their nets and containers. Lisa did the same.

Rafe positioned himself behind one of the tables in readiness to receive the full containers and empty them into the correct coloured barrels. Rafe didn't get this position easily. When he stood behind the table, a Gatherer came alongside him and applied his body weight against Rafe to move him out of the way - clearly trying not to draw attention to what was going on. However, Rafe wasn't going to be pushed out of the way by anyone. As the person pushed again, Rafe did the same. There was a silent stand-off. The person tried again, but this time Rafe pushed back more forcibly. When he felt the same response, he quickly shifted his body weight forward causing the Gatherer to push against thin air. Rafe's opponent fell sideways behind him, prompting immediate action from one of the huge roving Defenders, who pulled out a baton and hit the Gatherer, dragging and shoving him to the other end of the table. The Defender marched down the line and his vicious voice boomed into the night air,

"The penalties will be harsh. No more antics!" He kept his baton in his hand to reinforce his intention.

Rafe slowly turned his head to see if he could recognise Lisa. He hoped she was OK, but his search was almost impossible with everyone dressed the same and holding the same items.

The Defenders positioned themselves under the twisted trees. Everyone stood still. An unsettling silence descended on the entourage. Leaves fluttered and rustled as a sudden breeze wafted through the trees. The nets swung from side-to-side as the Gatherers held them in the air. They waited for the breeze to subside.

In sequence, the Defenders took out their golden batons, held them up above their heads while keeping the wooden batons lowered in their other hand. The rotation of the batons released a humming sound, which gradually became more intense with the rotation. At first, Rafe and Lisa wanted to cover their ears, but they dare not do anything that would risk giving themselves away.

Spores sprouted from the under leaves of the trees. They began to light up like electric bulbs. Ripping sounds echoed around them as the spores disconnected from the leaves and drifted into the air. A sudden descent immediately followed the gentle take-off, as the ground, which was dull and grey, gleamed and shimmered brightly with the fallen spores. Rafe and Lisa were grateful for the hood lining as it shielded their eyes from the extreme and intense brightness. The sound subsided to a rhythmic hum.

There was no time to concentrate on the noise once the action of having to catch and store the spores began. It became an organised, frenzied scene of action, sounds and colours - uncomfortable yet hypnotic.

In no time, the Gatherers had filled their containers. Lisa struggled at first to place the spores in her container. She wasn't releasing the lever at the right time to keep the spores contained. This inadequacy helped Rafe to spot her, and he silently encouraged her to catch up with the others. Eventually, she got the hang of it, working out that if she tapped the rim of the net on the edge of the container it released the spores more quickly and effectively.

Rafe was now having problems of his own. He found it difficult to take the spores out of the bowls and place them into the barrels. He was cautious, and treated them delicately. He didn't want to crush them. The Gatherers worked quickly, pushing and jolting Rafe as he moved slowly. Then he observed that the others handled the spores with no hesitation, as if they were solid objects. They swiftly placed them in the matching coloured barrel and returned the emptied containers for the collection to continue. Rafe carefully observed and rapidly matched the skill and competence of the Gatherers.

The twirling of the batons slowed, the sounds diminished and the releasing of the spores eased. The lights dimmed; the few spores that were still ascending left a trail of light in their wake. Eventually, the moonlight took prominence, illuminating the remaining spores that had hit the ground; the soil would soon absorb them. By daybreak, there would be no sign of them and the area would return to normal.

The absence of hypnotic sounds brought a deafening silence, soon interrupted by the snorting of the horses and the clinking and clanking of the equipment, as the packing away commenced.

The horses became jittery and kept moving backwards and forwards; this motion swung the cart out of place, and the contents started banging against each other. The Gatherers who still had items in their hands stepped out of the way. It took three more Defenders to assist the handlers to calm the horses and try to position the cart again. A Gatherer decided that this disturbance would assist his planned escape. He took the opportunity to dash across the clearing towards the woods. Two Defenders made after him. They were rapid, but he made it past the clearing to the dense part of the wood.

The other Gatherers were compelled to complete their tasks and not watch the escapee.

As the Gatherers finally lined up behind the cart, distressed cries rose from the direction in which the Gatherer had fled. They all turned in the direction of the cries. This time, the Defenders didn't deter them from taking a look. The Defenders dragged the escaped Gatherer between them and every couple of paces they hit him in the back with their wooden batons, a fizzing sound accompanying each hit. The Gatherer cried out in pain.

Lisa shook with fear. Rafe couldn't believe what was happening. They hoped this was not going to be their fate.

Chapter 19

Hidden Places

Wheels creaked, boots stomped, the agonizing moans of the Gatherer faltered along with the convoy. The woods became dense and it was difficult to see the stars or the night sky. The moon managed to work rays of light between the branches and leaves that scraped at the sky.

The track got narrower, the ground polished and worn. As they moved along, just above their heads, a layer of twigs, branches and creeping vines hung low. The horses manoeuvred through, and dipped their heads instinctively at the low branches. Rafe just about managed to avoid a low hanging branch. It only served to remind him of the blow to his head, which he had received some days ago. He became more alert in this darkness to avoid another incident.

They entered a hilly area. The track coiled its way downwards and then a sharp right turn sent them into the final ascent. It levelled out gradually, the canopy disappearing behind them, a rocky hillside to the right of them. The trees on the left side of the track served as camouflage to deceive passers-by of the steep drop that lay beyond.

The horses came to a halt followed by everyone else. The handlers moved the horses forward slowly, settling the horses and cart on a levelled circular area, enclosed by grey hillside.

Two Defenders held the delinquent Gatherer in front of the craggy rock face. The other Defenders shoved the Gatherers into two lines with Defenders positioned at the front and back of each line. The lines ran back up the gradient, ensuring everyone was able to see what was going to take place.

"Halt!" a Defender bellowed, ushering in an unsettling silence.

The hillside rumbled as though it had a hungry inner belly. The Gatherers clamped their hands to their ears as the grating sound escalated. The Defenders stood resolute, offering no reaction to this noise. Two ledges appeared out of the craggy rock, suspended outward into the night air like roughly carved bookshelves. One stood almost at the top of the hill face, the other about five metres below.

As the rumbling subsided, the Defenders pushed the Gatherer towards the slope. The Gatherer stumbled up to the first ledge. The Defenders returned to the level plane.

"Kneel," one shouted.

The Gatherer slumped down.

"The other way," another Defender yelled as though it were a game.

The Gatherer turned to face the sky, which overlooked the dangerous view below. His head bowed and visibly shaking, but no moans or sobs came. The moon peered around the hillside as if to investigate what was going on. It created a severe silhouette – the dark, crumpled, figure of the Gatherer against the moonlit sky. A large blue-grey owl flew onto the top ledge and surveyed the scene.

The cart creaked, the horses occasionally snorted. The trees rustled and whispered over the heads of the stunned convoy.

Above the bowed head of the Gatherer, a robotic voice resonated out of the hillside. It was strong and clear, enough for everyone to pay full attention. Its intentional and authoritative tone made the lined Gatherers shuffle closer together. The lone Gatherer tensed.

"You – have – dishonoured - the - great opportunity - that - you - have - been given. Many envy your position of light. You - have taken - advantage. You - have - disgraced - your family. You - have - tarnished - your - fellow Gatherers."

There was a measured pause.

Gatherers nodded in agreement. Disagreement wouldn't be tolerated. Lisa held her breath then exhaled slowly. She didn't want to see anything horrible happen to the kneeling Gatherer. Rafe wondered whether Tia had witnessed something similar and perhaps this made her more determined to help.

"What - should - we - do?" boomed the voice, cynically. No one dared to answer. The voice laughed a chilling cackle. "What - should - we - do?" This time the words came with false thought and contemplation. "Remove the platform is MY suggestion."

The Gatherer who was kneeling murmured something, but no one heard because of the next bout of cold laughter.

"If the platform is removed, you – will - have a wonderful trip. It will be days before anyone finds you – alive or dead."

Silence.

"Remove the platform...? I say, remove... remove... your hood," the voice demanded.

The Gatherer fumbled to release the lining. Head raised, the hood slumped backwards as the shoulders and head of the Gatherer shook ferociously to reveal a brown-haired boy about fourteen years old, his pale face frozen with fear. He bowed his head again and closed his eyes.

The Gatherer's shaky voice was low. "Forgive me...,"

"Is that all?" the voice coaxed menacingly.

"Forgive me for my disgraceful actions. It has brought shame upon my family and tarnished the Gatherers." The words stammered out.

"And again!"

The Gatherer repeated the statement.

"Again!" the voice took pleasure in this repetition.

The Gatherer repeated it three more times, each time having to say it louder. His voice became hoarse.

"What is the motto of the Gatherers? - *to be as excellent as I can be, to become a Defender when the time is right for me...*" The voice was taunting and severe, "Could you ever be a Defender? Could you? Could you?"

It was not expecting an answer.

"Repeat your motto. Raise your - disgraced head, and proclaim it! Your family's livelihood depends on it."

The voice was satisfied after three more repetitions of the motto. Then, as though nothing had taken place, the voice changed its tone, becoming more human, almost friendly.

"You may all enter. Well done for your job tonight. Your families will live well."

The voice ceased.

The owl took flight.

A relieved, but worried silence lingered in the air.

The Gatherer came down off the ledge. He stood, weak-kneed, between two Defenders. Almost immediately, the ledges withdrew as loudly as they had emerged. The hill-face that sat on the levelled area opened up like a giant beast yawning soothingly. The top jaw rose, emitting well-needed warmth, providing entry to the space within. The horses led the way.

*

The convoy moved into a wide, dimly lit passageway. Two large archways carried the signs 'Loading' and 'Unloading'. They all followed the horses into the unloading bay. It was a cavernous space - still dimly lit,

208

stacked high with barrels and boxes all grouped into alphabetical zones.

They stopped in a clear area to unload everything from the cart. The sounds of unpacking echoed throughout the area.

The horses left smelly deposits on the ground. Many of the Gatherers speedily moved away. The humiliated Gatherer received a small shovel to clear up the mess, watched by a few Defenders, amused by the use of such a small implement to remove such large deposits. It would take some time for him to get rid of it and the horrendous smell. Everyone else made their way into the main warehouse.

*

Rafe and Lisa stared intently at everyone's movements to see if they could spot each other. Some of the Gatherers had started to remove their gauzes and hoods. This worked to Rafe and Lisa's advantage, as it increased the odds of them finding each other. Rafe was glad to see they were all human, but the missing face of the Defender, the other night, still haunted him. The Gatherers were a mixed band of children - girls and boys between the ages of ten to sixteen. Rafe saw two Gatherers make their way past him. One of them was the same height as Lisa. This figure seemed to want to linger a little longer and hadn't removed their hood, so Rafe made his way across to them. He unzipped the top of his garment a little just in case he needed his pendant, but when he put his hand on the arm of the Gatherer he thought was Lisa, they pulled away roughly and marched on. Lisa, who was behind Rafe noticed this altercation and caught a glance of his pendant. She quickly moved towards him with relief.

"Rafe."

"Thank goodness it's you. I was beginning to think you had vanished off somewhere."

"No way, I wouldn't leave you alone in this place," Lisa was adamant.

Rafe was pleased with the growing sense of loyalty Lisa had shown over the past few days; they had developed a bond, something neither of them had thought possible at the beginning.

"Quickly, over there," Rafe said.

They both made sure no one was looking and slipped into an aisle of neatly stacked boxes.

"I'd prefer to be invisible now, especially after what happened to that Gatherer. Wasn't it awful?" Lisa gasped as she took off her gloves and removed her gauze.

"The hillside character massacre… Nasty." Rafe shuddered as his hood fell to his shoulders.

"Can you imagine how cold and dirty it was out on that ledge, and then that voice? What did he do to deserve that treatment?"

"Well, escaping is definitely a no no, just as Mrs Peri had said, which means we have to be quicker and very clever about how we go about this."

"Aren't you scared?"

"More determined."

"Tia said you're a martian artist, so I guess you're not that scared."

Rafe started to chortle. "Martial arts, Lisa."

Lisa felt embarrassed, yet glad it lightened the mood.

"I may have some fears, but not enough to deter me from what we have to do. Don't worry." Rafe smiled at Lisa and placed a supportive hand on her shoulder. "Look how well you did collecting the spores."

Lisa brightened. "Didn't think I'd be able to do that."

"But you did, and did it well, even if you did fall a couple of times."

They both started laughing, forgetting where they were for a moment.

211

"And I had to get rough with another Gatherer to keep the spot I wanted."

"Really?"

"Yep, showed him a bit of Rafe's rope-a-dope." Rafe punched twice into the air and laughed. "And now we're both here, safe. So, it's time to find the others."

"We need to look at the book, see if there is a map or any clues to this place," Lisa said, unzipping her all-in-one enough to take the book out of the concealed pocket. She handed it to Rafe.

"For a moment there, I thought you were going to find the map."

"I'm not totally changed." Lisa joked.

Rafe flicked through to the back pages. He couldn't see anything that resembled the warehouse. Lisa pulled out some of the loose pages she had in her pocket and handed them to Rafe.

"I don't think there is anything here for this warehouse, but there is a hill marked on here with corridors, dorm rooms, dining rooms and tunnels."

"You keep all of them; they're more useful with you."

"No, it's best if you keep yours. Mine is in much better shape." Rafe handed them back. "However, those loose pages can be kept close to hand to find our way around. We just need to get out of here."

"Perhaps if we use our pendants…," Lisa began.

"Use a what?" A girl stepped into the aisle. She was of similar height to Rafe, with deep honey coloured skin and wore her curly black hair in a ponytail. Rafe and Lisa fell silent. They had no idea how long this girl had been listening to their conversation.

Chapter 20

Warehouse

"You're new." She smiled at Rafe and looked over Lisa with a furrowed brow. "I'm Izzy," she said to Rafe and extended her hand towards him. They shook hands.

Lisa was not impressed. "I'm Lisa."

Izzy smiled at Lisa, then turned back to Rafe, "What were you going to use?"

"None of your business," Lisa said, folding her arms in defiance.

Izzy looked directly at Lisa. Her brown eyes found amusement in Lisa's hostile manner. "No need for the aggression, small fry."

"We were thinking of a way to avoid facing any of the humiliation we saw outside." Rafe hoped he'd done a good enough job to change the conversation.

"He was trying to escape. You'll be punished if you try to do anything like that," she warned.

214

"Where was he trying to run to?" Rafe asked unaware of the sizing up process going on between Lisa and Izzy.

"Anywhere," she announced then lowered her voice. "As long as it's not here."

Rafe lowered his voice too, "Will he be OK?"

"Yeah. It's his first attempt." She smiled at Rafe as though he were the only other person in the warehouse. "We'd better get a move on – we'll miss snacks before lights out and get locked in here, and that wouldn't be pleasant, not with that smell lingering – unless you like that sort of thing." She chuckled as she brushed past Lisa.

Lisa screwed up her face, not sure whether to push Izzy or make rude faces behind her back – she opted for the latter. Rafe shook his head curiously at Lisa's reaction to Izzy. However, they were both concerned about how much she had heard, if anything, but neither of them would ask. The one upside was that she could show them how to get out of the warehouse, after which they could go in search of the others.

As they turned the corner, a large, wooden door came into view. Bronze squares with protruding steel shapes of varying sizes lined the outer edges of the door.

"Quick!" Izzy said and started jogging towards the closing door. Rafe was close behind her. Her jog turned into a sprint as the doors slurped shut. She yanked at the horizontal handle. It wouldn't open. She curled up both her fists and banged three times on the middle of the door. The sound reverberated around the walls. Izzy began to count as Lisa finally caught up with them. Rafe and Lisa were mystified as to why she was counting.

"If you don't bang – ten, nine, eight – they won't open – five, four." It was as though she had read their minds.

A hooded Defender, whose sheer size and presence was intimidating, opened the door. A blue stripe embellished his hood and cuffs.

"Thank you," said Izzy, her posture straight and respectful. Lisa and Rafe followed suit.

He gave them permission to enter the corridor.

"That was close," Izzy whispered. "Muck would have been our snack tonight."

"We'd have been locked in?" Lisa grimaced.

"Well done – clever. Another few minutes, and we'd have been there for the rest of the night."

Lisa wasn't sure if that was a back-handed compliment, so she refrained from responding.

"Surely there's another way out." Rafe hoped he'd find out about other exits.

"No, that's the only way from the warehouse into here. You can always go back to the warehouse. It's not guarded."

"I thought, after their display tonight, they didn't want anyone to leave," Rafe said.

"If you want to go back you can. The only way out is back down the hillside. Who wants to risk that? Best to stick to the rules." Izzy was firm.

"Don't worry we will," Rafe said, making a mental note that this entrance could be an escape route regardless of the consequences.

Chapter 21

Refreshments

They walked swiftly along, white rugged walls and limestone underfoot. Lanterns lit their way as they passed a series of corridors where, eventually, they heard voices ahead of them. Their feet slapped against the ground as they jogged the rest of the way.

They entered though swing doors into a large dining room. It had wooden shutters along one side of the room. One of the shutters was open, revealing a serving hatch. Some of the Gatherers were still lining up, waiting for their snack of hot chocolate and biscuits.

There were rows of long tables, most of which were set with coloured tablecloths and breakfast settings. Two tables had Defenders sat around them. They had finished eating their meal of meat pie and vegetables and servers brought them hot drinks and cakes. They were older than the Gatherers, eighteen years old upwards; their gloves placed in a holder on each of their chairs and their wooden batons in another. The golden batons remained on their belts. They were having a great time, relishing the treatment and actions of the disciplined Gatherer.

"Noisy," Rafe remarked.

"They can be. They have the authority," Izzy said, as she glanced over at the Defenders. "They're not so bad. It's the ones who keep their faces covered at all times – especially those with blue stripes – that you need to look out for."

As Rafe queued up, Lisa made sure she went in front of him to put a little distance between her and Izzy.

"I haven't seen you around. Where have you been?" Izzy asked.

"You haven't been looking hard enough. It's so hectic here, there's not enough time to get to know anyone," Rafe replied. He hoped he could convince Izzy he was familiar with the surroundings.

"You're right about that. I've been here three years and it gets harder and harder. I was so glad when I was selected to gather the lights… I mean spores," she shrugged. "Some say spores, others, lights - who cares it's just great to get out," she smiled, lifting her voice.

"Why are you called Gatherers?" Lisa asked, not really wanting to get into the conversation, but she just wanted to know.

Izzy looked at Lisa as if she were brainless, "We gather... the lights. You're a Gatherer too." Her tone was severe.

"She only asked," Rafe said, in defence of Lisa.

"Yeah, well it seemed a bit of a dumb question."

"There's no harm in asking questions. She's not going to know everything."

"Sorry. It's just that recently we've had such a changeover of Gatherers, it's hard to keep track of who'll be with you on the night." That was Izzy's excuse, but the apology was only for Rafe. Lisa knew this, but was pleased Rafe didn't side with Izzy.

They moved along the line and collected a plate with two honey filled bread rolls, and a hot drink. They followed, as each Gatherer filled the long table in sequence. Lisa managed to get the last seat on the table. Rafe and Izzy started a new table, where they sat on their own. Lisa rolled her eyes, as she saw Izzy start to engross Rafe in conversation. Lisa sipped her drink, which tasted like a weak version of hot chocolate. She didn't quite like the taste, but she was thirsty and still quite cold. She wrapped her fingers around the cup to allow the warmth to comfort her. She scanned the faces of the Gatherers sat around her and listened keenly to the conversations, especially the boy sat next to her who was doing most of the talking; his red curly hair hung just above his eyes and bounced as he spoke.

"Did Asham say he was going to do that?" he asked.

"No, not to anyone," replied a girl whose afro hair was neatly held back in a ponytail. "What will his family say? It's such a disgrace."

"A real disgrace…," someone else said.

"And bold…" The curly-haired boy smothered a smile.

"Rowhan, don't say that too loudly. It's not a good thing." The girl shook her head in disapproval and continued to drink.

Lisa gazed at the walls, past the shutters, to the walls with pictures and large bronzed plaques with names or quotes in gold lettering. She bit into her roll and enjoyed the sticky sweet taste of the oozing honey. It enhanced the flavour of the drink.

"I think someone knew Asham was going to run." Rowhan turned to Lisa, as the rest of the table had started a conversation about tunnels. Lisa wasn't sure what to say.

221

She didn't want to get any unwanted attention from the table of rowdy Defenders.

"Why do you say that?"

"Because those guys were too prepared, they were on him before he got a chance to get to the inner woods."

Lisa was captivated with the way Rowhan's curls bounced as he spoke.

"Does it normally happen?" She glanced at the table of Defenders where two of them were having a competition, trying to balance a cup on their heads. Lisa focused again on Rowhan who looked at her strangely. On seeing his look, Lisa decided to explain herself, "It's my first time. I was shaken by it all."

"Oh. I see, first timer." He finished his roll and sipped his drink then licked his lips. He was clearly enjoying it. "My name's Rowhan." He extended his hand, Lisa went to shake his hand but he withdrew it and pushed his nose instead accompanied by a snorting sound. "Works all the time," he chuckled. Lisa wasn't impressed. She turned away and looked to Rafe, who glanced over, smiled and returned to his conversation. Lisa rolled her eyes, she felt like she was sandwiched between annoying Izzy and the even more irritating Rowhan.

"It's my party piece – an ice breaker for the new kid."

"I'm not a kid," Lisa scoffed.

"Lighten up. It's a joke." Rowhan took the last gulp of his chocolate. "Sometimes working in this place gets too much. You've got to have a laugh, you'll see."

"I think I'm beginning to understand. It's quite dismal here."

"But it's to help the village, more importantly those who work in the mines. That's what our job is, surely you know that?"

"Do we really help the miners?"

"Are you silly or something? Course we do. How would they be able to see? How would they get around - breathe?" He looked at her as though she had lost a couple of brain cells. "I think the lack of sleep must be getting to you. Tell you what, I'll guide you to the female sleeping quarters," he said, sarcastically.

Lisa gave him a hard stare. Rowhan, uncomfortably, averted her gaze and turned his attention to the others around the table.

A gentle chime rang out. The Defenders were the first to gather their belongings and leave the dining room. The Gatherers all stood, waiting for the Defenders to depart so they could start clearing the tables. Lisa swiftly placed her cup and plate on the serving hatch and was soon by Rafe's

223

side as he put his crockery away. The lights in the dining room began to dim.

Rafe lowered his voice and spoke quickly as they walked slowly to the door. "There are separate dorms for boys and girls. You find Tia and I'll find Ben. We'll meet back here. Exit through the warehouse."

Lisa nodded.

As they stepped out of the dining room, girls filtered left and boys filtered right into grey, stone corridors with limestone flooring. Electric lanterns lit their way.

"OK," Lisa said, weakly. On seeing her apprehension, Rafe tried to steady her nerves. "Remember - use your pendant if you don't feel safe. And if you get back here and don't see me, head to the warehouse and hide amongst the boxes closest to the exit wall."

"What if it takes longer?"

"Head out of the warehouse, back the way we came, to Mrs Peri's."

"I hope I remember the way."

"I'm sure you will. Use the book. You'll have Tia with you, she's good with outdoors stuff. Remember she has been this way before. I'd prefer that you are both safe, so don't worry." Rafe could see Izzy lingering at the bottom of the girls' corridor.

Lisa furrowed her brow. "I really don't want to follow her."

"She's not as bad as you think. She'll take you to the girls' quarters." He gave Lisa a reassuring hug and they both headed in opposite directions.

Chapter 22

The Search

Lisa took courage from what Rafe had said and hoped she would do the right thing. She walked along with Izzy, not saying a word, a group of girls laughing and talking just ahead of them.

"Here we are," Izzy said, as they approached the dormitory door. It was easy to distinguish as it had a plaque with a black silhouette of a female stood beside a bed. They went into a well-lit area with wooden flooring, which housed shoes, bags and jackets on pegs. Another door led into the sleeping quarters. The lanterns began to dim.

"Night Lisa."

"Night," Lisa replied as calmly as she could.

Izzy went in the direction of the sign for toilets, stopped and returned to Lisa.

"Can you remember where your cubicle is?"

Lisa was annoyed that Izzy actually sounded concerned. "Yep. I'm fine."

"OK."

As soon as Izzy was out of sight, Lisa pushed her pendant. She felt relieved, as she didn't know what she would have done if Izzy had decided to escort her any further. Lisa opened the door and closed it quietly behind her. Her eyes took a short while to adjust to the darkness in the sleeping quarters.

It was a huge square hall with partitions creating cubicles. Lisa couldn't see over the partitions. They were tall but didn't meet the high ceiling; releasing the sounds of the beds creaking, as the girls turned and moved as they slept. There was a narrow strip of carpet along each aisle. Although worn, the carpet was soft under her feet, which was a welcome change to the hard floor Lisa had encountered so far tonight. A subtle smell of wild flowers and wood led the way.

Carved into each cubicle entrance was a number. These ran in numerical order. Lisa peeked inside the first one. A girl's hand was flopped over the edge of the lower bunk; no one was in the top bunk. Two full height lockers, a desk, chair and waste paper basket lined the compact space. Tucked in the corner was a shabby settee. There

227

was a curtain to the right of Lisa, which could provide privacy, if needed. Lisa quickly moved along.

After getting to the thirtieth cubicle, Lisa began to feel despondent. She prayed her invisibility would last until she found Tia, but she had no idea how long it was going to take, as the cubicles seemed endless. Lisa heard footsteps shuffling along a stone surface, coming from the far end of the hall. Compelled to follow, she passed three aisles of cubicles. The footsteps descended a set of stairs, accompanied by a lantern's dim yellow glow. Lisa followed the light to the end of the hall and came to an un-carpeted aisle leading to a staircase. Three narrow oblong windows, the full length of the stairway, let in some much-needed moonlight. The footsteps shuffled along carpet ahead of Lisa. There were more cubicles on this level. Lisa's heart sank. *Another set to investigate*!

"Come now, you'll be fine tomorrow. Drink this and then try and get some sleep," said a kind voice from one of the cubicles.

"Thank you," the recipient replied.

Lisa's heart skipped, she knew that voice - Tia.

Lisa stood out of the way as a woman with a lantern, dressed in a purple housecoat, her hair wrapped in a scarf, brushed past her and went back up the stairs. Lisa ran to the cubicle. Tia was sitting up on the top bunk, sipping from a mug. There was no other occupant. Lisa stepped into the cubicle.

"Tia, thank goodness. Rafe's going to be so pleased."

When Tia saw Lisa, she almost screamed out with joy. She hastily handed Lisa the mug and jumped down off the bunk missing three of the steps, she threw herself at Lisa. They hugged each other as Lisa tried not to spill the contents of the mug.

"Are you OK? Why are you crying?"

"Keep it down," someone yelled. "I need my sleep even if you don't."

Lisa and Tia lowered their voices.

"It's so sad here. Where's Rafe?"

"He's gone to find Ben. Quickly, get changed."

*

Rafe entered a similar environment to Lisa. The main difference was the odour that hit him as he entered - smelly feet and sweat. *'Busy day,'* Rafe thought. He too had used his pendant and it didn't take him long to find Ben, fast asleep, snoring loudly in competition with the boy on the top bunk.

229

Rafe gently shook Ben, but he didn't respond. Rafe thought how he might wake Ben without disturbing the other boy. He briefly pinched Ben's nostrils together. Ben inhaled deeply and half opened his eyes.

"Ben," Rafe whispered, shaking his shoulder. Ben woke with a start and lashed out. "Get off," he yelled. Rafe stood back as Ben sat bolt up right, and stared into the darkness.

"Ben, its Rafe."

"Rafe?"

Rafe then realised Ben couldn't see him, because he didn't have a pendant, so he pressed his pendant and, fortunately, he reappeared.

"Sorry Rafe, I thought you were one of the Defender creeps."

"Quick. We need to get out of here. Where is Alamo?"

Ben swung his legs out onto the floor. "The snorer." Ben pointed to the top bunk with his left thumb.

Rafe raised an eyebrow. "You weren't doing too badly yourself."

Ben opened his locker and pulled on his jeans. He was still wearing his top from that day. Alamo was still sound asleep. Rafe called his name.

"I need more sleep, mom," he muttered. Rafe and Ben started sniggering.

"Come on big boy, wakie, wakie," Rafe jested.

Alamo's eyes flashed opened. "What are you doing here?"

"No time to waste. We really need to leave ASAP."

"What?" Alamo sat up.

"Your mom said you should come with us, if you haven't found Evan and Meela."

Alamo bounced out of the bunk. "Whoow, I know where Evan is. Can we get him first?" He had on pyjamas, but in no time, he had flung on his clothes from the locker.

"We need to meet Tia and Lisa."

"I must contact my brother first."

"We won't have enough time," Rafe said urgently.

"I don't want to be here any longer than I need to. It's nothing like the brochure, if you know what I mean – It's no holiday camp," Ben interrupted.

"OK," Alamo said. "Where are you meeting them?"

"In the warehouse."

"You get them and meet me at storage room three. You can hide there."

"I haven't a clue where that is."

Ben was excited that he could contribute to this break out. "I do. I'll get us there."

231

"Good. Evan can get us out of here." With that, Alamo dashed off in the opposite direction to Ben and Rafe.

They made their way swiftly down the empty corridors. Ben spoke quickly.

"Those pendants are great. I really wished I wasn't so off with Arabella."

"Rude was how I heard it."

"Lisa can be too loose with the truth."

"Lisa can talk – a lot!"

Ben smiled. "So, you know my little sister."

"That's true, but we've got on really well."

Ben was surprised. "So, two peas in a pod?"

"Not quite, but we're getting there," Rafe smiled, thinking back to how Lisa used to annoy him.

Their humour was short-lived. As they approached the dining room, a Defender was standing guard. Ben and Rafe stopped abruptly and plastered themselves against the curve of the wall.

Chapter 23

Cell

Rafe and Ben backed up the corridor slowly without looking around. They hit what they thought was a pillar. They jerked their heads around to see the tallest Defenders they had ever seen. They towered above them. Both had their hoods up and silver mesh in place, their blue stripes proudly on display. Ben wished with all his might that he had his pendant. Rafe wanted to press his pendant, but felt it wasn't right to leave Ben on his own to deal with whatever punishment would lay in wait for them.

Ben smiled weakly. "Hello guys."

"Come with us," they both said, in synchronised, robotic tones.

There was nothing they could do except follow their instructions. Rafe and Ben were marched along a myriad of corridors and thrown into a musty cell. The walls were rugged, cold and grey. Threadbare blankets lay on top of three planks of wood posing as beds - these were the total

233

sum of furniture in the tiny space. A small window let in a sliver of light along with the cold night air.

"Well, this looks like the height of their hospitality," Rafe said, as he peered through a hole in one of the blankets.

Ben slumped onto the other bench, it felt hard and cold. He sat on top of the blanket and heard something crunch under his weight. He dared not look. Even if it were a bug, it wouldn't make the seating any more comfortable.

"Have you spoken to Tia?"

Ben shook his head. "Nope. Well, only before we separated when we got here. She went to the female quarters."

"Was she OK?"

"Yeah. She's tough."

"Sometimes…anyway, I hope they've made it to the warehouse. I just hope they haven't been caught."

There was a long pause as Rafe tried to work out how to get out of this mess. They both looked around the room as though they might find a way out.

Ben broke the silence. "Why are you dressed like those mug heads?"

"We got here by posing as Gatherers. Alamo's mom helped us. They almost threw one guy off a ridge out there."

"No way."

"They're off their heads." Rafe held his head down as he remembered the scene.

"Gatherers or Defenders I think they're all the same – always trying to get one up on someone. Those who don't have stripes want stripes. Those who have them are keeping them to be control freaks," Ben said.

"I thought the Gatherers were better?"

"When you're down the mines, no one is better as far as I'm concerned."

"You've been in the mines?"

"I tell you this Rafe, I was excited when I heard about those games. I had no idea the conditions in here were so bad. And as for the mines..." Ben squeezed his face together, as though he had sucked a bitter lemon. "Alamo told me he wanted to win the games so he could join his brother and sister. Once we got here he told me he wanted to find them and escape."

"That sounds about right," Rafe confirmed, while Ben still seemed shocked.

"His mother told us Evan had escaped and left them with a map, and the map is similar to ours, but I believe Evan has more information."

"Oh no," Ben groaned.

"What's the matter?"

"We have no map. I have no pendant. We're in trouble." Ben sighed despondently.

"I have my book."

Ben brightened.

"But, it doesn't have all the details to this place."

"It looks like Arabella has messed us up again." Ben stood and dug his hands into his jeans pockets.

"Come on Ben, if you and Lisa hadn't done what you did…"

"OK, don't rub it in."

"I'm not. Where's your book?" Rafe asked knowingly.

Ben looked down, embarrassed. "I don't know… I think I must have lost it, again."

Rafe decided to break the news. "Lisa has it."

"What?"

"Long story, anyway it's safe."

"She's so sneaky."

Rafe cracked a smile. "I think you're both similar."

"To be honest, my sister is quite clever; I just don't like to admit it."

Rafe reflected again on the mines and got serious. "What do you do in the mines?"

236

Ben thought for a moment. "I've only been there a short while and I don't want to go back, because, well…. it's a strange one. It looks like what we're doing isn't really what we should be doing."

"Sounds ominous."

"You sound like Tia with her strange words."

"It's not a made-up word, it means worrying, sinister."

"Well, I'm not sure if it's sinister, but it's worrying, because I can't see how we provide water for the village. I think we need to speak to Evelyn," Ben said, with some conviction.

"Why? I can't see him helping," Rafe scoffed.

Ben sat down. "I think he will. When we first got here we went to a banquet at Hill House."

"Now you tell me. I thought it was all doom and gloom."

"Well, it was great. He, Evelyn, told us how great our efforts would be. I think he hasn't got a clue what's going on."

Rafe didn't have the same confidence in Evelyn. "There's something about him."

"You wait until you meet him, you'll change your mind. He's so down to earth."

"Too down to earth, perhaps."

237

"Don't write him off yet. He may be able to get us out of this scrape with those Mafia type beings."

"Perhaps Arabella is our only hope."

"Arabella? No way - I've tried to call her and she hasn't shown up. I think Evelyn is more helpful, he listened to all I told him about you guys and …"

"You told him about us?" Rafe was on his feet.

Ben's words started to falter. "He asked… who I came… with,"

Rafe shook his head and slumped to his seat. "This is bad…,"

Ben tried to redeem himself. "We were all having a great time. The man was giving us a good feed and…,"

"I don't know what it is about you and food, but it really needs to stop. Think. Think. What questions did he ask? Did he ask anyone else?"

"I can't remember, but don't worry - he's fine. You'll see."

Ben's reassurances fell on deaf ears, Rafe wasn't pleased and now he felt they were imprisoned because, somehow, Evelyn was behind it all.

Chapter 24

Evelyn

A shaft of morning light threatened to brighten the dark, dank cell. Rafe and Ben were asleep huddled under the threadbare blankets when the door hit the wall with a bang. Light shone in from the corridor. Rafe was the first to stir; he sat up slowly, his head felt groggy from his lack of sleep, worrying about Tia. He moved his legs to the ground to sit on the edge of the plank; the blanket clung to his clothing, his eyes barely opening.

Two Defenders marched in.

Ben sat up and stretched.

They took the drinks the Defenders thrust towards them and the Defenders marched out and locked the door.

Rafe sniffed the drink then cautiously sipped a little.

"Is it OK?"

"Drinkable…hot water and grassy," he said and took another sip.

"Better than nothing I suppose, you'd think they'd at least give us something to eat," Ben moaned.

Rafe rummaged in his secret pocket and pulled out one of Arabella's bars. He broke it in half. Ben leapt off the plank to get his half, almost spilling his drink. He slowed down as he felt stiffness in his muscles. "Those beds are no joke."

"Tell me about it."

"But this bar is amazing, tastes like a breakfast all rolled into one."

"I don't know how she does it, but the bars taste like the meal you would have at the time you're eating it."

"Who?"

"Arabella. She gave them to me and Lisa."

"Sometimes, when I think she's a total waste of time, she leaves me having to think again," Ben snorted. He gulped at the rest of his drink, "I think I'll call her now to see if she can help us or find Evelyn, to get us out of this mess."

Rafe was about to stop Ben when the door was flung open again. The shadows of the Defenders entered the cell. The boys didn't move. The Defenders stood at the entrance and spoke in unison: "Evelyn would like the pleasure of your company."

"Great," Ben said and plonked his cup on the plank beside him.

"Perhaps we'll get some answers," Rafe muttered.

Once out of the cell, one Defender marched in front of them, the other at the rear. Their footsteps echoed down the maze of grey, oppressive corridors, and then a set of white corridors. Eventually, they came to a locked wooden door embellished with carvings, which lead to a brightly decorated passageway, with natural light flowing through windows above them. The passageway opened up into a small reception area with three doors.

The Defender opened the middle door facing them. It had a capital A and E engraved into it. Rafe leant slightly towards Ben. "Here's hoping it's not Accident and Emergency."

"No talking," the Defender behind them growled and shoved them into the grand reception hall. Black and white diamond shaped tiles covered the floor.

Ben gasped with pleasure. "We're back at Hill House...,"

A swift thump with a baton to his back halted him in mid sentence. He stumbled forward in pain. Rafe stopped him from hitting the ground.

"Stand still. Straighten up!" the Defender barked.

Regardless of the throbbing in his back, Ben reminisced how jubilant he felt when he first arrived at Hill House. All the winners had a special breakfast with Evelyn, after which they had time to relax in one of the many luxurious rooms before their introduction to the mines. Ben felt it was all downhill from there.

There were a number of doors off the hall and a wide staircase led to a balcony area, with another set of ebony doors. The large windows allowed great amounts of light and sunshine into the area. It made it feel warm and inviting, whether you were welcomed or not.

The Defenders left them standing at a door with an inscription in gold stating '*Dining Room.*'

They looked around nervously.

The door opened before them. A banqueting table sat in the middle of an elegant cream and gold room, stocked with jugs of fruit juice, jams and toast. Elaborate flower arrangements swamped the table with four strangely carved animal ornaments.

Tia and Lisa grinned at them from across the table, while tucking into breakfast. Rafe and Ben ran around the table, past an amused Evelyn who sat at the head of the table, and hugged the girls in turn.

"I'm fine," Tia whispered. Rafe sighed with relief.

"Welcome." Evelyn smiled revealing his perfectly set veneers and icy eyes. He put down his knife and fork, wiping his mouth with a blue cloth napkin. "Help yourself to anything." He nodded towards a table, which ran half way along the back wall. It had platters of fried and boiled eggs, plantains, sausages, other cooked meats and a pot of porridge. Ben quickly plated up his breakfast and headed to the table. He sat opposite Tia and Lisa. Rafe took a little more time, eyeing the room wondering how to escape, although he felt extremely hungry.

Three thrones sat on a platform at the head of the room. Floor to ceiling windows arched the platform providing views of the woods on one side, the hills and a partial view of the water wheel on the other.

Harp and violin music was playing in the next room. The soothing music eased the tension in the room, at least for a while.

Tia looked up to say something to Rafe as he got to the table, but she caught Evelyn's stare, so, changed her mind, and continued to eat. Rafe had to move an oasis of holly to find room for his plate next to Ben. He placed the oasis on the back table and returned to his seat.

243

"Thoughtful," Evelyn commented. "Eat up, as much as you like."

"Thanks," Ben said, with his mouthful of toast.

"Please feel free to speak. My female company have been very quiet," Evelyn said, glancing at the children as he ate.

No one said a word.

They ate under Evelyn's concerned gaze. After a few minutes, Ben complied with Evelyn's wishes.

"This is great, thanks."

"It's a pleasure. I've been told you are one of our best workers."

Ben smiled with pride, much to the others discomfort.

"I know you haven't been here long, but you have impressed many."

"So why did they throw us in a cell?"

Evelyn looked astonished. "A cell?"

Ben nodded. They all looked to Evelyn. He leant forward, picked up his napkin. "That must have been an oversight. I'm so sorry to hear that." He wiped his mouth with his napkin and leant back in his chair. "I hope this was not your plight," he said to the girls. "We encourage the health and wellbeing of all our workers. Tia and Ben can

244

testify to that. The reception you received for being winners?"

"Yes," Ben said, keenly.

"I'm saddened that you seem to have developed the wrong impression of Hill House. I'm trying to show you that you have come to the right place. You weren't all given the right reception. Well – Tia and Ben can testify to that?"

"Yes," Ben said, quickly.

Tia was a bit slower to say anything. "We had a good time," she said, looking up from an empty plate.

"My Defenders do a good job in keeping everything running smoothly but sometimes they get over protective. As soon as I heard you were here, I sent for your release," he said, pleased with himself.

"What about the Gatherer…," Lisa began. Rafe cut into what she was going to say, "The Gatherers certainly do their job." Rafe didn't want Lisa to say anything about the Gatherer on the ledge. He had also caught sight of a picture of the owl that had landed on the ledge that night; the picture hung on the back wall.

"Everyone works hard here. Everyone knows providing water for the village is a difficult task and we all have to be supportive of each other. I make sure of this, as the father of them all. Parents rely on me for the well-being of their children and the village. I'm in contact with the other kingdoms and they help where they can."

Rafe said, "We need to go."

Evelyn was startled. "Go - of course you can - but before you do, consider this. We need help."

They all flashed anxious looks at each other.

"So, I hope you will stay. In fact, I insist on it. You will stay, won't you?"

Evelyn's menacing grin told them this was not a legitimate question.

Chapter 25

Suspicious

"We can't stay here," Rafe slammed his utensils on the table as he shot up.

Evelyn calmly got up from the table and walked over to Rafe. "Please sit down." He placed his hand on the back of Rafe's chair as though Rafe needed to know where to sit. Rafe hesitated then sat.

Evelyn spoke to Rafe, but gestured to all of them. "You came here to rescue Tia, she who vowed to serve our village - a noble gesture." He smiled at Tia. Tia kept her gaze on Rafe. "She is quick and clever. She can't just leave. You were willing to take her away from me and not do anything yourself; not even be patient enough to take part in the games."

Rafe tried to protest, but Evelyn elevated his voice so it resonated in the room as he strode onto the platform. "You're a strong lad Rafe, may even be quick. You could be another asset, but I question your loyalty." He looked

247

out of the window overlooking the woods. He paused for a while. "Please complete your meal. I need time to think." Evelyn didn't turn around. He continued staring out of the window stroking the beads on his goatee. However, he was really watching the children through the reflection in the glass.

Ben looked at everyone else to urge them to continue eating. He hadn't lost his appetite, but they had. Lisa and Tia looked at each other, not knowing what to do. Rafe took a gulp of juice. The music stopped for a brief moment, then started up again, playing a jolly tune.

Rafe leant forward. "Are you OK?" Although aimed at Tia, Lisa nodded as well.

Ben stretched over a flower arrangement to get a jug of juice. As he pulled the jug towards him, his hand caught something sharp in the arrangement. He dropped the jug and some of the juice slopped onto the table.

"Idiot," Lisa said.

"I'm not."

"You are!"

"It's bleeding," Ben said, as he thrust his wounded hand in Lisa's direction.

"Yuk," said Lisa, as she saw drops of blood hit the table. "Don't keep your hand over the table."

Rafe handed him a napkin hoping this would stem the argument. "You'll live."

"Arguing with the wounded one…," Evelyn looked at them quite interested in their exchange. "What's your brother like?" Evelyn asked too eager for comfort.

Tia kicked Lisa under the table, as she saw her get ready to answer. Lisa said nothing but frowned at Tia.

"Changed your mind? I would imagine he can be a bit annoying," Evelyn said.

Lisa wanted to nod.

Evelyn continued to address Lisa. "He's only a year older than you and he thinks he can boss you around." He smiled. Lisa nodded. "And although he's annoying, you came here to help him. No, rescue him. I don't know from what. He does not need rescuing. He vowed to help the village. But you, Lisa, were plotting to change that."

Lisa lowered her head so as not to catch Evelyn's hypnotic gaze.

Evelyn turned towards the windows again, took two steps back and tilted his head as though he were getting a perspective on the landscape to paint it.

"This is a beautiful place. I have tried my best to keep everyone happy." He turned around and settled himself on the middle throne.

Ben had managed to stop the flow of blood. His hand still wrapped in the napkin, he pointed to the jug. Rafe reluctantly poured him a glass of juice, as the girls looked on in disbelief that Ben could still be enjoying breakfast.

Evelyn chuckled for a while, amusing himself with a private joke. "Many have tried over the years, none of them clever or intelligent enough." He tapped his head with his forefinger. "Nor quick enough to outwit me." A slimy smile crept across his face. He was enjoying himself, watching the children's horrified faces, as he uttered each word. He settled into the chair like a comfortable suit. "It's a beautiful day, a day which should be spent outside enjoying the open air, but you will be working to make me, yes me, feel proud!"

Lisa couldn't hold her tongue any longer, and with a firm voice she said, "Why should we make you feel proud?" She folded her arms in front of her.

Evelyn chuckled, his shoulders moving up and down like a pump.

"What's so funny?" Lisa asked.

"What you all have to realise is I know what the village needs. I have made sure we all live well. Water is in short supply here; anyone that can bring water to the village is highly favoured. It makes me proud. It makes the village proud, and it makes individuals - boys, girls, dogs, cats and even rats – proud." He announced sternly.

"Yep, keep quiet, Lisa. All the children that work here are extremely proud of what they do!" Ben scoffed.

"How do you know?"

"They told me!"

"OK you two, cut it out," Rafe said.

"Sorry Rafe," Lisa said and then turned back to Ben. "You need to listen to Rafe."

Evelyn stared at Rafe. "Well, thank you so much Rafe, for your help. You see you could be so great here. Answer a few questions… If you will?"

"Ask away," Rafe said, but he knew he wouldn't answer anything that was too intrusive and hoped the others would do the same.

"Where did you come from?"

"The village, Sanguel," Rafe said, nonchalantly.

"Really," Evelyn said and shifted in his seat, not happy with the response.

"Where did you come from before there?" He narrowed his eyes, directly at Rafe. Rafe didn't avert his gaze.

"Where else is there?" Rafe asked.

Evelyn drew in his breath, and breathed out heavily,

"One more question…" He paused. "Where is Arabella Marquelleth?"

The name hung in the air like a tight rope no one wanted to walk across.

"Arabella Marquelleth," he said, this time as a statement.

"What are you talking about?" Rafe wasn't going to say anything more.

"Where is she?" Evelyn shouted, his rage filling the room. They were all stunned at his sudden outburst. Two Defenders with blue stripes marched into the room and stood in front of the exit.

Ben whispered nervously to Rafe, "This isn't good."

"Play it down," Rafe whispered back.

Tia gripped onto Lisa's arm, hoping she wouldn't say anything that would give them away.

Evelyn stood with his legs apart close to the edge of the platform, as though he were going to leap at them in an instant.

"Where is she? Save me the wounded looks, as though you don't know who she is. I know you know her." He spat these words out.

Rafe stepped forward, containing his fear. He was willing to take any punishment that came his way as long as the others could get away.

"I thought you knew everything?"

"Don't toy with me," Evelyn yelled.

Rafe was adamant. "We don't know."

"Of course you do! How else could you get here? How else would Tia have that necklace, it's impossible without – Her!"

Lisa was glad her and Rafe's necklace weren't exposed. Tia covered her necklace with her hand then tucked it under her t-shirt.

Rafe didn't move. He felt stronger now, sensing Evelyn's fear of Arabella. Rafe kept his voice low and steady, "You can ask anyone of us, we'll all say the same thing. We don't know."

"Why do you want to know?" Tia plucked up the courage to ask.

Evelyn's rage seemed to subside. He put his hands behind his back and walked over to the window. As he did so, he raised his right hand. The Defenders marched onto the platform. He quietly issued them with instructions and they marched back down. As they headed off the podium, one towards Rafe and Ben, the other towards Lisa and Tia, the children held their breath. The Defenders marched closely past them and left the room. They relaxed – for a moment.

Evelyn leant forwards over the back of the smaller throne on the platform. He extended his arms out in front of him. He stared at the children then rubbed his hands together, as though he were wiping them clean.

"Is she helpful?" He asked calmly.

"No, not at all. She's unreliable and hopeless," Ben said.

"Why say that? Shut up!" Lisa reprimanded.

"It's true. She's no use!" Ben said, hurriedly.

Rafe didn't like the amusement on Evelyn's face. "That's enough Ben," Rafe said. "The point is we have no idea where she is. That's final."

Evelyn paused, listening to the music still playing in the background.

"Arabella will make you believe she is right. She had this kingdom many, many years ago, but she didn't do what was necessary to prevent the people from going hungry and thirsty. I am the saviour. She has always wanted her kingdom back, but I will not permit anyone to be thirsty or starve again. It may not seem appropriate, using children to mine the water, but it is the best we can do. These children are strong and determined. Even in hazardous conditions they thrive." His triumphant speech completed, he became solemn. "The conditions are out of my control." He calmly settled himself into the largest of the three thrones and pressed a concealed button on the underside of the arm of the throne. Within seconds, four gold-striped Defenders marched in.

"Let them get changed. Take them to the mines. It would be terrible to waste their talents." It was clear Evelyn had other things on his mind. He shooed them out of the room.

Chapter 26

Water Mines

Rafe, Tia, Ben and Lisa, were now dressed in white overalls and led down to the mines by the four Defenders - their mesh linings now removed, displaying their stern faces.

The overwhelming smell of soil and damp greeted them as they approached a set of six-metre wide iron gates, which marked the mine entrance. Two large Defenders with blue stripes stood in like manner (feet slightly apart, shoulders back) on either side of the gates, their faces concealed. They had batons on either side of their belts and a coiled length of rope.

Lisa and Rafe immediately noticed the lighting behind the gates.

"The lights are in see-through balloons," Lisa whispered.

One of the sharp-eared female Defenders explained: "They're not balloons, they are orbs. They contain the

256

spores, which combine together to provide light and oxygen, and they stop the dazzling effects of the individual spores."

The orbs hovered freely close to the roof of the cave, the gravity in the tunnels kept them buoyant. The spores in each orb were all the same colour. This tunnel had gold and green orbs along its length, which provided the area with maximum light.

"There are no lanterns," Rafe observed.

"Don't get any ideas about bringing lanterns down here, they simply don't work. Now stop talking," the male Defender demanded.

Rafe raised an eyebrow at this revelation. They passed through a maze of passages of varying height and width. Each passageway echoed with noises or voices not clear enough for them to understand or identify. This made them feel uncomfortable.

Tia recognised a Defender approaching them, short blonde hair and stern blue eyes. She wasn't known for her mild or pleasant manner. She didn't introduce herself. She nodded in Tia's and Lisa's direction. "You're with me," she said roughly, and shoved both of them towards a tunnel.

"OK, no need to be like that." Lisa pulled herself away from the grasp.

"Save your energy. You're going to need it," Tia warned.

"That's right Tia. You tell your friend. She'll need all that energy." The Defender laughed cruelly. Rafe was powerless to do anything. Tia looked back at Rafe and mouthed: *'We'll be fine.'*

Once through a short limestone tunnel, their ears met sounds like a hundred rats scratching under floorboards. What came into view were three levels of scaffolding, with a ladder at either end of the metal frame, and a slide down the middle of the top platform. On each level stood rows of children between the ages of seven and eleven wearing white overalls, rubbing the rugged walls with dark cloth.

They wore masks to cover their mouths and noses, their eyes were weary from the work, their arms and legs bruised from grazing against the rugged walls. Peeling skin was a natural hazard of the job. Severely torn and deeply grazed skin often became infected. These wounds were cleaned, treated, bandaged and the injured party sent back to work. The smoother the walls became the less injuries ensued, but their skin would become callous-ridden.

There were crevices and hollows in the walls where the smaller children had to crawl in and clear any debris. The debris would then be placed in small sacks and dumped into wheelbarrows at the base of the scaffolding. Once full, the older children would push them to a holding bay. A sign over the top of the entrance stated, 'AUTHORISED ONLY' in bold red lettering. A Defender would collect the wheelbarrows and empty the contents down a chute. The child would return with the empty wheelbarrow and the process would start all over again.

Dust particles floated in the air. Lisa and Tia began to cough. None of the workers paid any attention to them.

"What are they doing?" Lisa coughed. Her eyes began to water.

"Priming the walls for when the water comes down this way."

"I've not seen this part," Tia spluttered as she covered her mouth. The dust still danced around her eyes and started to coat her throat.

The Defender handed them a facemask each. They happily received it.

"It's a job with great rewards. You are always rewarded when you work for the village," the Defender said, proudly.

Tia cleared her throat. "Why do the walls have to be smooth?"

Lisa touched the wall. It still felt rugged to her.

The Defender didn't like the enquiry. "For the water! Smoothness is what is required." Her tone was sharp but this didn't deter Tia.

"Water runs along any type of surface, doesn't it? It only requires an opening and …,"

"Enough. Follow all signs and instructions. Evelyn put them in place for our safety and protection. We need to appreciate that we all contribute here."

Tia knew it was time to be quiet. She wished she could speak to Rafe. She knew he would be able to make sense of this. She looked back to see some of the small children crawling out of the hollows in the wall. A Defender had a dispenser of water, which he took over to where they were and gave them a small cup of water to share. Tia shook her head. She had only been in that atmosphere for a few minutes and her throat was dry. She couldn't imagine how sharing a small cup of water was going to help.

*

Rafe and Ben had stopped just past another set of children rubbing down a wall. Rafe had asked a similar question about water not requiring a smooth surface. He was given a very similar response to the one Tia was given. The situation worsened when two Defenders with

260

their hoods and lining intact pushed a cart through a heavy plastic door opening. The cart rumbled to a standstill. All the children on the scaffolding came down the ladder or the slide and placed their used cloths into a container that was on the cart and collected a new cloth. Rafe stretched out and touched one of the cloths as a little boy walked by him.

"This is coarse!" he said, expecting it to be smooth or even soft. The little boy walked on as though Rafe was invisible, and ascended the ladder. The container was sealed and the cart rumbled back towards the doorway.

"It's going again! Run," a boy yelled and slipped down the slide. Some of the other children panicked and did the same, or skirted down the ladder. Others stopped for a brief moment, looked about them and then continued to work.

"Get back to work," the Defender with the water dispenser shouted. "It's not collapsing."

The Defenders who were pushing the cart stopped and returned to the mini frenzied scene.

"I'm sure I felt it move." The boy's eyes filled with fear. He pulled down his mask and had a coughing fit. The other children, now on the ground began to check to see if he was alright. The Defenders put their hands on their batons.

The children immediately scattered and scurried back onto the scaffolding.

Once they were back to work, the Defenders pushed the cart back through the doorway. The little boy who had raised the alarm received a severe lecture, followed by a small drink of water and then shoved back to work.

"What just happened?" Ben asked.

"Occupational hazard," the Defender replied and moved Rafe and Ben on.

Rafe lowered his voice. "This isn't right."

*

The four of them completed their tour in the quarry. All around them were steep hills and slabs of slate and rocks. It would be near impossible to climb out.

They were all grateful to be in the open air. The cool breeze and sunlight gave them a good feeling despite the grim, noisy scene they had just experienced.

At one end of the quarry, the start of a tunnel was visible. Drilling sounds came from inside the tunnel. A number of older children wearing grey overalls were clearing the rocks and debris from this entrance. They transported some of the rubble directly to an adjacent tunnel by hand-pushed carts or mules and carts. The cartwheels shrieked and rumbled against the rickety tracks that joined the two tunnels. The workers dressed in white overalls split large deposits of rubble into smaller pieces with pick-axes; others separated them into piles and transferred them from wheelbarrows to the carts on the tracks.

"This is where you will work. Wait here."

"This place is not nice," said Lisa.

"It gives me the geebies," Tia said. Her eyes were sad. "I don't believe Evelyn. Why would children want to leave their parents? Where's the water?"

"In the dispensers," Rafe said, not amused by anything he had seen.

"Yesterday I worked in the mines in a different section. It was exciting 'cos you had to go through things like the obstacle course to get to where we had to work," Ben said. "But when we got there it was quite wet and really dark. They used those green light spores to light the area. It was still quite dark, so it was as useful as a candle in the snow. We chipped circular rocks out of a wall."

"Why circular?" Rafe asked.

"No idea. How is that going to produce water? Yet we could hear running water. And with so little light, after a while I felt like I was in a trance." Ben sounded exhausted as though he had just carried out the activity.

"You could have been close to the water wheel," Tia said. Ben shrugged.

"But, back there," Rafe gave a quick nod in the direction they had just come from, "they are rubbing the walls in preparation for water...It doesn't make any sense. Is it really about water?"

"It must be. The village needs water. Everyone, so far, has told us that," said Lisa. "They must need more or else they wouldn't be doing all this." Lisa spread her hands out, her elbows tucked into her hips to display the surroundings.

"I think Evelyn wanted us to have this tour for two reasons. One," Rafe stuck out his forefinger, "so we would be impressed with what he has produced."

"Well I'm not impressed," Lisa said.

"Nor me," Tia seconded. They gave each other a high five.

"And two," Rafe stuck out his middle finger and held his two fingers together, waiting for Tia and Lisa to listen, "it really has little to do with you guys vowing to help the village. He wanted to frighten us."

"Why would he want to do that?" Ben asked

Tia went around Ben to stand next to Rafe. "It's a strange place. And Evelyn is a creepamologist."

For the first time that afternoon, they all had a good laugh at Tia's new word. They hadn't noticed the Defender returning with someone they knew, dressed in a grey overall and carrying a face mask with goggles.

"I'm here to give you instructions," Alamo said aloud, as the Defender walked away. They were all glad to see him, but reserved their greetings. His stern face gave nothing away. "Follow me."

Chapter 27

Quarry

Alamo was professional. He showed them how to split the quarry debris and cart the rubble along the old tunnel to the chute. They were put to work with the other children. Defenders marched in and out of the quarry to check on progress.

By the afternoon they were all ready for their break, they sat in shaded areas to get some relief from the sun. Defenders gave them a spoon, water, a bowl of mashed potatoes, an unidentifiable piece of mushed meat and vegetables and left them alone.

They all relaxed.

"Sorry about the other night," Alamo started, as the last child got up from the rock where they were all sitting together. Alamo's voice was low to avoid anyone in the surrounding area listening in on their conversation. "But I saw the Defenders head in your direction. I couldn't warn you. I returned to the dorms because they would have done a check on everyone. I had to wait it out."

"We got caught hiding in the dining room," Tia said.

"Why didn't you hide in the warehouse like I said?"

"We heard someone coming out of the warehouse, so we hid under a table. We waited for ages, didn't we Tia?"

Before Tia could respond, Ben interrupted. "What about the pendant?"

"Pendant?" Alamo inquired

"We'll tell you later… go on Tia," Rafe said.

"So, there were footsteps going in and out. Shutters opening and closing. It wasn't safe to move. I guess we fell asleep. The next thing I knew we were being yanked to our feet by a Defender and led to Evelyn," Tia said.

Ben sighed. "That was better than our cold, miserable cell. I thought Evelyn was a good guy."

"It looks like that on the surface," Alamo said. "All my family thought so. My dad is one of his loyal followers."

Lisa and Rafe nodded, understanding what Alamo meant.

"My family's reputation is a good one, even though Evelyn is displeased with Evan, he was a great worker - so was my sister. That's why I got this position of trainee Defender."

"Grey overalls for trainee Defenders?" Rafe said. Alamo nodded.

"The problem is I still don't know where Meela is. Evan said she may have been taken to another kingdom, but we're not sure."

There was a brief sad silence. Rafe hugged Tia.

"Look," Rafe said, determined to lift the mood, "we need to do something about this. We know something's not right. Isn't that what we're here for?"

They all nodded.

Alamo scanned behind him to make sure the Defenders hadn't returned. "Can I really trust you all?"

They all nodded earnestly in response.

"Your mom told us," Lisa pointed to Rafe and herself, "that we could trust you and Evan."

Alamo smiled with confidence. "I don't know all the details, because I was more concerned with finding Evan and Meela. I now know that part of the problem is to do with the water supply. I'll be meeting Evan tonight to discover more. If you're willing, I'll find out if you can come with me to the meeting place."

They didn't hesitate to say yes.

"Now, if Evan agrees, I'll take you tonight. We'll be sleeping in the quarters behind there." He pointed to an area just behind the used tunnel. "There are temporary log cabins, male and female sleeping quarters. We'll be safe enough to come and go quickly. Do enough today but don't weary yourself. Anyone who can't wake up stays sleeping."

"Could someone give me a nudge?"

Rafe raised his eyebrows at Ben, while the others furrowed their brows.

"What? I'm a heavy sleeper...," Ben said, sheepishly, "come on Lisa you know that."

Lisa giggled. "Don't worry, I'll wake you up."

"I don't like the sound of that," Ben confessed.

"Like I said, anyone sleeping stays sleeping."

They all nodded again, sensing the seriousness of it all.

"Come on let's get back to work before the Defenders give us more duties."

Lisa and Tia jumped up. They didn't want that to happen. As they left the lunch spot, Ben said, "Could someone, and not Lisa, make sure I'm up. Please?"

*

Work had stopped in the early evening due to the threat of a storm. The angry clouds rode the sky with furious winds. The wind whistled around the cabins, but inside there was a cosy atmosphere. The cabins were basic, a small area for a wooden table and foldaway metal chairs. Bunk beds filled most of the room. Footwear kept at the door, spare footwear kept under the bunks and spare overalls hung on hangers close to the toilet facilities. Narrow lockers housed very few personal items.

The hostile weather hadn't upset the mood of the workers; they were grateful for the break. Most of the workers sat talking together, playing games with pebbles and stones. Tia and Lisa opted to go to bed after their evening meal to get a good night's sleep in readiness for the adventure ahead. The boys were fortunate - Alamo had managed to get them into a cabin, which only had one other resident, a mouse searching for food.

The next morning Rafe and Alamo were up early. Ben was still sleeping, although Alamo and Rafe had tried to wake him. When the girls crept into the boys' cabin, Lisa immediately poured cold water into a cup and dripped it on Ben's face. Ben shot upright and shook his head. "I told you not to let her wake me."

They all laughed.

Rafe held his hands up. "We tried, but you kept falling back off."

Ben got dressed in the bathroom rapidly while listening to Alamo's final instructions.

"The Defenders will definitely be guarding the tunnels, positioned just inside the entrances. They believe that escape is difficult from here, but not impossible. Ready Ben?"

Ben pulled on his last boot, "Yes, let's go."

"Remember, keep low and to the right of the rocks. Don't move until I give the all clear." Alamo swirled his fist in the air as the signal.

They slipped out of the cabin and hid behind a mound of broken rock and rubble. Alamo looked out a few times just to make sure they weren't seen. They all shivered a bit as the night air caught their faces. It felt much colder here than in the village at night.

"Should we look at the book?" Tia quickly whispered to Rafe. She tucked herself beside him as they crouched low, near to a formation of rocks, Lisa and Ben close behind and Alamo just ahead.

"There's no time. It'll be difficult to look at it now."

Alamo gave the signal for them to stop where they were. Lisa and Ben now crouched with Tia and Rafe.

They waited.

Alamo peered out from his vantage point.

271

"We could have stayed inside a few more minutes instead of freezing out here," Ben complained.

"Don't be so rude." Lisa stared hard at Ben between blowing into her cupped hands.

"I'm not rude. I'm saying...."

"Just be quiet. You're making us look bad! It's cold not freezing."

"You make yourself look bad."

"Well you don't need any help in that department."

Rafe intervened, "OK, you two. Enough. Enough."

Rafe shuffled forwards to Alamo. "Is everything OK?"

"Yes," he said, with some relief in his voice. "Here he comes now."

Coming towards them was a muscular young man. Crouching forward, he ducked into a crevice and beckoned them to follow him. Alamo sent Rafe, then Lisa, Tia, Ben. Finally, Alamo made it to the crevice.

"Evan!" Alamo said, eagerly. "These are the ones I told you about."

"Alamo." They shook hands like comrades. Evan wasted no time in leading the way through a narrow exit into a small opening by slate piles.

"Put these on." Evan's voice was low, clear and firm. He had pulled out blindfolds from his pouch that hung to the side of his hip. Everyone did as they were told without questioning.

"We'll lead you. No harm will come to you, as long as you follow instructions. Listen - no talking."

Their hands placed on the shoulder of the person in front. Evan led the way followed by Rafe, Tia, Lisa, Ben and Alamo at the rear. As they moved along, the rubble and pebbles under their feet, felt like balls and boulders wanting to trip them over. They stumbled a few times, but no one fell. They all relied on each other to be as sure-footed as possible. After what seemed like hours, although it was only fifteen minutes, Evan instructed them to take off their blindfolds. They blinked repeatedly to adjust their eyes to the shades of darkness. The quarry hills were still visible behind them, but from the weaves and turns they had taken, they knew they were some distance away.

"Be careful along here. Follow me."

Evan started walking along the side of a hill with a sharp drop to his right, the dark greenery of shrubs and trees led to a valley below. Sharp rocks protruded through the greenery. The moon emerged from the darkness, illuminating the rain threatening clouds. It cast shadows along their trail. As they followed Evan they refused to look down, keeping their eyes firmly placed on the person in front, their bodies as close to the hill side as possible; they breathed deeply. They were relieved to see Evan turn into a camouflaged cave entrance that was clearly familiar to him. There was no light, so when Evan stopped abruptly they stumbled into each other.

"Get off my feet," Ben protested, thinking it was Lisa.

"Sorry," Tia replied.

"It's OK," Ben said, hastily. "I thought it was Lisa."

"Typical, blame it on me."

They were silenced by the sound of bolts being shunted across a door they couldn't see. A golden light penetrated the darkness ahead of them. It came from a lantern secured by a chain at the top of the cave. They stepped into a passageway, cooled by air seeping through small cracks in the rock. Their footsteps echoed about them.

"Wait here," Evan said. His sturdy, brown eyes beamed.

Evan pulled back a heavy, dark curtain and he and Alamo entered a room. The curtain swung back into place before they could see the contents or occupants of the room. The others looked at each other enquiringly. They could hear muffled voices from the other side of the curtain.

Chapter 28

Water Mine Plot

They entered a section of the cave converted into a meeting space with another door leading off it. A large group, all dressed in dark clothing, ranging from ten-year olds to some in their twenties, sat on cushions and crudely made benches and chairs. The room was warm and comfortable.

Rafe recognised Izzy. She smiled but didn't draw any attention to herself.

Lisa sighed.

Evan introduced the newcomers and signalled to them to sit on a curved, stone ledge that housed large cushions. The four made themselves as comfortable as possible.

Evan took up position at the front of the gathering. "I am overjoyed to welcome you here. We have heard about you. We are the REAL Defenders – we call ourselves Guardians, the ones who will save our village and children from the evil powers of Evelyn." He paused as the group nodded and gave shouts of support. "We have kept our plans a secret and now we are ready to execute them."

"What can we do?" The assured voice came from Tia, which surprised Rafe and the others.

Evan smiled. "I like your boldness." He perched on a tall stool behind him. "Let me explain. As you know, the village has prestigious games, games that select the fastest, strongest and fittest children. This selection process is said to help the village maintain its water supply. We were told many years ago that the water supply had to be sourced from further away. A delicate maze of tunnels had been constructed, but men and women couldn't do the work because they had to run their households, tend to the animals and crops and defend us in battles."

"The crafts people were also blamed," someone added.

Evan nodded. "True. At first, the villagers refused, but then the water became in short supply, even when it rained. Crops died, the soil wasn't being replenished and the risk of drought and famine was becoming more of a threat. Reluctantly, villagers gave in. One by one, they gave their children to the work. These families received barrels of water as a reward; their crops seemed to fare better, which convinced more families to offer their children. It got so bad that fights would break out between families battling to make sure their children were selected. The games ended these fights and brought even more rewards to the families and a sense of pride for those who work at Hill House, which is fine for the children that do. However, it has almost been forgotten that it's in the dangerous mines that most of the children work; and unfortunately, the conditions are not highlighted, just the prestige and rewards."

Ben whispered to Rafe, "That's awful."

Evan pointed to Izzy, who stood up and said, "The work is much harder than could be imagined. For some of us, we have never seen water unless there has been an explosion or accident. Still children work for the pride and reward it brings to their families. Yet all of us work in fear of punishment or death. Many parents believe their children are dead because Evelyn has informed them of this, rewarding them with various honours and plaques of tribute. Neither the parents nor Evelyn know that some of these children are alive, that we managed to rescue them and they now serve in secret to rescue others." Her voice was low and her face sombre.

Evan continued the account as Izzy sat down. "We haven't got enough time to go through all the details, but what we do know is that Evelyn is a deceiver."

277

Ben looked at Rafe in disbelief.

Rafe's response to Ben was a look of '*I told you so.*'

"Yes, we all know now that the water has been dammed. Cutting the water off from the village has given him the cloak he needed to get workers to mine the gold and precious minerals that have made him rich. We know he had help from others in the surrounding kingdoms. We're not sure who or why, but that is not our concern at this moment. Our main priority is to release the water, which will free the children and our village from Evelyn's deceptive grip."

The room exploded with applause and cheers. However, Rafe was still trying to place one last part of the puzzle together. He interrupted Evan's account to ask a question. "Why is Evelyn so troubled about Arabella?"

The group turned to face Rafe with astonished murmurs.

"You know Arabella?" Izzy exclaimed.

"How?" someone else shouted out.

"We all know her," Lisa said, smugly, using her finger like a compass to point out the four of them sat on the ledge.

"Because... they have met me before...many times." Arabella's voice seeped into the room, as blue glistening

278

leaves outlined a ledge higher up the rocky wall behind Evan, where she was standing with the aid of an engraved walking stick. She lowered herself onto a seat behind her.

Evan, Alamo and a few others laughed with solidarity. They weren't surprised by Arabella's appearance.

Rafe, Tia, Lisa and Ben could not believe their eyes – they all wanted to say something, but did their utmost to withhold their emotions.

"These are the children I spoke to you about some time ago. It's taken a little while for them to arrive. Nonetheless, they are here now. They have the last remaining pendants – except one."

"Can we see them?" someone yelled with anticipation. The children proudly pulled their clothing from around their necks and placed the pendants on the outside of their garments. Each pendant glowed with a freshness they hadn't seen before. For a short while, the three of them felt like very important people. Ben tried his best to hide his embarrassment as soon as everyone noticed he didn't have one. Evan and an older boy called Sam managed to get the group settled.

Excitement filled the air.

"Do they work?" someone else called out.

279

Arabella looked across the room in the direction of the caller. "Do you believe those pendants, have only ornamental value in something so, so precious?"

The caller lowered his head.

"Let us see how they work," Izzy said, as she smiled at Rafe. Even Lisa couldn't resist the chance to show off, as much as Izzy was the person requesting it. Rafe, Tia and Lisa looked at each other. On the count of three, they pressed their pendants. Gasps of amazement filled the room as, fortunately, they vanished. Rafe pressed his pendant again and reappeared. Lisa and Tia took a while longer to reappear, deciding to cause a bit of mischief by tapping a few of the group and quickly return to where they were sitting. This went down well, as the tap on the arm or back made the person turn around, only to realise no one was there. As Lisa was going back to her seat, she decided to do one last tap – this time on Evan's back, but Evan reached out and managed to grab her arm. She reappeared with a surprised look on her face.

"I felt your breath and heard you giggling," Evan laughed. The whole room enjoyed the prank.

"Evan has great hearing and swiftness – it is difficult for anyone to beat him on that," Alamo said, proudly.

Lisa smiled, feeling a little overwhelmed with Evan.

"You see," Arabella said, in a mild voice, "you can have a great gift, but it's how you use it that matters. As I have often told you and your brother – you give yourselves away far too easily. Pace your breath, be swift but gentle on your feet. You could learn a few lessons from your friends."

"Is it true that the pendants offer more than invisibility?" Izzy asked Rafe, as she settled down next to him. Arabella's ears focused in on the question,

"The pendants will enable other giftings, but it has to be treated well and gradually the gifting will be revealed."

This stunned the wearers – *why had Arabella not told them this before?*
It was also clear Arabella wasn't going to elaborate on the point, even with questions being fired at her. She held her hand up and stood unsteadily to her feet, holding on to the walking stick. She addressed the group. "My time is limited. I am growing weaker. Evelyn knows I am here."

Rafe thought back to the banqueting room and realised this may have been why Evelyn was pushing for information about Arabella. He wanted to tell Arabella that neither of them said anything to put her in danger, but it was not the time to do so. Arabella had started to explain what they needed to do and everyone listened intently.

281

"… As you can see - it needs to happen a lot sooner than you had planned. Evelyn is moving quickly. We have to get ahead of him. He will put more lives at risk and he will not have mercy on any of you. Now I need to speak to the newcomers."

*

As the room cleared, Arabella settled herself back into a seated position.

"Come closer."

They moved to the front line of chairs.

"Evan, Alamo. Do not leave," Arabella said. They closed the curtains and sat with the others.

"I'm sure you four have a lot of questions to ask me, but please…only one question from each of you. I'm very tired."

They were disappointed, as they had expected Arabella to answer their many questions. Lisa began to open her mouth. Ben turned to her, "Remember you only get one chance." For once Lisa didn't argue. She thought for a moment longer as did the others. They could see there was something different about Arabella. She wasn't as animated as they had known her to be.

282

Ben was the first to say something. "This isn't a question. I want to say something first." He waited for her to give the go ahead. She nodded her head once, slowly. Ben stood up. "I'm very sorry for how I behaved. I didn't know it was all so serious and so many people were in danger. Sorry."

Arabella's crooked smile appeared and Ben was sure he could see a slight watering of her eyes, or *was it the light?* They huddled together as Ben sat down to agree on the four questions. Arabella sat upright to signal her readiness for their questions. She cleared her throat.

"First question?"

Lisa raised her hand, then stood up, "Are our books still useful?"

"Yes. They hold maps that you will need."

Tia stood as Lisa sat down, "Can we rescue all the children before Evelyn does something awful?"

"I'm not totally sure, but the plans will work if we act quickly tomorrow."

"What is this?" Rafe took out what he now believed was a weapon.

"A tuber," Evan gasped, "Can I?" he extended his hand. Rafe looked at Arabella for the go-ahead. She nodded. Evan removed it from Rafe's palm and immediately

283

extended it with a flick of his wrist and swiped it in the air like a sword.

"It's a magnificent weapon." He struck a chair on its seat. It tore through the cushion and severed the wood. Evan struck the top of the chair and it separated in half. They were all amazed. Lisa immediately grabbed hers out of the secret pocket Mrs Peri had provided. Tia opened her overalls and pulled her tuber out of her waist bag.

Rafe was in awe. "If I knew this, I would have sliced through those Defenders when they took Tia."

"Why didn't I get one?" Ben blurted out in dismay. As the others attempted to flick the tuber open as Evan had done.

"Ben, you know why and there goes our last question," Lisa said, as she finally flicked open her tuber with satisfaction. They turned their attention back to Arabella.

"Remember, these tubers work with you, not just as weapons, but you will learn how else they can assist you. They can work in the hands of others but they are more effective and stronger in your hands. I need to rest now. Tomorrow we take action." Arabella said goodbye and vanished.

Chapter 29

Explosions

As they got to the quarry, dawn was breaking and everything was peaceful. They were still wary of any lurking Defenders.

"Did you feel that?" Rafe asked. Before anyone could answer, a thunderous bang blasted into the sky. They automatically ducked and ran for cover from a hail of debris. Evan directed them into a gap, which limited the deluge of debris.

Once the shower subsided they waited for a few more minutes then edged their way back out into the open.

"Are you OK?"

"I'm fine Ray."

"What on earth was that?" Rafe asked, as he dusted himself off and shook his head. The others followed suit except Ben who was spitting bits of grit out of his mouth.

"It's an explosion. How's everyone?" Evan asked.

"Fine," Lisa said, shakily.

"You've got something on your cheek," Ben said to Lisa. Lisa wiped her left cheek, then her right. She was startled. "I'm bleeding."

"Let me see." Alamo went over and immediately saw the wound just above Lisa's ear. "It's not deep, but you got caught."

"I've got a tissue," Tia said, as she rummaged in her waist bag and handed Alamo a tissue. He gently dabbed the cut then told Lisa to apply pressure to stem any flow of blood.

"I knew one of those things you carried in there would finally come in handy," Rafe said.

"I told you," Tia smiled and patted her waist bag.

Ben gently squeezed Lisa's arm, "You'll be OK."

Lisa smiled weakly. She felt a little dazed but didn't want to say anything, plus she was enjoying the attention she was receiving from Alamo. Her legs weakened and her head began to spin. "I feel sick." Alamo led her to lean against a stump of rock.

"Why would there be an explosion?" Tia asked worriedly.

Evan explained with some urgency: "Sometimes they want a tunnel to move on quickly, so they'll start early and

286

use explosives. The trouble is it causes a lot of injuries and in some cases loss of lives."

Ben was alarmed. "We need to see what we can do."

"No. Not yet," Evan warned. "Evelyn's mob will rescue the wounded – those they think are worth saving. It's the ones who are left behind that we need to do something about."

"You mean they could be buried alive?" Tia braced herself for the answer.

"Yes."

Tia buried her head into Rafe's side. He held onto her. The others couldn't believe what they were hearing. Evan continued, "We make sure we get them out - that's why we have a growing group of followers. When they realise the so-called Defenders aren't going to rescue them, they begin to understand their fate - that's where we step in – we're their only help."

"But how do you know when…? They could all be dead," Tia sobbed. Evan went over and knelt in front of her. "We are not unkind. That type of experience does something to everyone in here." He put his fist to his heart. "This makes everyone more determined."

287

"Has she lost someone?" Evan said, softly, looking up at Rafe. Rafe nodded. He looked back to Tia, who had wiped her tears.

"I'm not scared," she sniffed.

"I know. You are strong. You offered to help with no thought for yourself. We have watched the way you helped the others in the mines when you came. For someone so young, you have shown great spirit." He touched her on the cheek and got up.

"But why not rescue them sooner? What if they have serious injuries?" Ben said.

Evan's eyes narrowed. "Because those who get rescued too soon betray us!"

"It – just seems a – a bit harsh," Ben muttered.

"If I or Alamo got caught by Evelyn, I don't expect anyone to rescue either of us, because Evelyn is sure to kill me or anyone else who attempts to rescue what he considers to be down-graders – not fit for purpose."

"But we would save you, if that should ever happen," Rafe said, firmly.

"Evelyn would see that as a weakness and use it against the rest of the Guardians. If he captures one, he is sure to seize the others, and then get rid of all of us. He has made it clear that we, the runaways, are seen as the enemy. The children, especially the young ones, would report us rather than help us. They would rather see us die to halt their own punishment or risk family shame. That is how strong his grip is on the kingdom."

"Let me show you something. They won't notice you're missing because the explosion will keep them occupied for a while. Come with me."

Evan looked at his brother. In that moment, they acknowledged an unspoken secret.

"Alamo will take you. I will meet you later."

*

The early morning sky was full of birdsong as the small group walked through a secret passage, out of the dusty quarry, across a rope bridge to another hillside. They followed Alamo down the hillside to a lush green valley, brightened by delicate and robust flowers.

Fresh air filled their lungs. As they hit the bottom of the valley, they heard the magnificent sound of rushing water. They finally saw a fountain of water gushing out of the hill into a steady stream.

"This is a Guardian's secret place," Alamo said, with a smile.

They strolled along the edge of the embankment. Ben cupped some of the water and drank. He encouraged the others to try it. It was the most refreshing water they had ever tasted.

"Not even Evelyn knows this exists. Arabella has managed to safeguard this gem for decades." Alamo wiped his wet hands through his hair.

"It's beautiful," Lisa gasped.

Tia was taken aback too. "Crazygreat!"

"The quarry hides it away. For the villagers to even attempt to come this far is thirsty work and dangerous. Wild animals and Evelyn's inventions roam these parts. It's too risky. They would be killed before they got to the quarries."

"What types of inventions? Sounds exciting," Ben said.

"They're not cuddly. I'm told they are like wild beasts, but some say they are more like vicious creatures." Alamo walked away to be alone for a while.

"Not tactful, brother," Lisa said.

"I know. I got a bit too excited. I find those things interesting."

"More interest less excitement," said Rafe, as he walked past Ben towards Alamo.

They all eventually joined Alamo, standing at the side of the stream and watched the waters run through an archway of white and purple blossom trees until it was out of sight.

Rafe broke the silence. "Could this water be used by the village?"

"It would be too difficult to channel the water from here for a number of reasons. However, we know the true village water source has been dammed," Evan said. He and Izzy had quietly joined them by the water's edge. They had bags strapped around their waists, which contained supplies for the injured.

Rafe immediately went over and greeted Izzy. Lisa nudged Tia.

Evan paused for a moment and looked down the stream. "We bury the dead here." He took a long, deep breath and exhaled slowly, "They are sent down the stream to freedom, freedom from the mines. Their belongings and a letter recording their contribution to others are in a box for their families. One day they will receive them."

A peaceful sadness swept over the group.

"What happens when you get too old for the mines?" Tia inquired.

"Some serve as guards or get a position at Hill House. Many serve in hideaways, processing the gold and minerals. Some help with Evelyn's inventions," Evan said.

"Others get sent to other kingdoms and a new life is set up for them, as long as they don't speak against Evelyn," Izzy added.

Rafe was adamant they had to release the water for the village, to eradicate so much sadness, and get rid of Evelyn. "Where is the dam?" he asked.

Evan replied, "We have searched but it has been hidden well."

Ben walked over between Rafe and Alamo. He was glad for the change in subject. "Rafe, didn't you say that Alamo's mom said the map was similar to the one that Evan had?"

"Yes, that's true."

"Arabella had provided me with such a map, but it was destroyed by Evelyn – you have one?"

"Yes, Lisa, Tia, come here," Ben called. "Have you got your books?"

The three of them produced their books. Lisa knelt down to spread her crumpled pages out. Ben helped. Evan joined them on the ground as Alamo viewed Tia's book and Izzy shared Rafe's.

"Isn't it amazing that after all the fuss about the book, it's the maps that are most important," Ben said, as he spread the loose pages from Lisa's against his stomach and then on the ground.

"Some pages are blank," Evan said.

"Oh yes. I can't really see it all. I've left my glasses behind."

"It's a long story, best left for now," Rafe said. Lisa looked up and gave a weak '*thank you*' smile.

Evan looked at each map and his eyes sparkled. "You have maps of the different kingdoms!" he exclaimed. "I can see the village of Pershe. Here, that's us. The kingdom of Sheham and Clover covers more area than I thought. I have never heard of the kingdom of Tashem. These markings here are the quarries. My goodness, there are more water markings than I had imagined."

"Would Mrs M – Arabella not have told you?" Lisa enquired.

"As you could see, she is becoming frail."

"Oh, I see. Now I know why she's been offhand with me," said Ben.

Evan laughed. "No Ben. She likes you all, but for some reason you seem to irritate her. I see it as a good thing, it keeps her spirits high." Evan patted Ben's back.

Tia handed her book to Evan. "Look at this. Isn't this the dam?"

"Yes, yes, this is great. The map shows exactly where it is. We thought it was closer to the kingdom of Clover."

"Now we know exactly where to go!" Izzy cheered.

Everyone was jubilant.

"We can find the dam tomorrow. This is so much sooner than we ever thought we would be able to do this, but first we must help with the rescue operation," said Evan.

Chapter 30

Orbs

They headed back to the mines. Evan had used secret passageways to get as close to the explosion site as possible. They met with two older boys, Sam and Bruno. Both were taller than Rafe and Evan. Sam had cornrows and Bruno a Mohawk. They had briefly met them at the night's meeting. Sam was in charge of identifying any survivors. "We are still rescuing survivors. All Guardians are engaged in this task."

"How many have been rescued so far?" Evan asked.

"Ten and there are still more on the way. We have a problem. The Defenders must be on the look out for intruders and have sealed any new tunnels," Bruno said

"How do we get in?" Rafe asked.

Bruno explained. "It wasn't just one blast, there were two, both detonated at the same time. There are some children trapped in two other caves. At this point, there is no way of knowing how many. The list of workers in those areas was deliberately destroyed."

"Sounds like something that creep would do," Rafe grunted.

Evan agreed. "This makes our job a lot harder."

Sam continued with urgency. "All the green orbs have diminished with the blast. The air is already tight. We're against the breathing time."

Izzy whispered to the others, "That's the amount of time those trapped can survive."

Their hearts began to pound. They wanted to get started on the rescue.

"The other problem is this area has a high content of gold fragments, which means the blue Defenders are in charge – you know how ruthless they can be." Sam's tone indicated the danger level of the task.

Sam and Bruno marched up the passageway. Evan indicated for the others to follow. They got a few feet up the passage when Sam, Bruno and Evan began tapping a section of wall. The others observed with interest. A section of the tunnel walls cracked open. Bruno lifted it out of the way and Sam pulled out a square block of wood. Bruno and Evan lifted the fake section back in place as Sam stood on the block and fished a small horn out of his pocket. He manipulated it into a curve and placed the larger end on the roof of the passageway and the other to his ear. They all stood quietly.

He returned the horn to his pocket, extended both hands to the roof and twisted something above his head. The fake section slowly slid across the entrance to a space above. A subtle white light streamed into the tunnel. Sam swiftly pulled himself up through the gap. In a matter of seconds, a rope ladder descended. Izzy was the first to start the climb up, as Bruno steadied the ladder. They each climbed up leaving Bruno behind to secure the ladder for a quick decent.

Lisa and Rafe recognised it to be the warehouse.

"So," Rafe whispered to Izzy, "there is another way out of here." Izzy nodded. "Some things are on a need to know basis – now you know," she smiled.

Sam was already opening boxes, which contained the orbs, and Bruno was opening the spore barrels. Bruno and Sam both had their hoods pulled up and mesh across their faces. Izzy, Alamo and Evan did the same.

"We need clear, gold and green – the green will provide more oxygen," Evan whispered to the others as he pulled his gloves on.

"But we don't have gloves," Lisa said to Rafe.

297

"Don't worry. Let me show you," Izzy said. She picked up the flat, clear, balloon like membrane that had a thin-corded thread, which ran around the opening. "Pull this cord; it will open the seal so that the others can fill it with the spores." Izzy pulled it with ease. "You don't have to be gentle, they're quite tough. The others will fill them with the spores. Once they're inside, Ben and Rafe can re-seal them by pulling the cord again and there we have it – orbs!"

Lisa began to warm towards Izzy.

Once filled, Ben and Rafe sealed the orbs and wrapped the extended cords around their wrists to stop them from floating off. Instead, the orbs hovered above their heads.

Sam and Tia deposited some of the completed orbs back in the passageway. Tia returned quickly and gathered more. After the umpteenth time, Sam stuck his head out of the hole.

"I believe we have plenty."

"Already?" Evan was surprised.

Tia smiled. "With Sam's weight, I could fly up and down that ladder."

"Steady on with the weight thing. I just happen to be a big lad," Sam chuckled.

The other also saw the funny side.

"Let's get moving," Bruno urged.

They all descended the opening back to the secret corridors.

*

Sam explained as much as he could to the intrepid rescuers as they made their way along the secret corridor to the blast site. "You'll be fine at this point. Unfortunately, the blasts took out some of our secret tunnels so be extra vigilant, Defenders are everywhere. Some of the Guardians have managed to use the old cloth trick like this one." Sam pointed to a dark length of cloth hanging from the side of the tunnel, held down by a line of rocks. It gave the illusion that a wall was still present.

"We'll head to the other passage now. Guardians," Sam saluted by banging his fist against his chest twice. Evan and Bruno followed suit.
Bruno and Sam secured orbs to their belts and swiftly headed down the tunnel, out of sight.

Evan turned to the rest of them, "This is where it gets really dangerous. We need to be as quiet as possible and move quickly. I'll check the area is safe. Rafe you come with me. You can use your pendant, should anything go wrong, to get back to the rest and head to the meeting room along that tunnel; just turn left." Rafe had no problem with what he had to do - the Barrades had trained him to be ready to handle emergencies.

Evan and Rafe edged towards the cloth, their feet avoiding the rubble along the way. Evan knelt down and pointed to a rope. Rafe went towards it while Evan put his ear to the cloth. He carefully peeled it back enough to view the dark vacuum below. Rafe handed him his torch. Evan was more than grateful for this. There was no sign of movement. Evan handed the torch back to Rafe and signalled to Izzy. She came forward with two green orbs. Evan wrapped the cords around his belt. Rafe unwrapped a rope with knots along its length, attached to a metal bar, which had been driven into the side of the tunnel earlier.

Evan popped his head down through the gap again. The others watched as his body balanced and swivelled to analyse the condition below. He raised his head, "They have marked the area with red orbs. It's clear they didn't expect anyone else to survive." He descended the rope once Rafe had lowered it.

"Why just red orbs?" Tia asked

"They mark danger, but don't provide much oxygen," Izzy replied.

"We'll take all the green lights and a few gold ones," Rafe said, as he went down the rope.

Izzy immediately took the clear lights from them and began to clamp the cords under a rock. The others followed and took the green lights with them down the rope. Izzy was the last to get down into the blast site with three gold orbs
. She carefully stepped down onto the irregular ground.

They were able to observe the devastated area. An eerie silence lingered in the air along with a dusty metallic smell. Bent, twisted, metal poles and planks of wood jutted out of a huge mound of rocks and debris, which blocked one of the caves.

Alamo and Rafe went up the tunnel to keep watch. Evan and Alamo would signal each other for impending Defenders with a whistle. Tia, Lisa and Ben stood at the bottom of the rubble and watched as Izzy and Evan climbed carefully up either side of the mound to investigate the small gap - they positioned orbs as they went. The small group's hearts pounded in their ears.

When the climbers got to the top of the wreckage, Evan called out into a small opening.

"Is there anyone there?"

Izzy removed some of the rubble and pushed her last green light through the gap. They still couldn't hear anything.

Evan called out again.

Eventually they heard faint movements below.

"Please help," came the faint cry.

Chapter 31

Survivors

Evan looked back at the rest on the ground. "We need four green and two gold orbs."

There was no hesitation from Tia. She tied the cords to her wrist and started the climb. Using both hands and feet, she tested each footing as she went, rubble slipped beneath her. Lisa looked at the height and made a loud gulping sound.

"Here," Ben said and tied two cords to her wrist. "You can do it. Go carefully," he encouraged. Lisa followed Tia's example and clambered on all fours. She hated the feel of gravel and dirt under her hands, but she knew she had to do this. She slipped a few times, but on each occasion, she stopped, composed herself and started again. She made steady progress with Ben's support.

Once they got to the top, Evan and Izzy detached Tia and Lisa's orbs and pushed the orbs through the gap. Immediately, the darkened area brightened and illuminated a large cave with holes, crevices and piles of rubble splattered about its surface. The mound they stood on extended into the cave below in a gradual slope. At the bottom were three small children. Two of the children were lying on the ground, one with their head in the lap of the girl who sat staring up at the gap, her long dark hair and face covered with dust. Her eyes watered at the adjustment of the light.

"What's your name?" Izzy asked.

The girl began to cough as she opened her mouth. She put her dirty hand to her mouth, trying to control the coughing. She swallowed hard and wiped the tears from her eyes, which smeared the dust along her cheeks. She looked up again, and said something, but her voice was absent.

"Take your time," Izzy encouraged.

"My… My," she coughed uncontrollably again, gulped and coughed her name: "Sa...fia." Her small voice seemed to float up in their direction.

"I'm OK… Micah's arm hurts…. Hannah is …scared." Her voice quivered as she spoke.

"Don't worry. We are here to help you," Evan said.

Safia bowed her head and started to cry.

304

Tia was doing her best to hold back the tears. "We are going to help you don't worry."

Evan sat on the mound his back to the gap and in confident tone asked, "Izzy, can you make it in there?"

Tia was desperate to help, seeing the fear in the little girl's eyes. "I'll go. I've done first aid."

Evan didn't know what first aid was, but admired Tia's willingness. "Let Izzy go first, check the stability of the slope and whether we can get them through here. Then you follow."

Izzy had already cleared the gap to make it wide enough to get through.

"Lisa, you and Ben get us more orbs. Thanks."

Lisa nodded and carefully climbed across to the edge of the mound where it met the wall. She placed the palms of her hands against the cold, grey wall and used it as a means to steady herself down to where Ben was waiting. Ben pulled Lisa out of the way of falling debris as she got to him.

"Thanks."

"I wouldn't want anything to happen to you," he said and hurriedly added. "What would mom say if I didn't get you back in one piece?"

Lisa chuckled at Ben's cover up. "I know you care. Come on you, we need to get more of those light thingys."

"After you," Ben half nodded in the direction of the rope.

Izzy glided through the opening, the clear orb tied to the belt at the back of her waist. She slipped down the mound with a skilfulness she had used many times before. It disrupted some of the debris; puffs of dust rose and fell, setting them off in fits of coughs.

Evan turned to Tia. "Take this." He disconnected his water container from his belt. Tia took the container, pushed it into the front of her overall and rubbed her waist bag, remembering her mother as she slipped into the opening.

Izzy untied the orb and placed the cord under a rock so it hovered close by the survivors. Once on the ground, Tia helped to clear some of the rocks so they could tend to the injured.

Safia, comforted by their presence, spoke: "This is Hannah."

Hannah lay with her head in Safia's lap. She opened her scared blue eyes, smiled briefly at them and closed her eyes again; her white overalls now grey from the dust and debris.

"Micah." Safia laid her hand on the little boy's shoulder. Micah was lying beside them, his right arm held close to his body. Izzy noticed drying blood on his arms and hands. She gently touched his right hand - no response. She gently touched his left arm - he moaned in pain. She examined a bit further and realised his arm was broken.

Tia administered water to all of them as Izzy made her way back up to the gap.

Evan had been moving away rubble to open the gap, in anticipation that they could get the injured through.

Izzy reported her findings to Evan. "Micah has a broken arm, fortunately the bleeding has stopped. I'm not sure if there are any other injuries, but they are pretty drowsy from the shock and the pain. The boost of oxygen is helping. A few more clear orbs would help."

"Any other exits?"

"Only this one. There are a lot of nuggets and glittering gems in the rubble. Safia kept saying they said they would be back, but didn't return. I think..." she began to whisper. "Safia doesn't realise they're not coming back to rescue them. He wants them gone before he comes back. That's why there are no exits and they didn't provide them with oxygen orbs - or any orbs for that matter." She was disgusted, but not surprised.

Evan sighed, "We need Sam. He'll have a way of getting them out of here."

"Bring more water and bandages," Izzy called out as she slowly began her decent.

Lisa had made her way back up to the opening with three orbs. Evan told Lisa to follow Izzy, then he made it back down to the ground just as Ben was about to make his ascent. Evan whistled twice, summoning Alamo and Rafe. He explained the critical situation.

"I'm going to get more bandages and water. Ben, clear the opening a bit more so we can get the others out. Alamo and Rafe - get word to Sam and head straight back here. Remember the Defenders will be back for Evelyn's treasures. We need to move quickly."

Chapter 32

Rescue

Rafe returned to the top of the mound with a stretcher made of two wooden poles and a heavy linen cloth. Ben had opened up the gap in readiness for Alamo and Rafe's return. Evan had already returned and was assisting Izzy with Micah's wounds.

"Good job."

"Thanks." Ben admired his handy work.

"Where's Alamo?"

"We heard marching so Alamo went to check it out - there's so much going on out there. Give this to Izzy - it's to carry Micah. Let them know the Defenders are getting closer. Sam and Bruno have created diversions. Hopefully it'll keep the Defenders away for a while longer."

"OK."

Rafe lowered his voice as he peered down at the scene, "How's it going down there?"

309

"Pretty grim," Ben shrugged. "But they're doing their best."

Rafe didn't know what to say. He handed the folded stretcher to Ben and headed back to his look out spot.

Ben slipped halfway down the mound as he tried to carry the stretcher. He managed to gain his footing and made it safely to the ground.

"Thanks," Izzy said, as he placed the stretcher beside her.

Lisa greeted him with a hug.

"What have I done?"

"I'm glad you're OK. That's all."

Ben beamed and turned to the others, "Rafe said the Defenders are on the move, diversions are being set up to give us more time."

Everyone nodded and continued their tasks with greater urgency.

"Come and help us." Lisa pulled him over to the wall. Ben stumbled as he went. "We're trying to find a soft spot in the wall. Izzy said there might be one. Did you know that she was trapped like this before?"

Ben furrowed his brow.

Lisa wasn't waiting for an answer. "It was Arabella who created the soft spot in the rock and freed her. Anyway,

Izzy has worked, collecting lights ever since and helping the Guardians whenever she can. They have no idea."

Ben was surprised at Lisa's praise for Izzy. "You seem to like her now?"

"She's so brave."

"OK," Ben said, slowly. He was going to say something witty at that moment, but observing Evan and Izzy busily bandaging Hannah's head, he thought it best not to.

"My fingers are numbatized. I can't feel anything," said Tia

"I know. The walls are so cold my fingers are like icicles," Lisa said, as she blew on her fingers and went back to examine the gritty surface.

"It's amazing to think that this is gold," Ben said, as he dug away at a small nugget under the pad of his forefinger. It eventually came away from the wall. He blew the dirt away, scrutinised it and popped it in his pocket.

Tia looked back at the injured survivors. "I can't complain about cold fingers when they're hurt." She blew into her cupped hands. Lisa looked at the dirt on hers, shrugged and carried on.

"Put your hands in your pockets for a while. I'll continue," Ben encouraged, and started to check Tia's section of wall as she stood back. "I read somewhere that gases can accumulate in explosion sites and kill the occupants."

Lisa began to panic. "You mean we could all suffocate? Die?"

"No not necessarily," Ben said, in a nonchalant way. "The opening I've created should provide us with enough air flow."

"The orbs should be enough... shouldn't they?" Tia asked.

Rafe's voice broke the calm but critical atmosphere. "Run, Alamo, run."

They all looked up towards the opening. Rafe's legs appeared, then the rest of him.

"The Defenders are on their way, they're chasing Alamo. He's creating a diversion so we can get away."

Rafe was out of breath and feeling a little guilty, "I wished I could have helped him, they were so quick!"

"Don't worry. Alamo can look after himself. We need to get out of here," Evan said and stood up, after making sure Micah and Hannah's heads were resting comfortably on folded material.

"We can't find the soft areas," Tia choked. "We've tried our hardest."

Lisa put her arms around her friend.

"Don't worry Tia." Rafe went over to stand with her, while swallowing his sense of fear.

Evan called them together - he spoke in a lowered tone. "We have two options. We can all search the walls again or we go out the way we came. This will be more difficult as we'll need to stretcher Micah out of here. His arm is strapped up well, so we can move him."

Izzy remained seated on the ground with the injured children. "Is there a third option? Safia and Hannah are both weak and in a state of shock, I'm not sure if they're up to walking on the precarious surface without doing themselves more damage."

"Perhaps wait for Sam and Bruno?" Ben added.

"That may take a while with the Defenders creating problems," Rafe said.

They were so engrossed in trying to find a solution that they failed to hear the carefully placed boots of a small army of Defenders.

A shower of rubble rained down on them. They turned their attention upwards.

The haunting face of Evelyn glared down on them. His teeth appeared sharp and gleaming, baring what he considered a smile.

313

"Very touching." He was kneeling on one of his inventions - a padded board with spikes on the underside to anchor the board in the rubble. Evelyn leant forward, "It's nice to see you all together like this. It makes my job easier. The leader of the rebels - the unfortunate children and of course Arabella's Impostors!" He spat, paused and inhaled deeply, the dust having no effect on his lungs. "…amongst, my most treasured items." He selected a small rock with his gloved hands. Blew on the rock, and deliberately dribbled his saliva over it. Lisa looked away in disgust. The others screwed their faces in revulsion. He wiped his drool over the rock; his dull eyes began to sparkle as they caught sight of the rich elements that lay within the stone.

"Doesn't it look unassuming? Crusty, but treated delicately, it will reveal elegance, a true treasure." He looked at each one of them. They all stared back defiantly.

An orb drifted up to the edge of the gap and hovered beside his face. Tia and Lisa nudged each other, noticing the change of his hue to a vile green, never seen with anyone else near a green orb.

"Why are you being so horrible? Help us!" Tia yelled. Evelyn stared, unmoved by Tia's outburst. She wasn't going to hold back now, although Rafe tried to stop her.

314

She stepped forward, "Help the wounded children. Give the village back the water. They need it. You -," She pointed up to him, he grinned back, "You separate families - greedy!" She threw her hands in the air as though she were disposing of him.

Rafe clamped his hand over Tia's mouth, while Lisa smiled at Tia's confidence.

"My, my, Tia, you seem quite angry. Too aggressive for a sweet girl. Such energy should be used to release more riches. Never mind. I could give the village back the water, but it would wash away the village – hundreds would drown, homes lost, livestock killed," He tried to convince them. "So, the water will stay where it is, and the villagers will be proud of their children for saving their village."

Rafe wasn't impressed. "And you take riches from these mines, not water! At least be honest."

"I thought you were better than this," Ben added.

"Sorry to disappoint you."

"Weasel-dip," Tia shouted repeatedly.

"Weasel-dip." Lisa joined in.

Evelyn's patience had run out. His cold eyes returned and glazed over. "You can remain here. All of you," he said, as though it was a pleasant invitation. Micah began to moan, Izzy soothed him by wiping his brow. Evelyn was

315

unconcerned, "The next explosion you will hear is going to seal this entrance. When I send my Defenders back to retrieve MY treasures, you will be too weak to do anything. They may decide to save you – whoever survives. Now, how's that for honesty?"

No one answered. They were stunned that he was going to bury them alive.

"By the way, it won't be long before we find Alamo. We already have some of your rebel Guardians – real Defenders!" His laughter bounced off the walls in the imprisoned space. "They were sloppy. As for Arabella, she is no longer a threat. As I hear it, her powers are fading fast." His grin filled his evil face, "I have been exceptional in blocking all your interference. My only concern is to get everything back to normal. And, as for the explosions, a public meeting will quell any fears the villagers may have. My one regret… is that you are some of the best workers I have ever seen, wasted talents. Wasted." He moved away from the opening.

Two guarding Defenders came into view and carried Evelyn down the mound. Their mechanical legs had no problems negotiating the debris. Another Defender removed the kneeling pad and rummaged in the debris partially blocking the entrance again.

"Do you think he's really…," began Lisa.

"Quick - he's going to do what he just said. Move the children carefully. Grab the orbs. Everyone move," Evan shouted.

Rafe carried Safia, Ben and Evan stretchered Micah and Izzy carried Hannah. All of them moved to the furthest part of the cave. They could still hear Evelyn's wicked laughter accompanied by marching boots. Tia and Lisa jumped and grabbed the orbs that were close by. They huddled together over the injured children on the ground. Within minutes, the ground trembled, the mound shook. They squeezed their eyes shut. Pockets of debris spurted from the mound, the tremor intensified. They huddled closely together. The blast exploded into the area, rubble showered around them.

Chapter 33

All Good Plans

They succeeded in their attempt to shield the injured children from the main deluge of splintered rocks and debris. Those standing didn't complain about being struck. They considered their bruises to be minor. Their nostrils and throats were dry and irritated by the dust. They coughed as they raised themselves up.

As the dust settled, they could see the explosion had reduced the area to half its size. The mound had grown considerably and the opening was completely sealed.

Two green orbs hung low, their lights faded. A gold orb remained out of reach, but it was functioning properly. The rest of the orbs had either burst on impact or been buried by the fallen rubble. The exposed spores had leaked over sections of the wreckage.

Rafe cleared his throat, "Is everyone OK?"

The others coughed and spluttered as they nodded. Ben and Tia passed round water containers.

Evan inspected the green orbs. "We need to limit what we say – the air is decreasing; the orbs are leaking." He pointed to the available wall space about them and began to flex his hands over the surface, pushing and probing. They knew what they had to do, they worked side by side covering every inch – it was imperative they find the soft area.

Hannah took a small sip of water and snuggled herself back in Tia's arms. She couldn't keep her eyes open. Micah lay in between Tia and Izzy, unaware of what was going on. Izzy sat with Safia propped up on her lap as she gave her water. Safia drank and watched the movements about her through exhausted eyes.

"I think I've found it. Yes, I'm sure it's here," Ben's excitement gathered the others about him. Evan touched the area Ben pointed to and smiled as he patted Ben on the shoulder. "Now the hard work begins. Arabella would have burnt this through, but she is too weak to do this."

Ben began to worry that their efforts had been in vain. "So how...?"

Evan raised his hand to stop Ben from saying anything. He wanted everyone to be optimistic. "I think the tubers can do this. Rafe, use your tuber to follow the track of the soft area, but don't extend it. Don't stand too close."

319

The others stood back as Rafe marked the area. As he did this, a light blue glow came from the rock. Rafe, encouraged by this sign, continued to drag the tuber along the surface. Small gaps started to appear as the marked areas started to separate. Lisa looked at Rafe then back at the wall and then back at Rafe.

Ben gaped in amazement. "An archway!"

"Not quite," Evan said, "more needs to be removed."

Rafe extended his tuber and slashed the surface of the wall in a criss-cross pattern at the top of the arch. He stood back. Blue embers turned into an orange glow. They felt a gentle warmth as the pliable area began to disintegrate. The rock crumbled away like sand, leaving the bottom section intact.

Lisa got her tuber ready. "I'm willing to do the bottom."

Rafe nodded. "I'll concentrate on the top."

Rafe and Lisa hurriedly slashed crosses over the surface of the marked-out archway and stood back. The rock disintegrated again but this time a deep space became visible - enough for two people to stand side by side. They all smiled with relief now they could see a way of escaping.

Lisa and Rafe waited a few minutes to allow the rock to cool as they ventured into the space to mark the area again. On seeing this, Tia signalled to Ben to come and exchange places with her. Ben did so and cradled Hannah.

Tia didn't know if her idea was going to work, but she was going to have a good try. She picked up a rock the size of her hand and rubbed it with her tuber. Instantly, the rock started to glow. Tia could feel the warmth in her hand to the point where she had to drop it. She wanted to laugh and cry at the same time. Her idea had worked. She gathered some large stones and piled them close to where the injured children were. She rubbed the top of the stones with her tuber and sat back. The glow of orange and yellow lit up the grave chamber. The warmth made them all feel better and for once Safia and Hannah eventually stopped shivering and fell into a peaceful sleep. Ben and Izzy gave Tia a 'thumbs up' signal.

Rafe, Lisa and Evan were deep in the tunnel when they began to feel air coming through the rocks. The last groove they made took a little longer to burn through, but when it did, it opened into a maze of tunnels. Evan was in high spirits about this. "Let's get the others. We're back in Guardian territory."

*

Ben and Evan carried Micah on the stretcher. Tia walked alongside as Evan directed them back to the chambers of the Guardians. Lisa and Izzy walked with Safia between them, Rafe followed close behind with Hannah in his arms. Dimly lit lanterns marked their way along the narrow stone tunnel.

They took a right turn off the main tunnel into a short passageway with a wooden door at the end. Tia made a fist and banged at its centre. Bolts on the other side of the door shifted with a loud clunking sound. They were stunned to the spot as two blue striped Defenders, robotic faces revealed, gave them entrance. If it wasn't for the fact that they had the wounded children, they would have fought for their release. Instead, for the safety of the others, they went obediently to one of the chambers off the small entrance.

The chamber was warm with empty makeshift beds. It looked as though other wounded children had been in the room, as there were bandages and basins of water present. They laid the injured children carefully on the beds. The two threatening figures guarded the entrance. Evan wasn't going to let the injured die, shouting at the Defenders, "They need help now!"

The Defenders' beady eyes stared directly at him, but they remained in position, their stance the same, legs astride and hands behind their backs, facing straight ahead. Their mechanisms whirled and clicked. Rafe wasn't going to wait for a response. He flicked out his tuber, wielding it like a sword as he moved towards them. He struck the first Defender and it fell to the ground, writhing in mechanical spasms. The other Defender took a more defensive stance and held out his baton. It threw Evan to the other side of the room.

"Stop!"

Rowhan ran into the room and stood in front of the Defender.

"Get out of my way kid!" Rafe ordered.

Ben shoved Rowhan aside, but Rowhan jumped up and tried to grab Rafe's tuber as he yelled, "No – they're ours."

"Rowhan!" Izzy and Lisa called at the same time.

"What are you doing, get out the way!" Izzy cried.

"No. They're on our side," he said, trembling as he felt the heated glow from Rafe's tuber. Rafe wrenched his arm from Rowhan's poor grasp, keeping his eye on the Defender.

Micah began to groan. Tia ran to his aid.

"Explain yourself!" Evan said as he readied himself to tackle the Defender again.

"I rewired them, under Arabella's instructions – don't destroy them." He was near to tears, as he watched the Defender on the floor spark out.

"What is your name?" Evan addressed the other Defender.

"They can't talk. I couldn't do everything in such a short space of time."
Rowhan rushed his words. He turned to the Defender, "Stand down." The Defender stood back and took up his guard position at the door.

Rafe retracted his tuber.

"We need help for the children," Tia said, urgently.

"And for yourselves," Rowhan said, as he saw the abrasions on their hands and faces.

Chapter 34

Destinations

After a good evening meal, the injured children now sleeping soundly, the small group assembled at the front of the meeting chamber where they first met the Guardians. They listened as Sam gave an account of the day's events. "We are pretty thin on the ground. There have been many injuries, but they've all been tended to. Spirits are still high, not so in the mines. Evelyn has been exceptionally ruthless. Those in the mines are working round the clock. His underground workshops are under pressure to extract his gold and minerals, to get them stored or hidden."

"Underground workshops?" asked Lisa.

"Yes. He has a whole section dedicated to this operation." Sam noticed the other enquiring faces. "Wherever you see carts or wheelbarrows taken into 'Authorised Only' areas, they're heading to Evelyn's workshops and invention zones, where every item is cleansed to remove any gold or mineral elements - even

325

overalls. Punishments are given to anyone caught wearing their overalls outside of the mines."

"The more I hear, the more I dislike him," said Ben.

Rafe slapped Ben on the back. "Now you're talking my language."

"The problem we have is, he's found our woodland hide out, captured some of our more experienced Guardians and taken them to the holding cells."

As Sam continued to speak, Arabella appeared on the ledge where she had appeared before. Her usual animated character was more subdued.

"Thanks for leading us back here," Evan bowed his head.

"Really?" Ben whispered.

"Did you not see the flickers of the blue leaves through the burnt-out passage and tunnels?" said Lisa.

Arabella's voice was weak, but it held the same authority. "Evelyn is about to destroy all the goodness here. We need to act quickly. Tomorrow is all we have. He is going to parade Alamo and others as traitors and saboteurs of the water, which is now in short supply in the village."

Everyone gasped and started firing questions about Alamo and the water. They soon calmed as they saw Arabella waiting patiently.

"Alamo is strong," Arabella began. Sam and Evan both put their fists to their hearts in solidarity. "Evelyn has slowed the water wheel to make it obvious that someone or something has upset the equilibrium. He will blame this on the agitators and profess that he is trying to restore the water supply. Then he will make his escape as soon as he can. And the villagers will believe you had something to do with his disappearance."

Anger and disbelief filled the room.

"It's true. I saw it all on the circuitry of the Defender I re-programmed," Rowhan announced, as he entered the room, glad to be on the end of such disturbing, yet important information.

Arabella spoke directly to Tia and Lisa. "Come here, take my shawl." Arabella took her purple velvet shawl from around her neck. In their hands, it grew to the size of a blanket. "Place it over Safia, Micah and then Hannah."

They went to the back of the room, which had become a makeshift sleeping zone. They covered Safia with the shawl, which glistened with purple and red hues. Once

327

removed, the glow dimmed. They did this for the other two children and returned to the front of the room.

"You will all touch the shawl once I have finished talking. It will help you rest and gain enough energy to face tomorrow."

They all nodded and looked at the shawl, now resting in Tia and Lisa's lap.

"In the morning, I will let Safia know that she has to return to the village and tell them what has happened to her, Hannah and Micah. She must speak with each parent and tell her father what we know about Evelyn. Her father is on the council and is a good man. Ben and Sam, you must go with her. Ben, you have the gift of speech."

"Me?" Ben wasn't sure if Arabella was being sarcastic.

"Yes Ben, when it is done in the right way. Also, the villagers saw you win the games. That triumph was special. You must speak with Mrs Peri; tell her about Alamo and Evan. However, at all costs, do not speak with Mr Peri. He will only make the situation worse."

"With much respect, Arabella, I was hoping to find the dam."

"You mean; to see the beasts and other creatures?" Arabella said kindly. "They are not cuddly. They are aggressive and cunning. The pendants will be required to get past them."

Ben's shoulders slumped. "I'm sorry. I will do my best at the village. I'll help anyway I can."

Lisa looked at Ben with great pride. Her brother didn't seem such an idiot after all. (*Well at least not now, she thought.*)

"Sam, guide them back to the village and keep them safe. There are still Defenders out there trying to trip us up every step of the way. Rafe, Lisa, Tia - to the dam. Izzy, Evan…guide them." Arabella started to fade but not disappear. Evan moved closer and put his ear toward her.

He turned to the others. "We need to use the maps, don't let Evelyn's creatures outwit us."

"How will you get past them when you don't have pendants?" Rafe asked worriedly.

"Don't fret. We can get you to the dam quicker than if you went on your own. Our skills will help us negotiate some of the creatures. The point is you're here to find the dam and release the water so the villagers will have proof of the free-flowing water."

"I forgot to let you know, you cannot use the quarry to enter the woods. Evelyn has Defenders roaming that area," Rowhan warned.

Evan said, "We'll have to use the old passage. Let's not trouble ourselves about that now, time to get some rest."

They all gathered in and touched the shawl.

Arabella vanished - so did the shawl.

Chapter 35

New Followers

The next morning, Tia informed Safia she would be returning home. Safia was excited. She hadn't seen her father in over a year. She ran to tell Hannah and Micah and to find out if they had any messages they wanted her to give to their families. Tia went along with her.

Hannah was lying in bed; she was much better, but was feeling a bit tired. She asked them to hug her baby brothers and to tell her parents she loved them.

Micah was up and dressed. He wore a blue linen top and jeans, his left arm encased in a hardened, cotton tube. A sling held it to his body. He sat at a table finishing his breakfast. He was small for his age, but this didn't hinder him from being witty or fearless.

"I'm coming with you," he said.

"No, you can't. You need your rest." Tia was firm.

Micah held his encased arm. "No, I must. My arm is a bit sore, but I can walk. Look. I feel fine." With his good hand on the table, he levered himself off the chair with a

331

hop. "I heard what was said yesterday. I wasn't sleeping. They left me to die. I want my family to see what's happened to me. This arm is proof. It shouldn't be broken. I've fallen off things when I was small and never broke anything. They'll have to believe me. I can help. Please, please, please."

Rafe came in and heard the pleading. "Calm down. You've got a lot of spirit for one who's not fully recovered."

"I'm not ill, I'm fine. I'm eight not five, I can do it. I can."

Rafe knelt before Micah, "I think we should ask Sam; after all you would be travelling with him. You'd be his responsibility – and Ben of course."

Micah dashed out of the room in search of them.

*

The group made their way along a narrow, stone passageway, which hadn't been used in years. It was humid and the air was stagnant. Thick cobwebs, insects and moss inhabited the walls. The ground was gritty and dusty. Ground insects scattered as they walked through.

Evan and Sam cleared the protruding vegetation. Rafe and Izzy carried a lantern between them. Micah and Safia followed closely behind. Lisa and Tia shone their torches and used their tubers to spark any large insects that got

332

too close. (Lisa had started this, as she was not interested in any insect making a home in her hair, especially when she saw the size of them). Ben's lantern swayed as he chuckled at Tia and Lisa's antics.

The passageway opened into a U-shaped chamber, a wooden door overlaid with carvings marked its end. Creeping vines flowed over the door, hiding parts of its beauty. Evan and Sam hacked at the rubbery creepers with their knives and hauled the large bolt across the door. They pushed at the door, but it would not budge. Ben, Izzy and Rafe gave their lanterns to Tia and Lisa, who stood back with Safia and Micah. The others pushed hard at the door. It began to creak and groan, as if it had been disturbed from a peaceful slumber. They stopped, took a deep breath and braced themselves.

"On the count of three…," Sam said.

They gave everything they had when they heard *'three.'* They were groaning along with the door as it finally started to open. A fresh flow of air rushed through the gap. This gave them hope.

"Push," Sam yelled.

The door gave a metre and halted.

"I think that should do it." Evan wiped his brow.

They all followed as Evan squeezed through the

opening. On the other side lay a dusty chamber, shaped like a horseshoe, six metres in length. Although there was no vegetation within the chamber, brambles and small pink-flowered climbers surrounded its opening. The late morning sun penetrated the vegetation, producing the warmth and smells of summer.

They placed their lanterns on the ground. Sam and Evan took out their knives again and expertly cut away some of the foliage. Rafe, Lisa and Tia helped by practising with their tubers to remove the more stubborn thick brambles. They came out onto a hillside, which had spectacular views of the valleys and kingdoms.

Rafe wiped his brow, "It feels like it's going to be a warm day. Glad we're wearing these tunics instead of those overalls."

Tia laughed. "Fashion critic. You weren't saying that this morning."

Rafe shrugged with a grin. "Jeans were fine. Tunic's comfortable."

The Guardians had supplied them with leather pouches to carry their torches, tubers, maps and snacks. They hooked water canisters onto the pouch belts around their waists. Tia refused their pouch, as she wanted to keep her own trusted waist bag. Sam carried a rucksack with meals and water for those going to Sanguel.

"This is where we part," Evan said.

Everyone hugged and patted each other on the back. They exchanged encouraging words.

"So, you think you'll get to the dam before we get to the village?" Ben asked Evan.

"Hopefully."

As they started to depart, Lisa ran over to Ben. "Here, have this." Lisa gave Ben the book and the loose pages tucked inside.

"Sam knows the way to the village."

"Just in case," Lisa pushed it into his hands.

"Thanks sis."

Sam, Ben, Safia and Micah headed around the side of the rocky hill and descended into the pleasant green valley, dotted with small violet and white flowers. The others trekked down the craggy hillside. Just before they hit the levelled plains, the woods came into sight. Large robust blue and yellow bell-shaped flowers grew in groups around this area, their stems scaly and grey with spikes.

Izzy stopped in front of a cluster of these large plants, the bells a metre above her head, beneath a berry bush, waist high with tiny, light green leaves and yellow berries.

She pulled away handfuls of berries and started rubbing it on her face and hands. The berries left a watery smear on the skin that would eventually dry. Evan joined her and explained. "You have the benefit of the pendants. We need this – Berryscents - to disguise our smell, so we don't attract some of the animals."

Lisa joined them. "Me too, I'm not going to risk being eaten."

"Be careful, don't touch the stems of the Nightshades, your skin will itch for ages."

Lisa quickly stepped away with a handful of berries.

They all had a chuckle.

"Come on Tia," Lisa beckoned and offered her a handful of berries.

Tia held them in her hand and sniffed. "I'll rely on the pendant and my tuber, thanks. I can't stand that smell, yucky doo, pooh." She turned away and made sure she kept close to Rafe and away from the rest, as their smell was certainly an acquired scent.

Evan laughed. "Don't worry the scent fades."

The dense wood loomed in front of them, its forbidden secrets inside. They trudged on not knowing what was in store. One thing was certain, Evelyn was not going to make this easy for them.

Chapter 36

Mr Malik

It was noon when the small entourage arrived at the village. The journey didn't take as long as they had anticipated. Micah had kept his end of the bargain and travelled all the way, with only a few stops for water and something to eat, saying he had to keep his strength up. Ben kept looking at the map trying to work out how to get to the dam. He dreamed of being in on the action of releasing the water. Sam eventually had to tell him to put it away and concentrate on what they had to do.

Sam found the entrance to the passage Mrs Peri had led Lisa and Rafe through; they squeezed through the crevice and waited as Sam checked out the vicinity of the courtyard. The gate was ajar and the courtyard deserted. He signalled to the others to follow him in.

They made their way into the village.

"Do you remember where you live?" Ben asked.

"How could we forget?" Safia beamed. "Micah lives a few cabins away from mine."

Micah nodded in agreement, his large brown eyes welled with excitement.

Micah tugged on Sam's arm. "What about you Sam?"

Memories of home resonated in Sam. "It's been so long. I left when I was ten… nine years ago. I'm surprised at how different everything looks – yet it's the same. The paths defined; the cabins seem smaller… the smell of good food."

Everyone sniffed the air. It certainly smelt as if something delicious was being prepared for afternoon meals.

Children played outside, but none of them paid attention to the visitors.

They walked along a little further.

"There," Safia pointed. "My home." She ran to the door. Fortunately, no one was in the way, as the little girl would certainly have knocked someone over with her swiftness. She rapped on the door frantically. The others watched as a neatly dressed man opened the door; his black hair and beard sculpted to perfection. He looked stunned as Safia leapt into his arms.

"Papa, Papa."

Tears filled his eyes as he embraced his daughter. Eventually, still emotional and holding Safia, he greeted the others and gave way for them to enter his home.

"What are you doing here? How are you? We heard there was an explosion?" He said all of this while urging them to sit, pointing to the comfortable chairs. "Where are my manners...? I'm Mr Malik, Malna. Please call me Mal."

Ben and Sam introduced themselves. Mr Malik thought he recognised Sam, but he wasn't certain.

It was a small cabin, all on one level. Most of the villagers wanted Mr Malik to have a much larger cabin, as he was a respected member of the council. However, Mr Malik was a humble man and believed that the space was more than adequate for him and Safia. Most of all, it held fond memories of his wife.

They all sat in the area that served as the kitchen, dining and living area. A door led to two bedrooms and a bathroom. A small area behind the kitchen served as a tool cupboard.

Mr Malik served them drinks. "Little Micah, what have you done to your arm?"

"It broke in the blast. But I am fine."

"So, there was an explosion."

339

"Yes, no… I mean there were two. I was in the first one with Micah and some others. Some managed to get away with the help of the Defenders. We couldn't climb out. The Defenders said they'd come back, but they didn't return," Safia said.

"What?"

"Yes Papa."

Mr Malik sat down beside his daughter for a brief moment and placed a caring hand on her arm as she drank and explained the situation.

"We were finally rescued by these kind people," Safia smiled at Ben and Sam. She turned to her father. "Evelyn left us there to die."

"What?" He leaped up and paced the floor in disbelief.

"Yes, I saw him. I heard him and there is no mistake. It was him."

Ben and Sam nodded in acknowledgment.

"It is true Papa. The work is hard. We live a foul existence."

"We work in mines; some places are very dark and scary," Micah added. "But I didn't mind as long as I worked for my family and the village. Now I know it's not true." He looked at his arm and sighed.

Mr Malik continued to pace in front of the unlit fireplace as he pondered the information. "Yet, now Evelyn is hosting an impromptu celebration for the survivors of the explosion – why?"

"This is his usual practice. He is trying to hide the truth, but no more. It's time for the village to understand what is really going on behind Hill House," Sam said, looking at Mr Malik. He hoped he was on their side. In fact, they all watched Mr Malik as his pace slowed and he stood in front of the main entrance.

"I have heard of this before. Lies told about Evelyn, Hill House and those who defend us."

"They don't defend us," Sam said hesitantly. He wasn't too sure if Mr Malik believed them and was thinking about making a quick exit.

"I believed that Evelyn was a great man. I thought he didn't know what the Defenders were doing. I got my answer when he put us to work in the quarry and then left us to die in that pit of a cave. Why did he do it? His riches, that's why." Ben was adamant and stopped himself from banging his fist on the table for effect.

"Yes, Papa, it's all true." Safia ran to her father's side. He scooped her up and breathed out slowly. He stood for a while with his child in his arms, grateful she hadn't died.

341

Ben leaned over to Sam. "Do you think we should find out where Micah's parents are? He may not believe us."

Sam nodded and stood to his feet. "Mr Malik, we need to take Micah to his parents…,"

This jolted Mr Malik back to the here and now. "Please sit."

Sam reluctantly sat down. Mr Malik came back to the table. Safia sat on her chair next to her father and held on to his arm. "Your parents and brother are down in the field preparing," he said, paying attention to Micah. Then he addressed all of them. "I have to face what you have told me. We were told that everyone was safe and there were no fatalities. However, the evidence in front of me suggests otherwise. I know this isn't the first time. I have to admit that my fears of the past… I have to face them. We've all been deceived." He lowered his head, deep in thought. "It is painful to accept."

"So, you believe us?" Ben asked.

Mr Malik glanced at them and nodded. A silent relief filled the room. Mr Malik's gaze settled upon Sam.

"We can speak with Micah's parents. Sam, forgive me. You are familiar, what is your family name?"

"Stowic. Mr Malik."

"The Stowics…," Mr Malik held his head down for a moment, to prepare him for what he was about to say. "Your father hasn't been well, but has recently recovered considerably."

"I wrote to them every day."

"I don't believe they received your letters. Your mother is… she is no longer in the village. She left when she heard you had died three years ago."

Sam wasn't surprised by what he had heard. He knew that Evelyn confiscated letters, using any lie to hide the rise of the Guardians and the truth behind Hill House. All the same, the news was disturbing and sad.

Mr Malik inhaled deeply. "Evelyn gave her good money to start a new life in the kingdom of Clover. Your father refused to leave. They were both grieving in their own way." He could see the confusion on Sam's face. "Don't be angry with your mother, Evelyn is a persuasive man. Your mother promised to come back. She wrote to your father. I read the letters to him when he was ill, but her letters soon stopped."

"I need some air. I'll be back in a minute." Sam stepped outside.

Mr Malik decided it was a good point to energise them with food. "You must all be hungry; I'll get you something to eat."

"I'm just thirsty," Safia said, finishing her drink.

Ben wasn't going to refuse the offer of food. "I'm a bit hungry – if it's no trouble."

"That is fine. What about you little Micah?"

"Yes please."

"Good." Mr Malik poured out more juice for them. "The water wheel has slowed down." He sliced pieces of meat as Ben interrupted him to explain why the water wheel had really slowed down. Safia buttered chunky pieces of bread for all of them.

Sam re-entered the cabin. "Ben, we need to see Mrs Peri, I've just heard that Evelyn is giving his speech before the ceremony this afternoon."

"That's unusual. His speech for such an occasion is normally at the end of the proceedings," Mr Malik said.

Ben had a gulp of juice. "That means we need to hurry."

"We'll meet you back here before the speech starts," Sam said. He went over to Micah and knelt beside his chair. "It's best if you stay here and meet your parents later. If word gets out that you're here it may alert Evelyn."

Micah beamed back. "I thought you'd say that. I can wait."

"I'll make sure they are safe," Mr Malik assured.

"Will I have to wear a disguise?" Micah asked.

They all laughed. "Not a bad idea," Sam said as he and Ben headed to the door.

Chapter 37

Woodlands

Evan, Rafe and Izzy followed the route marked out on the map. Lisa and Tia followed behind. They drank plenty of water as the day got warmer. They were extra vigilant, looking out for any rogue beasts, but so far had only encountered birds and inquisitive insects, much to Lisa's dismay. "I hate these flies, it's a pity they aren't bigger, I'd zap them with my tuber again."

Tia decided to divert Lisa's attention away from the wildlife. "Do you think Safia and Micah have been reunited with their families yet?"

"I hope so."

"Rafe's getting on well with the others."

"You mean especially with Izzy," Lisa chuckled. "I could tell she liked him from the first time they met."

"Really? Tell me more."

They arrived at their next cooling spot - a shaded area, with a gathering of large stones and fallen trees. They made themselves as comfortable as they could. Lisa looked up and was astonished to see an owl fly off into the upper regions of a tree.

"Rafe, that night - the ledge - the voice," Lisa stared wide-eyed. They all looked upwards but couldn't see anything, wondering whether Lisa was confused.

However, Rafe had also caught sight of the owl and knew exactly what she meant. "When we posed as Gatherers, one of them tried to run away, but he was soon caught and punished," he said, remembering the awful event. "An owl made an appearance and it stayed until the voice, which was shouting terrible, humiliating instructions stopped."

Lisa was still looking up warily.

"I know that owl very well," Evan said.

"It belongs to Evelyn, doesn't it?" Tia asked.

"Yes, it does, how do you know that?"

"Evan, the man has a nasty picture of it in his banqueting room."

Lisa was surprised. "Really? I didn't see it."

"You were too busy scoffing his food." Tia gave Lisa a friendly nudge.

"How do you know of it?" Rafe asked.

What Evan had to say was going to be painful for him to relay. He took a deep breath, "I was punished in the same way. However, I had the added misfortune of having my flesh pecked by that creature - I'll never forget it. Evelyn took great pleasure in it. His owl –Tulisa - needed very little feeding for weeks. He thought it would make me comply with his wishes, but I promised myself, because of these marks," he pointed to his back but didn't raise his top to reveal the terrible scars, "I'd never let that man continue to deceive us any more."

"Imagine that nasty bird has part of my name."

"Don't take it personally Lisa. It's part mechanical. I don't blame the bird, I blame the owner, the way he manipulates people - my father being one of them. Who knows what has really happened to Meela."

For the first time, they saw sadness in Evan's eyes.

"That's why we're here," Rafe said, "It has to stop."

This rallied them back to the task and gave them a renewed strength to continue with purpose.

Tia opened her map. They all crowded over it. Rafe pointed to a distinctive black and grey area marked along a cluster of trees. "We need to find that ridge. The dam is just behind it."

Evan traced the route they were going to take with his finger. "We haven't far to go now, but the area we are going to is dangerous."

"Why?" Lisa asked.

"Because those orange bark trees mark the way to the ridge."

"They shield that area."

"Exactly Rafe, at night it can look like the place is about to go up in flames. Sam and I have seen it before and had to turn back – the heat was so intense. Arabella told us it's an illusion - the colours of the trees and the vegetation that lives on it, reflects in the moon light. If that doesn't put you off, the inhabitants will."

Lisa pulled out her tuber and held it firmly in her hand. Tia checked her pendant was easy to reach. Rafe braced himself.

"You have the benefit of the pendant and tubers, that will make a big difference," said Evan.

"Are we ready?" Izzy asked.

Lisa shuddered. "For the beasts?"

"Don't worry Lisa. We've done OK so far." Tia put her arm around her.

"Perhaps your book will provide more information about them," Evan suggested. "It may help to prepare you."

349

Rafe already had his book out. He thumbed through the pages. "There is nothing here about the beasts."

"Blank pages." Tia displayed her pages.

Izzy decided to impart what she knew about the beasts. "They are called mechagribea - Evelyn's invention, part mechanical and part animal." Seeing the horror on their faces, Izzy quickly added, "If you activate your pendants, they won't be able to see or smell you, but they are able to detect sudden movement. They are relentless in their pursuit and often roam in pairs."

Lisa's eyes widened with fear. "What do they look like?"

"They have orange fur, with…," Evan began.

Tia interrupted. "Large triangular ears that stand on end, metal teeth…,"

Evan was surprised. "You know them?"

Lisa shook her head in dismay. "Seen them in action, don't really want to see it again. Their howls alone are terrifying." She shuddered remembering the event at the library.

"Be brave." Evan put a comforting hand on her shoulder. "Over the years we have learnt how to outrun these creatures, but this preoccupation left little time for us to find the dam. With the maps and your devices, you can get to the dam. Leave the rest to us."

Rafe packed his book away. "We'll do our best, but how are you going to get away from these beasts?"

Izzy smiled, "Our gymnastic skills, wit and pace should get us through. In a clear field, they can outrun most things, but mechagribeas find difficulty scaling obstacles. Anyway, we have our batons - not as lethal as your tubers, but effective enough for us to draw them away to give you a chance to get to the dam."

Rafe nodded his head in admiration. Lisa and Tia nudged each other as they saw the growing fondness between Izzy and Rafe.

"Your task is to get to the dam and open it," Evan said.

"Are we ready?" Rafe stood and extended his hand in front of him.

The others followed suit, hands placed on top of each other.

"We can do this." Lisa chanted.

Tia placed her hand on the top of their hands. "Yes, we can."

"Are we ready?" Rafe's determined voice exuded a force from which they all drew courage.

Chapter 38

Hide

Ben and Sam were relieved to see Mrs Peri. She was just about to leave her home. They wanted to get indoors as soon as they could. Although the villagers were busy getting ready for the ceremony, some of them were taking a second glance as Sam walked by. At first, Mrs Peri didn't recognise Ben, but as he came closer, she was overjoyed. She immediately opened the door and ushered them in.

"How are you? How is Alamo? Did you meet with your friends and sister?" She hugged Ben.

"All doing well. Thank you. Where is Mr Peri?"

"He is down at the field preparing."

"Good," Sam said.

Mrs Peri looked at Sam again. "My goodness... Samuel Stowic, could it be you?"

"Yes."

She grabbed him into an embrace. "Thank goodness, you're alive. Your father will be overjoyed. What a fine man you have turned into, it will warm his heart." She released him, and smiled with hope.

"Thank you."

Ben and Sam quickly told her what they could. Evan's exploits brought tears of joy to her eyes. They prepared themselves to give her the difficult news about Alamo. Sam pulled out a chair for Mrs Peri to sit down.

"…And Alamo?" Her voice quivered.

Ben and Sam looked at each other.

"You might as well tell me. I know something is wrong. I can feel it."

Ben sighed. *Where was Lisa when he needed her?*

"He was…. Errrmmm."

"Evelyn has captured him," Sam said. A heart-rending silence descended. Mrs Peri rocked from side to side to comfort herself.

"Evelyn will use him as an example. I know he will. He threatened to do so with Evan, but my husband pleaded with Evelyn to retain Evan's position at Hill House. And ever since, Omar has been indebted to Evelyn, believing everything he says or does."

Mr Peri's booming laugh could be heard through the open window. Mrs Peri sprung to her feet. "Hide. Quickly." Mrs Peri shunted them into the back room and slammed the door shut. A waistcoat fell off the hanger on the back of the door.

Mr Peri marched into the cabin, stomping the ground as if he were cold.

"They have done it this time. This time they have done it. We'll have less water in the village."

Mrs Peri wiped her tears away with her green shawl. Mr Peri was too busy stomping to and fro to notice the nervousness of her actions or the sadness in her expression.

"The explosion by rebels. REBELS! Why would anyone want to be a rebel? They have brought great shame to their families. Throw them out. Throw them out. They should be thrown out like that woman, what was her name - Stew, Stowic. Dam pests these rebels. If any of MY children were caught up in that nonsense, I'd disown them. Disown them." He yelled.

"Don't be so harsh. We don't know the full story. Keep your voice down."

"What more is there to tell? Evelyn is right. We live well. All of us."

"You don't have to try to convince me. Just remember what Evan said." She pressed close to her husband's side to stop him from stomping up and down. He shoved her away in frustration.

"Evan thinks of no one but himself!" He flared his arms, one of his dungaree straps fell from over his shoulder. He stopped to fix it. It gave him time to think.

"What's the matter?" he asked, as he examined the expression on his wife's face. She remained silent.

He continued to rant.

"Evelyn said we need to beware of strangers. Be aware. The last time there was an explosion, strangers were here. In fact, every time there is an explosion, strangers have been in our peaceful Sanguel."

Rays of sunlight beamed through the window. Mr Peri took this as a sign that he, of course, was right.

"If you see any of them, any of them, report them. I'll take them to Evelyn myself. I'll humiliate them in the village first." A grin stretched so far across his face it looked as though his face would split in two. "I'm sure we would be rewarded. Yes, rewarded…, well, handsomely." He chuckled.

His wife shuddered. "Don't you need to be going?"

"I came back for my waistcoat and penknife. I need it for the bunting."

Mrs Peri hurried ahead of him, "Why do you really need that knife. Use the one in the cupboard. It's much sharper."

"Don't be stupid, that knife ripped a slice out of my thumb, not again, definitely, not again." He stated as he tried to force his way past her. Mrs Peri stumbled forward, banging against the back-room door.

"Oh Reena."

"I'm fine." She deliberately took her time regaining her balance, but didn't move away from the door.

"You do fuss, too much fussing. Now, let me get my things then I'll be off." He squeezed past her, his stomach gently guiding her out of the way. He opened the door. Mr Peri saw the waistcoat on the floor. He snatched it up. The penknife fell out of the pocket. He went down on one knee to retrieve it and slowly rose back unto his feet with the aid of the door handle and a grunt. He popped the penknife into his pocket and went back into the living room. Mrs Peri glanced in the room and saw no sign of Ben or Sam.

"How does this look?" Mr Peri said, as he pulled the front of the waistcoat together. It didn't quite meet.

"You look fine," she said, dusting his shoulders.

356

"You're a wonderful wife, a little wilful at times, but a good wife." He kissed her on the cheek. "Remember, gathering in twenty minutes - don't be late. Don't be late, reputation is what we have."

He left the cabin, with long proud strides.

Mrs Peri hastened to the back room. "He's gone."

The chairs around the table scraped against the floor, as Ben and Sam pushed themselves out from the tiny space.

Sam stretched with relief. "There was less space than I thought."

"We heard you coming to the door. It took a mad moment of panic before we worked out where to hide." Ben chuckled.

Sam laughed. "The cupboard, the trunk, we were grateful for the tablecloth, with a few adjustments it did the job."

"Listen," Mrs Peri was serious. "It's best if you stay until the meeting is underway. If Omar sees you, he will hand you over to Evelyn."

"But we need to meet with the others," said Sam.

Mrs Peri tried to persuade them otherwise.

"We need to get back to Micah and Safia. It's best if we stay together," Ben said.

"Alright, but be careful. Evelyn will send his dreadful Defenders if he knows you're here."

"I doubt if he does or he wouldn't have changed his meeting. I think he believes that we died in his little explosion antic," Ben said.

Sam thought otherwise, "Or, someone has reported us missing and so he's moved it. We have to talk to the villagers before he gets to them with his misleading speech."

"Speak with Mal, he'll know which villagers to speak to. After all, you are living proof that things are not right," Mrs Peri said, giving Sam a reassuring squeeze on the arm.

Chapter 39

Mechagribea

It wasn't long before they saw the first of a cluster of distinctive trees. Their bark had brown, orange and red hues; yellow moss oozed through the cracks in the bark and branches. The leaves glowed with the same colouring. These trees towered above the other trees in this area, providing a tropical canopy. The undergrowth had a distinctive, pungent, burnt orange odour that was, at times, quite nauseating. Long grass irritatingly rustled about their knees.

"Is it getting warmer?" Tia asked, as sweat beaded her brow.

"No, it's no warmer than where we've just come from," Izzy said, as she walked alongside Tia.

Tia drank some more water.

Izzy beckoned to Rafe, who was in front of them with Evan and Lisa. "The area is affecting Tia more than the

359

rest of us," she whispered. "We'll need to find a suitable place to rest before she passes out."

Rafe slowed his pace to match Tia. Izzy caught up with the others to explain Tia's situation.

They tried their best to find a place to take a break, but within minutes of them stopping, they heard rustling movements around them. Birds screeched and took flight, as deep growls and grunts came from the undergrowth. The group jerked their heads about them trying to catch sight of whatever it was. They were not sure how close they were to the growls and grunts, but decided it wasn't a good place to rest. They continued their journey with even more vigilance.

They trekked on in the direction of the dam. Rafe and Evan pointed at the same time as the enormous grey ridge came into view. Both grinned at their find. The group cheered with excitement and relief. Tia took the opportunity to rest on a tree stump, as the others walked on to get a better view. In their excitement, they failed to take notice of the muted growl of the preying beast a few metres behind them, its movement subtle and effective. A mechagribea lumbered out of the undergrowth, attracted by their euphoric sounds.

Evan and Izzy caught sight of it.

"Stand still," Evan said, quietly. Tia being closest to the beast didn't hear what he said. Instead, she turned to run, tripped over a log and tumbled into the tall grass. She pressed her pendant as she tumbled. Rafe and Lisa pressed theirs too.

The mechagribea rose on its hind legs. It stood eight feet tall. Evan and Izzy slowly moved away from the others. It swiped the air with its front paws, its razor-sharp claws and teeth gleamed like polished silver. It let out two high pitch cries, as though it was calling for help, followed by a deep lengthy wail, as its large grey eyes tried to narrow in on the prey. Evan and Izzy had taken shelter behind a tree and stabilised their breathing to a steady calmed motion, waiting for a chance to attract the beast's attention while trying to avoid any harm to Tia.

Rafe wasn't about to leave Tia. He and Lisa remained motionless. They believed the mechagribea was calling for help and they didn't want to be taken by surprise again, if another one was in the vicinity. They breathed out slowly as if breathing through a straw. Beads of sweat trickled from their brow. Lisa held her tuber firmly, building up courage to use it.

The beast slumped down on all fours. Its orange body mass still looked large and intimidating. Its eyes roamed as its white snout sniffed the air. It wailed twice and thumped the ground with its large paws, repeatedly. Tia tried her best to keep still, but the pungent smell of the undergrowth, the disturbing vibrations and impending closeness of the beast forced her into action. As the beast lifted its head again and wailed, Tia couldn't bear it. She leapt to her feet and sprinted in the direction of the ridge. Rafe and Lisa followed suit.

Sensing the movement, the mechagribea wrenched its neck forward, then its body. Just as it was about to pursue the movement, Evan and Izzy jumped out, clapped their hands and yelled feverishly. This confused and distracted the beast for a moment. Once they got its attention, they ran in the opposite direction of the ridge. The mechagribea gave chase with long, powerful strides.

Chapter 40

Villagers

Ben and Sam made their way back to Safia's home. A small crowd had gathered inside the Malik's home. Others were outside, peering in through the opened windows and doorway. Ben and Sam weren't sure whether it was a welcoming committee or an angry mob. They decided the only thing they could do was to push through the crowd and find out what was going on.

"Is she sure there is a dam?" someone asked.

Another person called out. "There is plenty of water."

"This is not possible? Is it?"

The crowd murmured.

Ben and Sam saw Mr Malik stood behind the dining table with Safia. To his left were Micah and his family.

Safia's father settled the crowd. On seeing Ben and Sam, he announced, "These are the young men who saved my daughter and the lives of the others."

They greeted Micah's family and took up positions on the right of Mr Malik

"My goodness," a woman yelled, "is that not the Stowic's son?"

"You're seeing things - you old flake!" Someone else shouted. A few chuckles went up, but it soon changed as Sam spoke, a sober look on his face. "I am Samuel Stowic."

The crowd gasped in disbelief, chatter broke out.

"I thought they said he had died." A man shouted.

"It's a Miracle." The woman who had spotted him in the first place pushed forward towards Sam, clapping her hands in amazement. The crowd started to cheer. Some also pressed forward and greeted Sam and Ben, who were grateful that the table shielded them from the thrust of the crowd. A few of the villagers went around the table to welcome them.

The crowd bombarded Sam and Ben with questions about what was going on behind Hill House. Mr Malik waved his arms and raised his voice to calm the crowd. "One question at a time please."

Someone yelled over the top of the fading din. "Is it true there is water - in abundance?" The crowd fell silent, eagerly awaiting the answer.

"Yes," Sam said.

Loud gasps and clatter of voices.

"We can show you where the water will flow. It will come from a dam...," Ben said.

"We can't do that now." A large man's voice bellowed into the room. He was standing just inside the doorway. He was one of the guards from the courtyard. He wore his uniform proudly.

"Evelyn has called us together." The crowd parted as he swaggered forward. A few villagers scurried away from the assembly.

"It shouldn't take us long," Sam said, not intimidated by the threatening figure approaching them.

"We will go to the meeting first." He stipulated, as he stuck his chest out even further.

Ben felt a little timid, but he plucked up courage. "The water is needed here. Isn't that the most important thing?"

"Evelyn's speech first!" He clenched his fist.

Mr Malik stepped in between them. The large man stepped back in respect of Mr Malik's authority and reputation.

"We will attend the ceremony as planned. You can show us this place later," Mr Malik said.

"We must all leave now," the man roared and strode out of the room. The crowd parted like waves and obediently followed him. Ben wanted to protest, but it was no use. Mr Malik consoled him. "When Evelyn calls, we all have to be present, it's village protocol." He rested a calm hand on Ben's shoulder. "Sanguel was not built in a day. Your time will come."

Micah's mother held on to Micah's hand. "We are grateful you saved our son's life."

"The villagers who were here will tell the others who were not here, and everyone will have their own idea about what has taken place. We will do anything we can to help," Micah's father said, "but for now we will find out what excuses he has." He guided his wife and child out of Mr Malik's home.

Sam and Ben were intrigued to find out why the crowd had gathered.

"Micah's father came by for some tools to repair one of the benches for the ceremony. You should have seen his reaction when he saw Micah," Safia clapped and danced. They all smiled at her excitement. Mr Malik continued the story, "he called his wife, others came with them. Hannah's parents turned up and before we knew it, Micah and Safia were giving an account, a very good one, of what had happened to them."

"But many seem unconvinced," said Sam.

"On seeing you, there was further proof. We were told you were dead, but here you are fit and strong," Mr Malik stressed, tapping Sam on his sturdy biceps. "It will give them much to think about. We must hurry - go see your father. The gossipers may have already got to him. Then get to Evelyn's speech. It is best if you stay out of sight until we know what Evelyn is going to announce. From what you have told me, you will all be in danger."

Safia clutched onto her father's arm. "I don't like this."

"I believe it is time for the truth to come out." Mr Malik soothed.

The task was harder than Ben and Sam expected. They were still determined to get the villagers to the dried stream. They only hoped the others were having a better time of it than they were.

Chapter 41

Ridge

Lisa and Rafe finally caught up with Tia at the edge of the woods. She was bent forward gasping for breath

"I'm... so... sorry...," she panted. "I... just... had... to," she straightened up, hands on her hips. She exhaled, "run."

"It's OK." Rafe breathed deeply. "Let's catch our breath then get to the ridge. It's not too far now."

They looked ahead and saw a thin line of metallic trees with translucent leaves. They intermittently veiled the silvery rock side.

"I hope the others got away," Lisa panted.

"I'm sure they will have," Rafe said.

They began striding towards the ridge, vigilantly holding their tubers, their adrenaline still pumping.

"It was jaganormous!"

"It wouldn't have caught you," Rafe chuckled. "I know you're fast, but man, you legged it!"

"I simply couldn't lay there. I felt a real surge, my legs did the rest."

The smell of the undergrowth soon faded as they trudged over stony terrain and approached the rock side. They leant backwards to look up at the ridge. A white mist lingered over its upper regions.

"How are we expected to get up there?" Lisa said, as she stepped backwards, to avoid her neck feeling as though it was going to snap in two, "It's way too steep to climb."

"There must be another way up," Rafe said.

They decided it was better to walk under the ridge for shade and look for a way up as they went. Within a few minutes, they came upon a gap in the rock. Rafe shone his torch inside.

"It looks like this is a way in," he said.
Lisa wasn't too keen. "There may be another way further along," she said. "OK Rafe, I know what you're saying, that eyebrow of yours tells me this is it." She sighed.

Rafe pushed his torch back in his pocket and squeezed through the gap. It opened into a small irregular shaped curve, only big enough to fit two people. A shaft of light beamed in from an opening above. The space had crudely chiselled half circles up the wall and alternating iron rods embedded in the rock. Rafe used these to scale the six-metre wall.

Tia looked at Lisa. "After you."

"I can't wait till this is over; I don't want to see another crevice, cranny or tree." Lisa moaned, as she pushed her way through. There was a sliver of light around Rafe's frame as he climbed towards the opening. Lisa placed her right foot in the first half-circle, gripped the rods above her head and began her shaky ascent. Tia followed shortly after.

Rafe pulled himself up into the opening and inhaled, the air was refreshing. He observed the tranquil scene below the ridge.

"Help, please help me!" The voice was that of a child, accompanied by a rattling sound. It came from around the corner of the ridge. Rafe didn't hesitate to take out the tuber and sprint towards the cry. He saw no one, but could hear the rattling sound. He ventured further along the wide ridge - rocks on one side, a steep drop to the other. A thin mist gathered around him, he slowed his pace, continued around the bend and still saw no one.

Rafe thought perhaps he hadn't heard the cry, so he retracted the tuber and turned to head back for the girls. As he approached the bend the mist greyed, a strange shape was heading towards him. Rafe hesitated and stepped backwards, he couldn't make out what it was.

Slithering towards him was a double-headed snake, its grey, furry body extended proudly as its neck separated into two.

One head, covered with tufts of grey fur with green scaly patches, dipped forward and cried softly like a child. "Help me." A sly smile on its gruesome face sneakily covering its jagged teeth. It stood its ground and sucked in the mist. The other head and neck was now clear to see - clothed with blue scales, tufts of grey fur protruding around its emerald eyes. It glared down at Rafe and rubbed its paws together a slowly ripping sound emanated as two steel claws emerged from under the skin.

Rafe swallowed hard. He shuffled cautiously backwards against the rock face.

The creature dipped its heads a few inches away from Rafe, as though bowing in submission and rapidly jerked them upward. It grinned, revealing its sharp teeth. This time when the voice came, it was that of a gruff beast. "You won't pass!"

Chapter 42

Real Treasure

The villagers had gathered in front of the moat, under the gaze of Hill House. A few were scattered under trees or beside the food and drinks tables. Children were under strict orders - no running around until after Evelyn's address. Dogs sat obediently at their owners' feet.

Sam and Ben stood a short distance away from each other wearing caps, not to shade from the sun but to provide some disguise from Evelyn and his Defenders' gaze. Mr Malik made sure Safia and Micah were with him and both suitably disguised in the crowd.

Evelyn was dressed in simple attire, not like the flamboyant clothing he regularly wore in Hill House. He stood regally on a platform between two guards. Two blue striped Defenders guarded the door to Hill House.

Evelyn assumed a concerned expression and stepped humbly to the front of the platform. He adjusted the horned microphone to his lips and began.

"I have gathered you here to inform you of the unfortunate, regrettable events over the past few days regarding the explosion." He surveyed the crowed with feigned sympathetic eyes. It made so many of them feel an affiliation to him and his concerns for them.

"We thought it was an accident, but unfortunately it was more than that." His face appeared troubled. He began to pace thoughtfully, his hands behind his back, all done for dramatic effect to draw the villagers into his supposed dilemma.

"We have had some trouble. Trouble that we had no idea was developing." He twisted the beads on his beard. "We believed all children, all parents, even those who may have the misfortune of not having children, would be thrilled, contented, patriotic, to work for this harmonious community we have built for the survival of us all!"

The villagers nodded in appreciation.

"But this is not so." He stopped pacing. "Some members believed they should take matters into their own selfish hands." Evelyn swirled his right hand in the air. It was a signal to the Defenders standing behind him. One marched round to the side of the house and returned with another Defender, parading Alamo between them. His hands bound in front of him, he looked dazed, the wounds on his back concealed by a clean tunic. Another set of Defenders appeared, presenting three more captives to the crowd. Villagers cried out in shock. Some wept and held their heads in shame as they recognised their children.

"Yes. Yes. You know them!" Evelyn shouted. "They have disgraced us all. They tried to stop the progress of the water. Our survival!" He pointed to the motionless water wheel.

Some of the villagers started booing, ran to the edge of the moat and shook their fists at them. A woman ran forward and threw some rotting tomatoes and apples at them. A tomato struck Alamo on his face, the residue dripped down his cheek. Mrs Peri held a dignified pose, compassion in her eyes for her son. Mr Peri held his head in shame, pulled his cap closer to his eyes.

Evelyn held his hand up, to halt the flight of fruit. "We will not behave like them. Madam, save your beautiful fruits. They will have a more fitting punishment."

Aghast chatter broke out.

Ben and Sam didn't like the sound of that. "Here," Sam said, as he strolled past Ben and handed him a wooden baton that he had retrieved from his rucksack. He stood beside Ben and spoke quietly, "You'll need this. A good hard whack will weaken their limbs, a couple more and you can paralyse his mob."

Ben grabbed it, glad to have some form of defence. He had witnessed its use on the children in the mines. His Xplorers training in self-defence was going to come in handy.

"Time to take action," Sam said. They began to make their way around the edge of the crowd to some nearby bushes screening the left side of the moat. Everyone else focused on Evelyn's delusion show.

"They are rebels! Traitors! They have stopped our progress." He jabbed the air with his finger in the direction of his prisoners. His voice echoed across the field. He pushed Alamo in the chest. Alamo shunted backwards. "Not so gallant now." He sneered in his ear.

"What about the water?" A large man from the cabin meeting shouted.

Evelyn jerked his head around like an animal caught in headlights.

"It's hampered for the moment, but we will get it right once the damage has been assessed."

"Is it true there's a dam?" The man bellowed again.

Evelyn tilted his head in the air and twisted his mouth and brow, trying to mask his disdain and shock that such information would be known or aired.

"Is it true a dam holds our water?" Mr Malik shouted.

Evelyn's poise faltered. His eyes darted across the crowd to find the culprit, "Water? Dam?" He steadied his voice. "What is this about?"

"Tell them the truth," Alamo yelled. "Our water has been dammed!"

Evelyn swung around and struck Alamo on the face with the back of his hand. Contempt flared in his eyes.

Alamo's mother ran forward. "We were told there is a dam - it's not my son's fault. I beg you to release him."

Embarrassment forced Mr Peri to action. He lumbered forward as quickly as his weight would allow and pulled his wife away, ushering her back towards the gathering, making gestures of regret for her behaviour, saying 'sorry' repeatedly until they retreated into the centre of crowd.

Alamo was not discouraged. "Give up, Evelyn, the truth is out."

However, Evelyn had a few more tricks to unleash. "Who said there is a dam? Where?" Evelyn said it with such innocence, most of the villagers believed he had no knowledge of it.

"The new boy... I think his name is Ken, or was it Len. He was with Sam, the Stowic's lost...deceased child," an old woman said, turning to her husband to recollect Ben's name and the shock of Sam's appearance.

"Ask Councillor Malik, his daughter knows all about it!" someone else shouted.

Evelyn was astonished. He believed they were still trapped or even dead. He thought he was only searching for Arabella and her last few followers.

Some of the villagers turned to point out Mr Malik, but he had already left.

The crowd's attention was now drawn to the skies where a circling owl swooped low and landed on Evelyn's extended arm. The bird spoke to Evelyn in a language only he understood then flew off towards the woods.

Evelyn spoke abruptly to his guards and Defenders. A Defender headed back into Hill House. In no time, the bridge extended across the moat and the guards ran across it through the crowd in the direction of the village.

Defenders took the captives back to their cells.

Evelyn spoke with the returning Defender, composed himself, dispelled the idea of the dam, and emphasised the intended destruction of the rebels.

Sam and Ben had already made their way across the moat by means of a lengthy plank of wood, hidden in the bushes by the Guardians some time ago after a games event. They were far away from prying eyes, as Sam led the way through the secret route to the cells. A stone archway marked the entrance, the door was unlocked as no one was expecting intruders.

Ben and Sam hid behind opposite pillars in the dimly lit stone corridor. The door leapt open as two Defenders shoved the captives into the corridor. As the Defenders marched past, Ben and Sam dived at them and struck them to the ground. On seeing the fight behind them, the captives dashed to help. They seized the Defenders' batons and, with ropes intended for the captives, bound their arms and legs. They dragged them into the cells and locked the doors. The freed Guardians were ecstatic. They hugged and shook hands.

"Where's Evan and the others?" Alamo asked.

Ben was eager to tell them what had happened. He explained, quickly, who had gone to the dam, and that he and Sam were sent to convince the villagers of the truth.

Alamo was running on adrenalin. "The crowd was asking Evelyn some difficult questions when we were being led away - it's working. Although I heard Evelyn send his mob after Mr Malik and to the dam."

"I'll make sure Mr Malik is taken to a safe place. You three come with me." Sam charged out of the cells with the three Guardians.

Alamo slapped Ben on his back. "Come with me. You said you could ride?"

"Yes," Ben said, but when he had told Alamo this, he only meant he'd had a few riding lessons. The rest was on the bronco at the funfair. Now this *'yes'* was going to be tested.

Chapter 43

Dam

Lisa pulled herself through the gap, followed by Tia, both unaware that Rafe was doing battle with a devilish serpent.

"We're visible," Lisa groaned. "I wish this could last until we leave this place."

Tia dusted herself off. "No such luck. Where's Ray?"

The monstrous shriek of the serpent answered her question. Its head shot into the air dripping green slime along its way. Lisa and Tia clung to each other as they watched the head plummet over the ridge.

"Ray," Tia shouted. "You alright?"

There was no response, but they heard muffled sounds of clashing metal against metal from around the ridge. Tia and Lisa slipped their tubers into their palms, gripping them tightly as they made tentative steps around the bend.

Rafe jumped to the left and swung his tuber to the right. It missed the serpent's head as it lunged towards him. Claws ripped at him. Rafe stunned them into submission. However, he knew he had to remove the last head or the claws were going to do him some serious damage. With a final upward stroke, he struck into the weak part of the serpent's neck.

"Not fair." The face crumpled, the head grunted as it left its body and flew upwards, green fluid splashing the area. Rafe twisted away as it splattered against his back. The dismembered head bounced off the rock and rotated in the air over Lisa and Tia's heads, they both instinctively ducked and followed its path as it smashed into the trees below.

"Mega Mega."

"Hey, you two... meet my conquest." Rafe boasted, out of breath. He wiped the sweat from his face and directed Tia and Lisa to the body of the beast lying on the edge of the ridge.

"Are those really scales? Fur? Green glup or muck?" Lisa grimaced.

Tia stepped a little closer to investigate.

Rafe laughed. "Lisa can't stand the sight of it and you want to see more."

"It's fascinating. I might not see one of these again," said Tia, poking it with her tuber. "What is it?"

"Who knows? One thing's for sure it's Evelyn's," Lisa said.

Tia noticed small patches of blood on Rafe's face and arms. "Are you OK?" She went over to him and dabbed at the areas with a small cloth from her waist bag.

"I'm fine really, just grazes," he smiled. His reassuring tone comforted her. "One day you'll take a fridge out of that bag," he laughed.

Rafe used his tunic to wipe the green slime off his tuber, "These tubers are great, they stun, strike and cut."

"Don't walk too close to me. I don't want that muck on me."

"Well Lisa, that means you have to be really careful where you're going to step, because we're going that way." Rafe smiled and pointed to the ridge, splattered with the slimy green substance.

Lisa sighed. "In for a penny…"

*

The ridge led them into a short tunnel. Light poured in from the opposite end. The reverberation of thundering water filled their ears. It was an almost unbearable, but

382

pleasing sound. Gathering speed, they made it to the other side to view a magnificent scene.

The hillside was crammed with orange-bark trees. Water gushed into a massive basin made of stone. The water danced with bubbles and froth, a rainbow of colours shimmered in the motion. There was nowhere for the water to go except the few designated channels. Metal shutters sealed the other channels.

They made their way along the railed walkway, which ran the full perimeter of the dam, with exits every quarter of a section.

As they went through the first exit, the sound of the water began to dim. The corridors that ran beyond were white with coloured arrows providing directions to designated areas. They followed the direction arrows to the operation room, passing a myriad of corridors and doorways.

With tubers in hand, they approached the door. Rafe tried the handle. It was unlocked. He peered, cautiously, through the gap, "No one." He breathed out with relief and stepped inside.

A steady hum resonated from the equipment in the room.

"I thought they would be guarding this place," said Tia.

383

"Perhaps they thought we'd never make it this far," Lisa said, quite pleased that they had.

Rafe was cautious. "Let's be careful. We don't know what surprises Evelyn has in store."

They scanned the rows of workstations that ran around the room. The control panels had coded instructions surrounding the numerous levers and black and red buttons.

Lisa ran her hands over the panels. "Do you think we might flood the village if we pull the wrong lever?"

Rafe was mystified. "True, I'm not sure which lever to pull, or if the buttons need to be pushed in conjunction with the levers."

Tia was busy looking at the detailed diagrams of the dam on the walls. "Arabella, Arabella," Tia called earnestly, "we don't know what to do. Help us please."

Lisa gasped in amazement. "Words are appearing on the levers. Hill House, Village, Water wheel. Look!"

For a brief moment, they saw a tinge of blue against the grey walls. Arabella's voice broke through the hum of the room. "Firstly, push the village lever upwards and press the red then the black button. The water will take a little while to get to the release point. You will need to get to the west wing to discharge the water manually. You must move quickly." She repeated this again. The blue faded to grey.

"Ok." Rafe said, "let's do this." He placed his hand on the lever. Lisa's hand hovered over the red button, Tia's over the black.

It took Rafe a few attempts to crank the lever upwards. Once he did this, the screen in front of him flickered into life. Lisa pressed down on her button then Tia. Neither of them felt they could release their button until Rafe pointed to the information that flashed up on the screen: -

> First channel open
> Shutter open
> Second channel pending
> Shutter open

A counter displayed a clock counting down from 20 minutes

> Third channel pending
> Shutter sealed.

"Does that mean we only have twenty minutes to open the last shutter?" Tia asked.

"Nineteen," Rafe replied.

Lisa was ready. "Let's get going."

Rafe was impressed. "Go Lisa!"

They rushed out of the room. Rafe grabbed hold of a coiled rope that was hanging on the wall.

Tia ran alongside Rafe. "What do you need that for?"

"Not sure. I've seen ropes used in so many films I just thought it might be handy."

Tia attempted to raise her eyebrow.

They followed the directions to a spiral staircase that led them down a darkened, wooden, musty shaft. At the end of the staircase were two metal doors opposite each other. One of the doors had a wheel lock that would not open. The other door opened into a short passageway, which led to an outside staircase.

Lisa gasped. "I can't run anymore."

"Keep going. Mr Creepy's done this deliberately. He wants us to give up. Well we're not going to," said Tia.

They landed in a trench imbedded in the hillside. Trees adorned the rest of the area. Rafe stopped them as they rushed along the trench. "Look, shutters."

Sure enough, to the side of them, peeking through a tangled curtain of vines, were large wooden shutters. They pulled at the vines and banished the stubborn ones with their tubers. Lisa threw the vines in her hands to the ground and wiped her brow. "Why are these shutters wooden and the others metal?"

"Perhaps he made these first, to stop the water, then the metals ones as an improvement, who knows," Rafe said, "every madman has an alternative, just in case they have to use it …There has to be a lever of some sort around here."

As they sliced away at the vines at the bottom edge of the shutter, they heard a hissing sound, a blast of cool air released from a gap as the shutter rose slowly from the embedded soil. The shutter creaked and clattered as it wrenched upwards. They fled to the side of the trench to avoid a water deluge, but none came.

"Where is it?" Tia asked.

They felt deflated as they stared into the deep, dark, circular chamber. Lisa shone her torch inside. They could just make out another shutter to the right of them.

Lisa sighed. "I hope it's not shutter after shutter, we'll be here for ages. Poor Ben and Sam must be sat over the dry stream willing it to flow."

Kingdom of Sanguel – Secret Mission

As sunrays hit the lower inner chamber, a mass of screeching, red winged creatures swooped out of the darkness into the middle of the chamber.

Chapter 44

Ride

Alamo and Ben had made their way to the stables. Ben, with Alamo's help, heaved himself onto one of Alamo's horses called Calm. He was nervous, but tried to look confident by sitting upright and patting Calm, as Alamo mounted Dart.

Alamo took a last look at the map and handed the book to Ben. Ben tucked it back in his pouch.

"She's a great horse. Talk to her, she'll listen," Alamo said, as they trotted towards the courtyard.

Ben nodded. "You can do this," he told himself.

"Follow my lead." Alamo said. As they came to the open gates, he galloped away.

Ben held on for dear life as Calm raced after them.

A few metres into the woods, Alamo slowed his horse. Ben followed suit and thanked Calm for an exhilarating ride. Alamo put his finger to his lips; something had

389

unnerved his horse. They peered ahead of them, but only saw rustling trees and deep undergrowth.

"What's the matter?" Ben whispered, as Calm tried to turn to the left.

"Mechagribeas... I think," Alamo said.

"What?"

"Beasts," Alamo whispered. "Come on Dart. Are we OK to go any further?" Dart turned to the left. A mechagribea came bounding out of the undergrowth.

"Oh... one of them!" Ben yelled in a fit of excitement mixed with fear. The horses galloped away at full speed, as the beast gave chase and started to make up ground. Ben wanted to look around, but, at the speed they were going, he dared not, just in case he fell off. Alamo enjoyed the chase. He was determined to get away.

Dart and Calm leapt over a felled tree, clearing a dusty area. They slowed their pace to an eventual halt. The mechagribea was still in pursuit.

"We need to move. Come on Calm," Ben pleaded, pulling at her reins. Calm resisted.

"No Ben. Hold still." Alamo instructed and clapped his hands repeatedly.

Ben knew he wanted to see one of these beasts up close, but this felt too close for comfort. The mechagribea charged at them. It leapt up over the felled tree, but didn't clear the ground as the horses did. Instead, it hit the ground. The earth gave way and sucked the beast into a pit. It wailed and thumped the earth trap.

"No way." Ben cried in excitement.

Izzy and a Guardian descended from nearby trees. "Guardian trap…" she yelled.

"Climb up," Alamo said, extending his hand. Izzy mounted behind him and gripped his waist.

Ben almost slipped off his saddle as he tried to do the same for the Guardian. It was a good thing the Guardian was used to horses and was able to mount, even with the mishap.

"I know where the ridge is. Follow us," Izzy said.

Alamo turned Dart around. He had to wait a moment for Ben to do the same. Alamo had soon worked out that Ben's stories about horses were exaggerated. He chuckled. "Talk to her Ben, she'll make it easier for you."

"OK Calm, you know I'm not a real rider, but I like horses. Follow Alamo."

Alamo smiled. "On!" Dart was off.

Calm didn't hesitate. Ben and the Guardian held on as they shot through the terrain.

Chapter 45

Chamber

Rafe managed to pull Tia and Lisa down into the trench as the creatures fluttered over their heads and scattered into the sky. A trail of yellow vapour and droppings covered the ground. The smell was foul. They coughed and spluttered as the vapour dispersed about them. It became easier to breathe, as the wind swept the mist into the air.

The upper chamber was still dark, but the sunlight faintly marked out half of its flooring and walls of moss.

Tia peered into the chamber from the trench, then to Lisa and Rafe for reassurance. "Have those redwingies gone?"

"I'll find out." Rafe clambered into the chamber. "They seem to be gone," he shouted back. His voice echoed in the hollow space. Lisa and Tia entered, their tubers extended, their eyes wary.

"Be careful the ground's slippery in places. There are ladders over there, fixed to the walls." Rafe directed his torch light on them.

Lisa grimaced, "They're filthy."

Tia's nose twitched, "What a strange smell."

Rafe was unconcerned. "It's better than before."

"Stinks," Tia and Lisa said, in unison and then grinned at each other.

Rafe wasn't in the mood for jokes. He was feeling the pressure with the clock counting down in his head.

"We need to get a move on." He pulled at some of the moss, which came away easily. "Here it is." He stepped back and shone his torch on the area. "The shutter is between these ladders." He shone the beam upwards and criss-crossed the upper chamber.

Lisa stared upwards earnestly. "Is that railings?"

"Looks like it. These ladders lead that way...could be another way into the dam." Rafe's torch light shone over the creatures' nesting area. They were unaware that they had disturbed the last occupant. Their attention focused on finding a way to open the shutter, the previous method was not working. They could hear the faint rumblings of water behind the shutter.

"This is thirsty work Ray."

"Thank goodness for that breeze." Lisa straightened up and wiped her neck. She turned to face the relieving draught and screamed. The others shot around. Above their heads, claws, wings and protruding teeth attacked them. Its deafening squeal forced them back outside. Its hairy tail swiped after them. They jumped into the trench. The creature remained hovering in the chamber.

"Having a little trouble?" Evan grinned. He was standing in the trench as they dashed out. They greeted him warmly, almost forgetting the encounter they just had.

"Where's Izzy?" Tia asked.

"She's tying up loose ends trapping the other mechagribea."

"We've got the other problem," Rafe said.

"I thought so, I saw you all rush out of there. Is it the vultumis, Arabella told us about?"

"The winged rat?" Rafe said, "I had no idea it would be that big or that loud."

Lisa was indignant. "What about telling us?"

"Because, she got the feeling you wouldn't want to do it if you knew," Evan said, bluntly.

Tia couldn't believe Rafe hadn't told her about this discovery. She shook her head in disbelief.

Lisa put her hands up, "Yep. True. I wouldn't, but now I'm ready. So, what do we do?"

"We need to lure it out. If it's killed in there, the water will be contaminated for weeks. Drive it out and it will go back to the Serdal country where it belongs. Watch out for its tail. By the way, nice work with the serpent," Evan said.

Rafe gave Evan a high five.

"OK. It's not the time for male bonding," Tia said, tapping Rafe's arm. "So, we can use our tubers to nudge it in the right direction?"

"Yes, Tia, nudge not kill," Rafe warned with a grin, although he knew facing that creature wasn't going to be fun.

A stone, the size of a football, narrowly missed the four of them. Another came flying in and just missed Rafe. More stones of various sizes bombarded them. They ducked down in the trench.

"Between the devil and the deep blue sea!" Rafe exclaimed.

"His mom says that," said Tia.

"I get the meaning," Lisa smiled.

Evan spied across the trench. "I can see Defenders in those trees across there."

"Where? Where? I can't see them," Tia said.

"Ten to twelve."

"Thanks Ray, I see them."

Two Defenders were launching rocks from a vantage point in a tree house - tree houses were constructed at the same time as the dam for such eventualities. The tree houses had an ample supply of rocks and stones, with extra supplies secured in sacks tied to nearby branches. The launch apparatus was a large spring catapult.

"I'll head around the side and see if I can distract them. They have given you the ammo you need to force the vultumis out of there," Evan said, as he ducked down into the trench and moved stealthily toward the trees.

"I hope these pendants are ready to work again." Tia held her pendant and mouthed a silent prayer. Rafe pressed his pendant and jumped out of the trench, grabbing a large rock as he dashed into the chamber.

The Defenders ceased firing, unable to see a target. Instead, they aimed at Evan weaving down the gradient, using boulders and bushes as recovery points.

Lisa and Tia climbed out of the trench and ventured into the chamber. All was still, except the faint rumbling of water in the background. Rafe was poised, rock in one hand, tuber in the other, "I'm going to throw it up there. Are you ready?"

Tia and Lisa held their tubers with both hands and waited anxiously. They nodded in agreement, as they looked up at the area where the shadowy figure loomed.

"Here goes," Rafe said and hurled the rock into the darkness. The rock banged against the wall and crumbled. The remnants caught the prey. With red wings flapping and a deafening squeal, it flew towards them. Its black beady eyes couldn't see them, its back twisted towards them and its front faced the opening. They lunged forward and whacked it on its wings and back. Instead of going forward, it swivelled to face them. Tia slipped backwards and hit the ground. A sharp pain shot up her right arm on impact. The tuber fell out of her hand. Rafe swung his tuber towards the creature in an attempt to divert it. Tia quickly turned onto her front and grabbed her tuber. She ignored the pain in her hand and scrambled to her feet.

Lisa ducked under its wings and fell on the end of its tail. Her invisibility vanished. Its tail whipped around her body and squeezed tightly. She screamed out and dropped her tuber as it dragged her along, unable to take full flight. Rafe ran under the creature swinging his tuber like a sword, delivering several blows to its stomach until he got to Lisa, who was trying her best to wiggle free from its grip.

Tia whacked repeatedly on the upper half of its tail along with Rafe. The continued assault had the desired effect. Confused and unable to see its attackers the vultumis released Lisa. She staggered away from the

397

creature as it landed and stumbled backwards. Tia and Rafe took advantage of its dazed state and battered it towards the opening. The vultumis smashed its head against the mouth of the chamber, which stunned it for a few seconds, as it plunged lifelessly towards the trees. Just before it hit the tops of the trees, it regained some life, flapping its wings ferociously to gain height. As it did so, its tail caught the Defenders stationed in the tree house, knocking them out. The vultumis took off into the clear sky with a squeal and was soon out of sight.

They all breathed a sigh of relief. However, with no time to waste they gathered themselves and went back to open the shutter. Time was running out.

Chapter 46

Water

Ben and his group raced towards Evan on horseback. Alamo jumped off his horse to greet his brother. The others dismounted. Izzy noticed bloodstains on Evan's top. "You've been hit."

"I'm fine, a few of their missiles caught me," Evan said. "Fortunately, the winged beast took them out." He nodded in the direction of the lifeless Defenders a short distance away. One was slumped over a branch.

"That's what the ruckus was about," Ben said, "we caught sight of that thing."

"Impressive. Sorry we missed it. If it wasn't for Izzy and these horses, we wouldn't have got here." Alamo patted Dart, who snorted in agreement.

Ben was eager to get on with the job. "Defenders are on their way. Where are the others?"

Evan pointed to the rise. "They're inside that chamber. You and Alamo go and help them. We can hold the Defenders from their own vantage point."

"Great – they can't have all the fun. I need to stretch my bum," Ben said, rubbing his rear end.

Evan laughed. "Calm didn't go easy on you, I take it." He took the horses' reins.

"She got him here in one piece," Alamo chuckled, as he followed Ben.

Evan secured the horses then joined the Guardians up in the tree houses. They positioned themselves ready to do battle.

*

As Ben and Alamo entered the chamber, they could hear water beating against the lower end of the shutter. Rafe was heading over to Lisa and Tia. They had a rope tied to their lever. Lisa was pulling with both hands, while Tia pulled with one hand, her other hand injured from her encounter with the vultimis. Lisa was unhurt and determined to finish their task. They were thrilled to see Alamo and Ben. They wanted to ask them so many questions about what had happened in the village, but there was no time.

Rafe began, "Both levers need to be pulled down at the same time. The trouble is they are stiff. It's good to have a bit of muscle -,"

Ben interjected. "Ok sis, I'll help you, Tia, you rest for a while."

Rafe continued: "That lever is in the ready position, we just need this one to do the same and then release them together."

Alamo, Ben and Rafe pulled the awkward lever into position.

"Now for what we've been waiting for." Rafe was jubilant.

Once the two levers were in the same position, Ben and Alamo held onto one lever. Rafe, Lisa and Tia (who wanted to help regardless of her injured hand), held onto the other one. They all pushed down on the levers and released them. The levers rose above their heads then returned to their lower position. They heard the shutters rattle, but they didn't open. They pushed down again and soon got into a rhythm, like using a water pump. Gradually the shutters began to lift with creaks and rattles, a trickle of murky water slipped under their feet.

They all grinned as the trickle turned into a steady flow. The shutters started to shudder as the water became more forceful and gushed out.

The force and rise of the water took them by surprise, pushing its way into the chamber. They dashed for the ladders. Tia had difficulty gripping the rung of the ladder. The water lifted her off her feet. Ben managed to reach down and pull her up out of the water.

The entry of the water triggered a secret panel at the entrance of the chamber. The metal panel shot upwards from the ground with an ear-piercing screech, trapping the water and its shocked inhabitants inside. Green fluorescent lights flashed on and off at the roof of the chamber, changing the world of the chamber into an eerie waterlogged tomb.

Panic rose in all of them. The water surged upwards. Tia was just behind Ben and Lisa when her injured hand sent shooting pains into her arm, as she gripped the slippery ladder tightly. The pain ran jaggedly through her body, causing her to release her grip. She attempted to regain her footing, but her legs gave way and she fell backwards. The water wasted no time in pulling her in and tossed her away from the ladder, her screams swallowed up by the roar of the water.

Lisa and Ben were now safely on the ledge, which ran around the chamber. The railings along its side provided a safety barrier. Rafe and Alamo managed to make it up the other ladder. Rafe assumed Tia had made it to safety with Ben and Lisa, but was soon horrified when he noticed Tia was missing.

"Where is she?" he shouted, trying to transcend the roar of the water. Ben and Lisa looked around in a state of panic and frenzy at missing the obvious.

"She was just behind us," Lisa cried. Ben dashed back to the ladder and peered desperately into the surging water.

Rafe shone his torch frantically around the swirling water, fearing the worst. His clear torch light cut through the gloomy green flashing light. He caught sight of Tia clinging to something jutting out of the chamber wall a few metres below the ledge, the water battering her body. He yelled for her to hold on as he shot around the ledge to where she was.

Tia's head bobbed under the water a few times, but each time she mustered enough energy to raise her head just above the water before another surge came along. She was grateful for a small duct that ran alongside the

403

metal plate she was holding onto, as it drained away some of the water.

Alamo made his way to what was the creature's nest. Ben helped him to dislodge it, kicking it into the water. Once they saw that it was buoyant, they got in. Disregarding the smell and the prickliness, they held onto the edge of the ledge and began their manoeuvre towards Tia. Alamo had rescued a broken branch from the nest to use as a paddle to steer the makeshift boat.

Rafe made his way round the ledge close to where Tia was positioned; lying flat under the perimeter rails, his head and hands over the ledge, he adjusted himself a number of times trying to grab hold of Tia, but he was unsuccessful.

"Hold on Tia!" he yelled.

Tia was getting weaker. Her hands began to slip away from the plate.

"Don't give up!"

She tried to hold on, but she was exhausted and the pain in her hand was beyond what she could imagine or bear. As her hands slipped away, Alamo managed to get hold of her shoulders before she began to sink. Ben jumped into the water and grabbed her legs, which helped Alamo to pull her into the nest, out of the torrid water. They were grateful when the nest wedged itself against the metal plate. Rafe leant forward in relief as Alamo lifted Tia towards him. Rafe pulled her onto the ledge away from the rail. She immediately started to cough and spat out water; she lay back against Rafe. He held her in his arms, grateful she was still alive.

Alamo helped Ben back into the nest. They felt a mild tremor beneath them, prompting them to get out just before the nest began to splinter and drift away.

The water level started to reduce.

"How is that possible?" Ben asked, "The water's going down?"

Alamo looked over the edge.

The green light stopped flashing and stayed on.

Lisa ran towards them smiling proudly. "I found the reset button - just by the exit."

Ben went over and hugged Lisa. "Good one, sis!" The rest nodded in agreement.

"And I know the way out," she beamed as she knelt beside Rafe and Tia.

*

They eventually made their way to the exit, and found their way back to the well-lit shaft. They climbed the spiral

405

staircase, feeling the water rumble beneath them. They felt free. Tia took her time as the others ran to the grassy embankment and lay in the sunshine, breathing deeply.

A loud crash resonated in the air. They jumped up and ran to look over the mound, where they saw the remnants of the wooden shutters flowing out of the chamber mouth, guided by the rushing force of water into the trench stretched out in front of them.

"Wouldn't you like to see Evelyn's face when the water gets to the village?" Rafe laughed. The others joined in the excitement.

Chapter 47

Arabella

A search party of Guardians, led by Sam, were about to leave the courtyard when they saw the tired but happy group approaching the village gates. Alamo rode with Tia sat in front of him. She held onto the reins with one hand as Dart strode gently. Lisa rode with Evan, holding onto him tightly. The others walked behind the horses.

The Guardians ran to greet them. Excited chatter escorted the ecstatic group into the courtyard. Water gurgled in the once dry well and the statue carrying the buckets now had water flowing through the holes in the bucket.

They dismounted, taking special care of Tia.

They all talked over each other about the reaction of the villagers to the water when it entered the wells, the creatures they had encountered and how Evelyn and his Defenders ran into Hill House for refuge.

There were shouts of joy as Mrs Peri rushed forward and embraced her sons and then the others. She cried tears of joy, "I'm so glad you're all safe. Thank you for all your help... but I must know, where is Meela?"

"We believe she is fine. She got married and moved to the Kingdom of Princes." That was as much as Evan would say. He was not totally convinced that this was true. However, he knew he couldn't inflict any more pain on his mother until he found out for sure.

"Where is father?" Alamo asked.

"He's rescuing the rest of the children from the mines. He couldn't believe what Evelyn had done. Now, no more talk of Evelyn until later. You need to get some rest before the celebrations. I have clean clothes for you and something to get your appetites going." Mrs Peri led the way to her cabin.

*

The following evening, the rescue party were dressed in fine clothes provided by the villagers. The whole village made a special effort. Everywhere sparkled with decorations as the entourage made their way into Hill House. The bridge was permanently in place, lit by miniature lanterns. The water moved peacefully in the moat. Some of the villagers stood admiring it.

Rafe, Tia, Lisa and Ben entered once again into the great hall. This time it was much brighter. Evelyn's picture collection was gone. In its place were images of the true royalty of Sanguel.

Music played.

An array of flowers and food covered the numerous tables. The main table was set up on the platform. A full-sized, rejuvenated Arabella stood at the head of the table.

"Sit down, sit down," she greeted them with a wide smile. The hall fell silent. The music ceased. "Let us celebrate the freedom of Sanguel," she announced proudly.

Everyone applauded. Arabella awarded accolades to Rafe, Tia, Ben and Lisa. Alamo, Evan and the other Guardians received medals for their bravery. The villagers thanked them for reuniting them with their children and helping them to discover the truth about those who had died. Arabella signalled to the musicians. They promptly played and the servers brought out lavish food. The atmosphere was magnificent.

Arabella sat proudly, smiling at her guests. "I am so glad you completed your task. A bit rocky at first - however, you have freed my kingdom from my wicked uncle."

"Your uncle?" Rafe scorned.

"Family should look out for each other," Rafe said, as he sliced Tia's meat up for her. Her bandaged hand was still quite sore.

"Not all families do that," said Arabella, "some people are driven by greed, power or control. He was driven by all three. He found out that the mines contained precious metals and minerals. I refused to help him with his devious plans, so he persuaded the duchess from the Kingdom of Kings to banish me. The only way I could return was to be smaller than my original size; and my powers could only be used in limited ways. The ripping of the book sped up the fading process." Arabella didn't labour the point. "The only way to break the spell was to get help - children and young people to help children. Evelyn believed children would be too self-absorbed to even notice what was going on, and the parents too gullible to be aware of his deception."

"Really? I can't believe that."

"Oh yes, Lisa. Evelyn is very clever, with his purposeful inventions and his manipulative techniques. He almost got away with it."

"But surely some of them, like Alamo's mother, knew." Ben said, licking his fingers as he devoured his food.

"Yes, but like so many, his father was misguided. They were happy to receive the rewards of their children working at Hill House."

"Where is Evelyn?" Tia asked

"We have word that he escaped to the Clover kingdom. He'll have difficulty there, as the terrain is rough and the people are not so forgiving."

"I suppose he'll use his Defenders to do his dirty work," said Rafe.

"It's his way, but we will catch up with him. He only has two Defenders with him, the others debriefed. Their parents will do all they can to help. As for his robotic ones, Rowhan has a scheme to re-program them and the mechagribeas."

They talked on into the night as the celebrations continued.

Chapter 48

Home

The following afternoon they said their goodbyes to their friends. Rafe and Izzy had a touching farewell, as Lisa and Tia giggled and nudged each other without Rafe being aware.

Arabella took them by horse and cart to the crossroads. Arabella stopped at the post and laughed as she retrieved a crumpled box from under her seat and handed it to Ben. "Here Ben, this belongs to you. If you and Lisa had not argued so much, you would have had your pendant and got to the mines without Evelyn even suspecting that any of you had arrived."

Ben yanked the key out of the box and jumped down off the cart. He opened the chamber that Arabella pointed out.

The others were at Ben's side when he pulled out his pendant, the same shape and size as Rafe's. It glimmered

412

in the sunlight. Ben admired it. The thought of being invisible intrigued him.

"What about your tuber?" Rafe said. "How can you not want this?" He wheeled his in the air.

Arabella pressed her point. "My memory and strength were fading; the books were there to help you. They contained all the information you needed for the task - although the maps by themselves were important. Kept intact, you would have known about Evelyn and the situation in the village. However, you all ended up going the long way about it." She grinned. "Anyway, now it's time for you to return home. And remember... never overlook the details."

"Will our parents be looking for us? Can we tell them?" Lisa was eager to share her adventure.

"You can if you wish. However, they may not believe you. They may think it is just the Sanguel production that you watched in the library, or you got the story from a book."

They all looked puzzled.

Arabella wasn't going to say any more about that issue. "Don't worry. Follow the path. It will lead you to the library entrance."

"Will you be in the library?" Ben asked.

413

"Perhaps it's time for me to go."

"Why?"

Arabella was gone.

"I tell you what, she's still peculiar. You'd think she would just answer the question." Ben stood in disbelief at her disappearance.

They followed the path, laughing and chatting about what had happened, as they went.

"Do you think we'll be able to use the pendants in the real world?" Tia said, cheerily.

"Let's try it," said Lisa.

Rafe shook his head, "I'm not sure that would be a good idea for you two."

"Leave it to me and Rafe. We'll see." Ben boasted.

"Says the boy who just got his... You've got no idea what it's like – like a mini electric shock." Lisa winked at Tia.

"Yeah, electric," Tia said, straight faced.

"What electric? What do you mean?"

Lisa elaborated, "The first time you try it, you get an electric thingy as part of you disappears... until you get used to it and it gets used to you."

"That true Rafe?"

"Leave me out of this." Rafe stifled a laugh.

Ben took the hint. "Lisa, I hope the first part of you to vanish is your mouth."

They entered the library as two staff members were at the door seeing out the last visitors.

Tia asked them for the time.

"Six o'clock. The production ran over."

"Thanks." Tia said, as they stepped out on the front steps of the library. The evening sun provided a warm homely glow.

"That all?" Lisa and Ben sang together.

The time delay hit Rafe, "I get it - what's a second when you have hours, what's a minute when you have days? Remember Tia, that's what Arabella said when I asked what time will we get home? It only took a few hours! That's the answer."

"A few hours – it felt like weeks!" Lisa exclaimed

"More like months," Ben contradicted.

Ben and Lisa's mom shouted from her car, "Come on you two. You're always late."

Lisa hugged Tia and Rafe and dashed to the car. Ben said goodbye, and walked to the car, trying to contain his excitement. He said something to his mom and returned to Rafe and Tia. "Do you want a lift?"

"No thanks. We're fine," Rafe said and waved them off. "We need to walk so we can come up with a story about your bandaged hand, even though Arabella said it would be fine by the time you get home."

Tia giggled. "You're going to get it in the neck if it doesn't, so the story better be good."

"I think it has got to be better than we went to the kingdom of Sanguel."

"Or... I won a competition and got captured to work in a mine."

"I went to rescue Tia with some friends."

"We escaped and got chased by mechagribeas."

"But we helped to free the children working in mines... I killed a serpent, unleashed a vultumis, we opened a dam where Tia fell and injured her hand... and did I tell you she almost drowned?"

"Don't think they'll be convinced."

"Get thinking, little T, get thinking..."

End

About the Author

After many years working as a qualified social worker and lecturer, as well as completing a Master degree in applied family studies, Chalmere decided to explore her passion for creative writing.

When she's not working or writing, she enjoys sewing, needlecraft and listening to music.

Chalmere writes under the pseudonym of Alex Lee Davis for her children's and teenage fiction. Kingdom of Sanguel is her debut novel.

Contact the author: davis.fiction@outlook.com

Kingdom of Sanguel - Secret Mission is available in paperback and kindle version on Amazon.co.uk, Amazon.eu and Amazon.com

Printed in Great Britain
by Amazon

29486951R00239